DUBLIN MOON

Jack Dillon Dublin Tale 10

Second Edition

DUBLIN MOON

Jack Dillon Dublin Tale 10
Second Edition

Mike Faricy

Library of Congress Control Number: 2023920386
paperback ISBN: 978-1-962080-79-8
e-Book ISBN: 978-1-962080-80-4

Published by

MJF Publishing
https://www.mikefaricybooks.com

ACKNOWLEDGMENTS

I would like to thank the following people for their help & support: Special thanks to Nick, Roy, Julie, Mittie, and Toui for their hard work, cheerful patience and positive feedback. I would like to thank family and friends for their encouragement and unqualified support. Special thanks to Maggie, Jed, Schatz, Pat, Av, Emily and Pat, for not rolling their eyes, at least when I was there. Most of all, to my wife, Teresa, whose belief, support and inspiration has, from day one, never waned.

To Teresa
"You've driven me demented . . ."

ONE

As Dillon refilled Tara's glass he asked, "More wine?"

"Not too much. There's no telling what I'll be up to," she said and raised her eyebrows. She raised her glass in a toast. Just like the previous dozen times this evening, they clinked glasses. Dillon let the wine touch his lips then set his glass on the coffee table. Tara took a couple of audible swallows.

She lived across the lane from Dillon. They'd had an on-again, off-again relationship for a couple of years. She'd been gone for the past three weeks, minding her father in the west of Ireland following his heart surgery. Fortunately, he was doing just fine. Stubborn guy that he was, surprisingly, he was following the doctor's orders. Apparently, a heart attack can have that effect on you.

"Thanks for bringing dinner over tonight and for minding the lawn while I was gone, Jack. You didn't have to do that."

"No big deal. I'm just glad your dad's doing okay. From what you told me, it sounds like it could have been a lot worse."

"You think? Chest pains for three solid days before he gives a call to the doctor, then he drives himself to the emergency room. Honest to God, we're lucky they didn't find him dead behind the wheel on a country road. A double bypass and I damn near had to lock him in his bedroom to keep him from tending the sheep," she said and took another healthy swallow of wine.

"You said you got a neighbor to watch over them."

"Aw, yeah. Alfie, he and his family have been next door for the last twenty years. Nice couple with four boys. They'll be taking good care of the sheep, and Alfie will be cracking the whip. He and his wife run a tight ship." She took another swallow of wine and raised her eyebrows again.

Dillon figured maybe a couple more sips, and they could begin what they were both looking forward to. He'd missed her, and although he'd never admit it to himself, he was thrilled that she was back in town. Hopefully, things would remain somewhat quiet in Dublin over the next seventy-two hours, and maybe they could get back on track.

"It's good to see you, Jack. I thought about you a good bit."

"Hopefully in a positive manner," he said.

"Most of the time. I really want—What the hell is that?"

"Oh, my damn phone," Dillon said, pulling his cell-phone from his pocket.

"I thought you told me you'd turned it off."

"I thought I did, I—"

"Well, don't answer it."

"Hello?"

"Dillon?"

"Yes, sir."

"Sorry to bother you at this time of night." DCI McCabe, usually unflappable. Tonight he sounded very upset.

"Not a bother, sir."

"There's been a tragic incident at Mountjoy Square. It's all hands on. We need you here."

"I'm on it. I'll see you there in fifteen minutes."
Click

"You're leaving?" Tara asked.

"I'm sorry, Tara, but I have to. There's been—"

"No doubt some dreadful situation you can't wait to get involved in. Well, go ahead. Off with you."

"It's not like that. I'm on call. That was DCI McCabe. He wanted—"

"McCabe is it? Well, when you see him, tell him to stop over. As long as you're leaving, maybe he'd be interested in coming over and attending to my needs. Hmm?"

"Tara, I'm sorry. Maybe if we hurried, we could—"

"You've got to be kidding. Save it, Jack. I've heard it too many times. Go on, git. If you stay here, you'll just be wondering what gruesome, grisly situation you're missing out on."

"Look, Tara, if there was—"

"Go on. Besides, this just leaves more wine for me," she said and grabbed the bottle. She emptied the bottle, filling her glass to the rim. The glass overflowed with a final glug, and she set the empty bottle on the floor.

"Okay, look, I'm really sorry. I'll call you tomorrow," Dillon said and stood. "Can I get a kiss goodbye?"

"Sure you can," she said and staggered to her feet. As she stepped toward him, she kicked the empty bottle under the coffee table. She smiled, placed her hands on either side of Dillon's face, and gave him a long, passionate kiss. As she pulled away, she rubbed both hands below his belt, smiled, and said, "Just to remind you what you'll be missing. Now go."

As he stepped out of her sitting room, he heard the TV come on. He crossed the lane and hurried into his place. He opened the cookie jar on the kitchen counter and took out a dog biscuit. At the sound of the cookie jar lid, Lucifer jumped off the bed upstairs and a moment later peeked around the newel post at the top of the stairs.

"Come on, Lucifer, outside," Dillon said and held up the biscuit. The dog hurried down the stairs and stood at the front door. Dillon opened the door, tossed out the biscuit, and closed the door behind him.

He raced upstairs, changed into a pair of pressed jeans and a clean shirt. He pulled on his shoulder holster and grabbed his brown leather jacket. He filled Lucifer's food and water dishes, let him back inside, and climbed in his car.

TWO

DCI McCabe's phone call had been more terse than usual, which was saying a lot. All Dillon knew was a body had been found in Mountjoy Square, down on Gardiner Street. "Need you here now," McCabe had said. No, 'Are you busy?' 'Sorry to interrupt,' or even a 'Please,' which was very unlike him.

On the ten-minute drive over to Mountjoy Square, Dillon tuned in to a number of different radio stations but never found any news. He sped down Drumcondra Road, which turned into Dorset Street. He took a right onto Gardiner Street, and two blocks later, just past St. Francis Xavier Church, the street was blocked by two An Garda Síochána squad cars. The officers were directing traffic onto a side street. Dillon pulled alongside and was fumbling to get his ID out when there was a knock on his window.

"You'll not be parking here. Now move on before we lock you up and sort things out in the morning. Hey, are you even listening, mate? Did you hear what I just said?" the uniformed officer said.

Dillon finally got hold of his ID and held it up as he lowered his window.

"Oh, sorry, sir. I didn't know. This situation is more than a bit upsetting."

"Relax, no problem. I just got the call to come down. No other information. What's happened?"

"Two of our lads, sir."

"Two Gardai? Are you sure? Two?" He shook his head in disbelief.

"Murdered, sir. Shot, apparently execution-style if you can believe it."

"Jesus Christ."

Now the officer shook his head and said, "I'm afraid Jesus was nowhere around when this happened. Let me move my car so you can drive past. When you find the bollox what did this, call me. I'll gladly kill the lousy bastard." He hurried into a squad car, turned it on, and pulled ahead maybe five feet.

Dillon backed up, gave him a nod as he drove between the squad cars and down Gardiner Street. Mountjoy Square was just that, a square park with trees, a children's playground, and St. Brigid's Daycare Center in the far corner. Lovely brick paths wound across the square. Developed in the late 18th century, the square was located in the middle of the city and bounded on all sides by four-story brick buildings that 250 years ago were homes to Dublin's wealthy. Today, the buildings have largely been converted to office space or multiple rental units.

Ahead, Dillon could see two emergency vehicles backed up to the sidewalk along the front of the square. The rear doors were open, and an officer was standing next to them. He pulled across the street and parked. As he climbed out of his car, he grabbed his ID and draped the lanyard around his neck. With the almost full moon, it was more like dusk than a dark evening.

The officer gave him a nod and said, "They're straight back in the middle of the square. Follow the route they've taped off."

"Thanks," Dillon said and hurried along the sidewalk. The park was lined by a six-foot-tall wrought iron fence. White plastic tape with blue letters in English and Irish, CRIME SCENE NO ENTRY LÁTHAIR CHOIRE NÍL IONTRÁIL, was strung on the wrought iron fence. About a third of the way along the sidewalk, the tape followed a brick path, five feet wide, leading toward the center of the square. Maybe twenty individuals were scattered along the path. A camera was flashing, and a number of officers were slowly walking along an area with flashlights illuminating the ground. A white nylon tent was erected halfway down and just off the path; that would be where the bodies were.

As he approached, a familiar voice called, "Dillon, over here." It was Paddy Suel, Dillon's partner in the Special Branch. Standing next to him was their boss, DCI McCabe, and next to McCabe was a man in uniform. Dillon recognized the man as Drew Harris, Garda Commissioner. As Dillon approached, Harris shook hands with McCabe, placed a hand on his shoulder, and said something Dillon couldn't hear.

McCabe nodded, and Harris walked over to the tent. Two individuals in blue hazmat suits stepped out of the tent. Harris said something to them, and they responded.

"Thank you for coming so promptly, Dillon," McCabe said and cleared his throat. "DI Suel, if you'd be so kind as to bring Marshal Dillon up to date. If you'll excuse me, I've a matter to attend to," he said and headed down the brick path to the street.

"Fecking hell," Suel said as McCabe walked away.

"What'd I miss? One of the guys directing traffic told me two Gardai were killed. Is that right?"

"Afraid so. Executed would be a more accurate term. One of them was McCabe's nephew, Liam. The chief is heading to his brother's house now. God, I don't envy him the task. New recruit, barely a month out of the academy, and this shite happens."

They watched DCI McCabe as he walked down the path and out of the square. "What do you know at this point?" Dillon asked.

Suel shook his head, "Feck all. Teams are out knocking on doors as we speak. Early reports are two shots. Based on appearances, both men were shot in the back of the head."

"Executed?"

"Certainly appears that way," Suel said. "No witnesses at this point. The lads patrol the general area on foot, do a walk-through every evening, standard procedure. They were both unarmed. I can't wait to get my hands on the bastard that did this. For the love of God," Suel said.

"How long ago did this happen?"

"Call came in, mmm, maybe a couple of hours ago. Report of two gunshots, nothing about victims."

"You think they saw something?"

"The victims? I suppose it's possible. What's the worst they'd see? A drug deal? Maybe a robbery? God forbid two young ones banging away. Why in the hell would someone shoot them? They were unarmed. Shoot them in the damn foot if you have to, but this, this execution. Feck all. We're going to get the bastard that did this if it's the last thing I do."

They spent the next three hours talking to the officers from the Fitzgibbon Street Garda Station, the section where the two officers were stationed. The Fitzgibbon Street station was just a block away from the square. Both victims, Liam McCabe and Jimmy Murphy, were walking their usual route back to the station at the end of their shift. Dillon and Suel would get confirmation tomorrow on the route they took by checking the CCTV camera footage along the way. Unfortunately, the square itself didn't have CCTVs. A Garda was on the scene within minutes of the shots being fired. A few minutes after that, the area was crawling with officers.

"I'd say there's not much more we can do until daylight," Suel said and glanced up at the stars and the full moon. It was close to midnight. "Clear sky, no rain forecast. Meet back here tomorrow, say seven?"

"Yeah, we need to get copies of CCTV footage first thing. I'm with you on this. It doesn't seem to make much sense at this point unless the aim right from the beginning was to kill a member of the force."

"This was their usual routine. They'd walk through here every evening at the end of their shift, same time. Even with the full moon tonight you'd maybe miss someone hiding behind a tree. Some idiot with a gun comes out, lines them up, and pulls a trigger. It could've happened in less than twenty seconds, start to finish."

Dillon shook his head. "Killing two would almost have to be intentional rather than them stumbling onto something."

"Afraid so," Suel said.

Dillon turned toward a squeaking sound as two gurneys were pushed up the path past them and over to the tent. A folded black body bag rested on each of the gurneys.

Dillon and Suel walked over to the tent and glanced in. The bodies were lying no more than a foot apart. The two men who'd pushed the gurneys were arranging the body bags on the gurneys.

An officer was in the tent taking photos with a digital device. Dillon recognized him but couldn't recall his name.

"Any shell casings, Sean?" Suel asked.

"Afraid not, Paddy," Sean said and snapped off a half-dozen more photos, each time adjusting his position ever so slightly. A young-looking guy in a blue hazmat suit stepped into the tent. The photographer took two more photos, raised his eyebrows at Suel, and said, "See you later, Paddy. Good luck here."

"Take care," Suel called as Sean hurried out of the tent.

Suel rolled his eyes at Dillon then faced the guy in the hazmat suit and asked, "Anyone else from the examiner's office around?"

"No, sir. I'm afraid you're stuck with me. You're not with the Fitzgibbon Station, are you?"

"DI Suel, Special Branch. We'll be working with the Fitzgibbon team, not that it's any of your concern. What can you tell me?"

Dillon shot a look a Suel, wondering where the sudden attitude came from.

The young man swallowed nervously and said, "One round in each victim— no exit wounds. I'd say it's a pretty safe guess whoever did this used a small-caliber weapon. Maybe a 25ACP or a 22 short. That's just a guess on my part at this stage. Residue on both victims suggests maybe eight-to-twelve-inch distance."

"How 'bout you leave the guessing to us, and you just give me the damn facts."

The man quickly nodded and said, "Officer Murphy was shot in the back of the head and Officer McCabe just above the left ear. That suggests Murphy took the first round, and as he's shot, McCabe turned his head. Maybe he attempted to fight back and was shot. Both victims were on their knees, just off the path here. I don't know. Once we recover the slugs, hopefully, we'll get a confirmation on the type of weapon. No signs of any altercation. I'm thinking one individual did this."

Suel shook his head and said, "Feck sake," just under his breath. "Contact me in Special Branch as soon as you have information. Clear?"

"Yes, sir," the young man said and nodded a number of times.

Suel stormed out of the tent. Dillon smiled and said, "Thanks for the information. Sorry for the attitude. This is hitting close to home for us. Appreciate your help." He stepped out of the tent and looked around for Suel.

THREE

Suel was partway down the path, just finishing up talking to the man who'd been taking the pictures. "Thanks for the update, Sean. We'll be back here in the daylight, early," Suel said.

"Good luck on the investigation," Sean said. He nodded as Dillon approached and headed out of the park.

"Let's do a quick walk around the square. There's only a couple of ways in and out of here," Suel said and headed out of the park without waiting for Dillon's response.

They walked around the square, looking, not saying much. After twenty minutes, Dillon was back near his car. He guessed it would be at least another hour before the bodies were removed. "I'll be back tomorrow morning. You still thinking seven?"

Suel nodded as he stared back into the square.

"Based on where the bodies are, it would seem someone was in there waiting for them instead of someone who just happened to pass them on the path. The place is unlit, dark. A normal sort, just out for a nighttime stroll, probably wouldn't cut through. They'd stick to the street with the lights," Dillon said.

"A bloody damn shame," Suel said and shook his head. "Now we've got that limp dick from the examiner's office in there mucking up the works."

"You were pretty rough on him, Paddy. He's doing his job. He's not going to be able to tell us much until they perform the autopsies. I know this is tough, and I'm just as determined as you to get whoever did this but reaming out someone we're going to be wanting information from tomorrow isn't going to help. Why are you so pissed off at him?"

"That's right, blame me, my fault. As if that plonker would mind. He'd love a reaming. Don't you get it, Dillon? He's a puff. Makes the whole lot of us a laughingstock. How in the hell they ever let him into the department when—"

"Wait a minute. Paddy? You were giving the guy a hard time because he's gay?"

"You're damn right. Everyone does. We don't want him associated with us."

"That's just great. He's hired because he's smart, probably was first in his class, but you don't like it because of who he sleeps with? Are you kidding me? You—"

"Save it, Dillon. You Americans, always looking out for everyone unless they have something you want, then you just march in and take whatever it is and call it your own. Whether it's oil, or land, or gold, or feck all.

Save the holier than thou attitude for someone that feck-ing cares."

"Okay, probably be a good idea if we both head home, cool down, and come back here tomorrow morning. We need anything from the medical examiner, maybe let me handle it."

"Fine with me. See how that works out," Suel said and headed down the street.

Dillon walked back into the park and made his way to the tent. The young guy was standing outside writing something on a clipboard. He looked up as Dillon approached.

"Hey, just wanted to give you one of my cards," Dillon said and handed him a card. "Give me a call when you have some information. Any idea when the autopsy will be?"

"Not exactly. I'll probably be assisting, but I'm going to be here for at least another hour, which means they'll be scheduled no earlier than eleven tomorrow morning."

He glanced at the business card. "Oh, you're the American I've heard about. The shooting a few years back at Dublin Airport, terminal two."

"Ancient history," Dillon said. "I'm sorry, I didn't catch your name."

"Oh, I'm called a lot of things," he said and shrugged, not really making a joke. "Umm, Hugh Healy, pleased to meet you, Marshal Dillon," he said and held out his hand.

"Pleasure is all mine," Dillon said.

"I'll call you tomorrow with the autopsy time," Healy said.

"Thanks, I'd appreciate that. I'll be back here first thing in the morning, and then we're going to be tracking down CCTV footage, so you may end up leaving a message. Don't take it personally. I'd like to get those results as soon as they're available. Will you be dealing with the Fitzgibbon Station as well? I'm guessing they'll be heading up the investigation."

"Maybe. I believe DI Kinch at Fitzgibbon will be in charge," Healy said. "Dealt with him once before. He'd prefer anyone but me. I'm used to it."

"Hugh, it's been a pleasure. I look forward to chatting with you tomorrow at some point. Get home and get some sleep."

"A few things to wrap up, and then I'll get some sleep. Thank you for introducing yourself. It was nice to meet you."

"Like I said, the pleasure was all mine," Dillon said. They shook hands, and Dillon walked to his car. At this hour, now approaching one in the morning, traffic was light. He kept thinking about Suel's reaction to Hugh Healy on the drive home and suddenly found himself turning onto his lane. He drove down the short hill, past Tara's house. All the lights were off, and he wondered where he stood with her after leaving the way he did.

He pulled into the parking area in front of his house and climbed out of the car. He unlocked the door, stepped inside, and quietly closed the door. He got the coffee ready for the morning, topped up Lucifer's food and water dishes, and headed upstairs to bed.

Lucifer was asleep on the bed and didn't so much as move when Dillon entered the bedroom. He set the alarm for 5:30, undressed, climbed into bed, and was asleep in less than a minute.

FOUR

Dillon woke five minutes before the alarm was set to go. He turned it off and headed into the bathroom to shave and shower. He dressed in the bedroom, and Lucifer never so much as moved. He quietly headed downstairs, turned on the coffee, and set about making a breakfast of scrambled eggs and bacon. At 6:30, he woke Lucifer with a half-dozen calls offering a biscuit. He finally heard him jump off the bed, and a moment later, Lucifer appeared at the top of the stairs.

"Come on, boy, treat. A nice biscuit, just for you," Dillon said, and Lucifer hurried down the stairs. He bounded out the front door when Dillon tossed the biscuit. Dillon filled his travel mug with coffee, turned off the coffee maker, and let Lucifer back in the house.

He climbed in his car and drove back up the lane. He looked Tara's house without turning his head as he drove past. There didn't seem to be any activity, but then it was only 6:45.

Gardiner Street was still blocked off, but now there was only one squad car and a very tired-looking officer directing traffic to the side street. Dillon slowed, raised the ID hanging around his neck, and got a friendly nod and wave from the officer.

He parked in the same spot as the previous night and headed into the square. The tent was gone, and there was only a handful of Gardai in the square. One of them was Suel.

"You able to get some sleep last night?" Dillon asked.

Suel nodded and said, "What about you?"

"I was out like a light," Dillon said.

"I just finished talking to a sergeant from Fitzgibbon Station. DI Garret Kinch will be leading the charge from there."

"Oh really," Dillon said and decided there was no point in mentioning Hugh Healy had told him that last night.

"Yeah, have you ever had to deal with him?" Suel asked.

Dillon shook his head and said, "Couldn't pick him out of a crowd of two."

"Bit of a plonker. Has to be the person always in complete control. Just a warning, let's be polite, smile, and keep things close to the vest."

"I'm with you. Any results from last night? A name or names? Type of weapon?"

"Nothing yet. It's still early. No shells found, which makes me think it was a revolver."

"Or they picked up the shells."

"Yeah, could be. One thing, the route the lads always walked was along Parnell Street to Hill Street. They would take a left on Hill up to Grenville Street then into the square. Kinch has someone rounding up the CCTV footage as we speak. Hope to be able to view that later this morning."

"Any history of threats against either one of the victims or the Fitzgibbon Station?"

Suel shook his head. "Nothing out of the ordinary. A woman charged with solicitation threatened to sue an arresting officer out of Fitzgibbon, and when that didn't work, she offered him a fifty percent discount."

"You're kidding, a discount to the arresting officer? How'd that go?"

"Not too well for her."

"They're going to conduct another search here in about thirty minutes. I've got a laundry list of CCTV locations along the route the victims were supposed to have taken. You interested in walking it with me?" Suel asked.

"Yeah, it'll give me a sense of the area. I've only driven through occasionally."

"It can be a bit dicey. There are some rough pockets," Suel said, and they headed toward Grenville Street. The street was one long block before it butted into Hill Street. On one side of Grenville was a relatively recent, as in maybe twenty or thirty years, five-story apartment building. "Council Housing," Suel said.

Across the street was a two-story white stucco structure that looked like it housed one-room efficiency units
. The exterior of the building was covered with graffiti
from the first floor up to the roof. At this hour of the
morning, there was no apparent activity at either building.

"It'll be quiet around here until noon. Why would
you get up if you don't have to go to a job?" Suel said.

Hill Street was more of the same, with a few busi-
nesses interspersed. Three and four-story apartment
buildings and a stretch of one and two-story commercial
establishments in hundred-year-old buildings, including
an Asian butcher shop. The traffic picked up substantially once Hill Street ran into Parnell Street. There were
more Asian grocery stores, Chinese restaurants, and a
noodle house. A number of commercial establishments
were housed in older two-story buildings along with restaurants and some bars. Parnell Street was busy even at
this hour, and Dillon figured it would be hopping on just
about any evening.

"You think someone could have followed them
from down here?" Dillon asked.

"Entirely possible. I'm not aware of any calls they
made to the station. Hopefully, we'll learn. Maybe they
had a run-in with someone, or they were spotted and followed. With the council housing and the state of the
buildings, I'd say sixty-to-seventy percent of the residents have had some interaction with the Gardai at one
time or another."

"That doesn't mean they'd shoot someone."

"No, of course not, but it also means there's probably more than one individual around here that's harboring a grudge," Suel said.

"You up for a coffee or a tea?" Dillon asked as they approached a coffee shop.

"You buying?"

"Yeah, I'll buy."

They headed into the Ming Coffee Shop and were greeted with a smile from the Asian woman behind the counter.

"You go ahead, Paddy."

"Just a regular coffee, nothing fancy," Suel said.

"Make it two," Dillon said.

The woman poured coffee into two paper cups, placed a plastic lid on top of each, and said, "Seven Euro."

Dillon handed her a ten Euro note and pocketed the change.

Once outside, Suel took a sip and said, "Sweet Jesus, but that's hot. Wow."

"Seven Euros for the coffee, we should have gotten a pint of Guinness and split it," Dillon said.

"Yeah, we'll do that next time. As long as I get to drink the first half," Suel said.

They walked back to Mountjoy Square along the same route. The foot traffic along Hill Street was beginning to pick up, largely people working in the various commercial establishments and the occasional older woman dragging a cart to the grocery store.

Grenville Street was still quiet. Twice as many officers were now in Mountjoy Square. They'd fanned out in a line and were slowly combing over the area, looking for anything. It appeared they were coming up empty-handed.

"Looks like they'll be done here in the next hour or so," Dillon said.

"Yeah, and still no answers," Suel replied and took the final sip of his coffee. "What do you think? Do you want to hang around and wait, or should we move on?"

"I don't see any point in waiting here. Do you see Kinch anywhere?"

"I'm guessing he's at the station. Let's walk over there. It's just on the other side of the square."

They headed across the square and then onto Fitzgibbon Street. Dillon expected a smaller station based on the two-story brown brick structures along the street. He was surprised by the large four-story red-brick building with the decorative stone entrance. A plaque listed the construction date as 1913.

They walked up the four stone steps and entered the building. Directly in front of them was a U-shape counter with four officers behind it. The oldest of the four, a bald man with a graying mustache and sergeant stripes on his sleeve, looked up and watched as they approached.

Suel was about to say something when the Sergeant said, "DI Suel, here to turn yourself in?"

Suel looked up and laughed, "Declan Tierney, I didn't know you were stationed here. And look, it takes three of these poor souls just to keep you in line." Everyone chuckled at that.

"I suppose you're here based on last night's activities."

"Unfortunately," Suel said. "The one lad, Liam McCabe, is the nephew of DCI McCabe heading up Special Branch. That's why we're here, although DI Kinch will be running the investigation."

"Mmm," Tierney said. "So what can we do for you this morning?"

"Well, if he's available, we'd like to see DI Kinch. Oh, by the way, my sometime partner, US Marshal Jack Dillon. Dillon, Sergeant Declan Tierney and I go way back."

"Oh, many's the pint, eh, Paddy? A pleasure to meet you, Dillon, is it?"

"Yeah, Jack Dillon. Nice to meet you, Sergeant."

"Likewise. I'd say you've got your work cut out for you," Tierney said and nodded at Suel.

"It's been a long time, Declan. You've been keeping well?" Suel asked.

"Yeah, twenty-three months and counting until retirement."

"Really, that's all? Oh, terrific, Declan. Really it is. So nice to see someone make it over the wall."

"Mmm, especially after an event like last night. God, if I could get my hands on the bastard who's responsible for—"

"You'd have to wait in line," Suel said.

"So, you said it's Kinch you're here to see. Let me place a call."

"We'll grab a seat," Suel said.

They hadn't taken six steps when Tierney called, "Paddy, I just left a message. No telling when he'll respond. You know how that bollox can be, so you didn't get this from me, but here's his cellphone." Tierney proceeded to write down a number and then handed the note to Suel.

"Thanks, Declan. You take care," Suel said, and they left the station.

FIVE

They were standing on the sidewalk outside the Fitzgibbon Station. "You hear anything from your puff friend, Healy?" Suel asked.

"Cut the guy some slack, Paddy. No, I haven't heard anything from him, but then he was working before we arrived last night, and he was working well after we left. We were both sound asleep in bed while he was still attending to details in the square. I do know that the autopsies won't be until 11:00 this morning, at the earliest."

Suel shook his head. "We're here, working. The square is full of teams working, and everyone was here last night."

"That's right, and none of us will be doing the sort of precise work that's required in an autopsy. I don't know. Maybe you'd prefer to have that carried out by someone who's functioning on three hours of sleep. Me, I think I want the people fully rested so they can get us the most accurate information possible. At this stage, there's no weapon and no shell casings. Be nice if we had knowledgeable individuals narrowing down the particular weapon we're looking for. On the other hand, if you don't think so, maybe we should go wake him up. It's almost 8:00. He's probably been sacked out for a good three hours."

"Ahh, there you go, taking his side again."

"No, I'm not. I happen to believe we've got a tough case on our hands, and we need the best information possible. Having someone so exhausted they can't see straight and making them perform an autopsy doesn't seem to fit that standard."

"Nice to know you're on his side and—"

"Paddy, it's not about sides. It's about finding out who the hell killed these two and getting their ass in jail. The quickest way to that end is accurate information. Back off on Healy. He's doing his job under very tough circumstances, and he doesn't need you, Kinch, or your pal Sean what's his name making life more difficult."

"Sean Donnelly," Suel said.

Dillon decided to change the subject. "Let's go back to the square. Maybe Kinch is there. We need to see the CCTV footage. If he's not there, let's head back to Special Branch. If Kinch is as big a pain in the ass as you suggest, maybe we can have McCabe bypass him and get us the footage."

In short order, it was obvious nothing was going to be gained by standing around in the square. Kinch wasn't there, which was maybe a good thing and possibly suggested he was lining things up to disperse information. They decided to meet back at the station. Dillon got there first.

As he entered the Special Branch section, he noticed the lights were off in DCI McCabe's office. The phone on Dillon's desk was blinking, signaling a message, and there were three used tea mugs and two plates left on his desk. He carried the plates and mugs into the break room and dumped them in the sink. He poured a coffee for himself and settled in at his desk. He fired up his computer and then listened to his phone messages. The first message was from Eric Bergman, Dillon's contact at the US Embassy.

"Yeah, Jack, give me a call when you've got a moment. Nothing urgent."

The second message was from Hugh Healy at the medical examiner's office. "Hi Marshal Dillon, Hugh Healy, it's half-past eight. We'll be performing the autopsies beginning this morning at 10:30. Hope to have some basic information for you by mid-afternoon. Don't bother returning my call. I'll have the phone taking messages until we have results. Talk to you later."

Dillon phoned Eric Bergman. He picked up on the third ring. "Hi, Eric, Jack Dillon, returning your call."

"Thanks for calling. Sorry to bother you. I heard the news this morning. I'm sure you're up to your eyeballs working this double homicide. Deepest condolences."

"Thanks, Eric, we're just getting started. Not much at this stage."

"This might be unrelated; in fact, it probably is, but I had a notification from a DEA friend waiting for me on my desk this morning. Does the name Kevin McBaine mean anything to you?" Bergman asked and then spelled out the last name.

Dillon thought for a moment. "McBaine? No, it doesn't ring a bell."

"Kevin McBaine, he's out of New Jersey. Arrived in Dublin forty-eight hours ago. Nothing concrete, but rumor has it he's put together some agreement with the Linnehan family. They're involved in—"

"In the drug trade," Dillon said. "Supposedly here, but aren't they operating out of Costa del Sol? I thought they were more or less driven out of Ireland maybe eighteen months ago. At least that's the story. A number of people were killed in an ongoing gangland disagreement between the Linnehan and Doyle families. The Linnehans basically lost, and they fled to Costa del Sol."

"Well, apparently, this McBaine is somehow linked to them. He arrived forty-eight hours ago, and suddenly you've got two officers murdered in Dublin."

"Sounds thin at best. Has he been over here before?"

"No, according to his passport, other than trips to Mexico, he's never left the US."

"Connections in New York?" Dillon asked.

"Supposedly. He's never been arrested. Lives a life that can only be described as under the radar. Officially, he runs a software business. No pending charges."

"So why were you alerted?"

"Well, no pending charges, but he's a person of interest in three murders and two robberies. Big time online robberies, the guess is a haul of one point five million in one and three million in another."

"And he's a suspect but never charged?"

"In both the robberies and the murders, no one has ever been arrested."

"You have a file I can look at or a name I could contact?"

"I have access to a file or at least a portion of a file. You got time today?"

"Maybe. Things are going to get crazy come afternoon. What's your morning look like?"

"I can make time if you want to come over."

Dillon glanced at the clock on his computer screen. "I'll be over in forty-five minutes, Eric. Thanks for the call."

"See you then. I'll put the coffee on."

Dillon gave a quick glance toward Suel's empty desk. He picked up his phone and dialed Suel's number. After three rings, it dropped him into the message center. "Yeah, Paddy. I'm meeting with Eric Bergman. He called with the name of an American who arrived forty-eight hours ago. Apparently, the guy is connected or wants to be connected with the Linnehan gang. I hope to be back by the noon hour. Also, Hugh Healy left a message. Autopsies are later this morning. He hopes to have information for us sometime this afternoon. The time now is 9:45. It appears DCI McCabe has not been in yet. Later."

SIX

The American Embassy, actually the Chancery, is located in the Ballsbridge area of Dublin. Dillon took the Samuel Beckett Bridge across the Liffey and eventually made his way to Pembroke Road. He drove past the Israeli Embassy and, two minutes later, pulled into the secure parking area at the American Chancery.

The Chancery, a three-story circular structure built in 1962, was deemed unfit for purpose in 2012, and plans were made to move. Nothings happened since. An Garda Síochána helps to provide security, and Dillon showed his ID as he pulled into the parking area. He wisely left his pistol in his glove compartment and headed into the building. He passed through three more levels of security before he was in front of a receptionist desk.

The receptionist summoned Eric Bergman. He appeared five minutes later and escorted Dillon back to his office.

"How does it feel to work in the ugliest building in all of Dublin?" Dillon asked.

"That's not even the biggest problem. Just the matter of security, not only in the building but from here all the way to the airport, is a constant headache. They began looking for a new location essentially ten years ago, and nothing has been accomplished as far as I know. If and when they do find a location, construction is estimated to take ten years. I don't think I'll ever see the thing."

"Yeah, well, me either," Dillon said, and they both laughed.

Dillon had been in closets that were larger than Bergman's office. There was barely room for his desk, let alone the two chairs in front of the desk. As Dillon settled into one of the chairs, his knees rubbed against the front of the desk.

Bergman got right to the point. "Okay, so Kevin McBaine flew out of Newark Liberty International Airport three days ago. He landed in Amsterdam and arrived in Dublin two days ago. Check this out," Bergman said and clicked some keys on his computer. An image suddenly appeared from passport control in Terminal Two at Dublin International Airport.

The image on the screen featured a dark-haired man with blue eyes who Dillon would have guessed at mid-to-late forties. He had neatly trimmed hair, was clean-shaven, and basically appeared to be what one might call average looking. The first page of his passport listing name, birth date, passport issue, and expiration date, along with the passport photo, appeared below the image. Dillon did the math on the birthdate. McBaine was forty-six.

"Looks like a nice enough guy," Dillon said. "Can you send me a copy of that?"

"Doing it now. I'll print off a copy for you, too," Bergman said and began tapping keys. "Let me bring up the file on 'this nice enough guy.' You can start to read it while I grab the printed copy from down the hall. You want a coffee while I'm up?"

"You going to have one?" Dillon asked.

"Yeah, here, let me bring this up." He typed a bit more then said, "Okay, take my chair. I'll be back in a couple of minutes." Bergman rose from his desk and squeezed past Dillon. "Read through this. It will give you an idea of what you might be dealing with. I stress the word '*might.*' Nothing is ever officially linked, although when you look at the incidents as a whole, you can't help but think there has to be something, somewhere. Anyway, I'd like to hear your opinion," he said and closed the office door as he left. Dillon settled into the desk chair and began reading the file on Kevin McBaine.

McBaine grew up in Newark, New Jersey. He attended high school in Newark and college at Princeton on a full scholarship. He graduated in the upper third of his class with a double degree in History and English. He attended graduate school at Princeton's Woodrow Wilson School for one semester and dropped out in 1999.

The first murder mentioned occurred in October of 2004. Justin Wilmont, a bank officer in Newark, New Jersey, was shot twice in the head as he climbed out of his car. The murder was committed in the driveway of Wilmont's home at 8:20 in the evening. Two weeks earlier, Wilmont had denied Kevin McBaine's mortgage application. It was rumored McBaine had threatened Wilmont at the time, but it was never proven.

The second murder occurred in Newark in 2011. The victim, Edward Malnory, was the owner of the commercial building where McBaine's software company was located. Malnory's body was discovered in the Passaic River four days after he went missing. He'd been shot in the head, execution-style. Interestingly, McBaine purchased the office building from the Malnory estate six months later.

The third murder was that of an undercover DEA agent, Salvatore Menendez, in 2018. Menendez was executed on a boat anchored in Gateway National Recreation Area on Staten Island. He was involved in the transfer of a thousand kilos of cocaine that disappeared, never to be found. Menendez was shot in the back of the head at close range. McBaine was again listed as a person of interest because Menendez had rented an apartment from him, and it was later determined that the apartment had been bugged.

At the time of the Menendez murder, McBaine had been in Playa del Carmen. It was suspected that he took a private jet from Playa to Allentown, Pennsylvania and back to Playa, but once again, it could never be proven.

Bergman stepped back into the office, placed a coffee mug on the desk, and laid the Xerox copy of McBaine's picture and passport information next to the coffee mug. "What do you think so far?"

"A lot of coincidental activity but obviously nothing you could prosecute," Dillon said and took a sip of coffee. "Oh, God, this is almost as bad as the stuff we have in our break room."

"You get used to it after a while," Bergman said, and they both laughed.

"You know, as I read this stuff, I keep thinking this is just the things that are known. What about all the things he may have done and pulled off that no one is aware of?" Dillon asked. He took another sip of coffee, grimaced, and set the mug down.

"Yeah, and don't forget he has that software company. Nothing is listed in that file, but the DEA agent who had the apartment that was bugged, apparently the bugging was so high tech that they never caught it until after the murder. They routinely went through the apartment checking for bugs and never found anything. The problem was, they were looking for bugging devices, and the technology was way beyond them."

"Yeah, okay, but the private jet supposedly flying from Playa to Allentown and back. How does that work?"

"A couple from Allentown was staying down in Playa at the same time. The woman's mother was assaulted in a purse snatching, and she ended up in intensive care. Nice guy that he is, McBaine had a private jet bring them from Playa up to Allentown. The pilot spends the night in Allentown and flies back to Playa the following afternoon."

"So, did they see McBaine on the flight? I mean, how big was the jet?"

"Not that big, and no, they didn't see him. But he could have been up with the pilot. Oh, and get this, the couple that flew back, the guy was a federal judge, and he insisted McBaine wasn't on the flight. McBaine's computer in Playa was sending emails to staff and clients. More emails than on any of the other ten days McBaine was in Playa. It's suspected he programmed the computer to send the emails. But the activity was sufficient to confirm his presence in Playa."

"What the hell happened with the thousand Kilos of cocaine? It's not like you can put that in your pocket and walk away."

"They found something like a hundred kilos left on the boat when they discovered the body. Every one of the kilos had a tracking device. The nine hundred kilos that were missing, not one of them had a tracking device."

"So inside information?"

"Possibly, or maybe they had a way of scanning each kilo to determine which ones had a tracking device.

It's suspected the nine hundred kilos went over the side and were transported underwater to another boat using an SDV."

"What the hell is that?"

"A swimmer delivery vehicle. It can transport a diver or divers. Navy seals use them. Someone could have made a number of trips throughout the night. Then the next morning, they just drive off in another boat and disappear."

"Sounds pretty far-fetched."

"Yeah, except that McBaine happened to purchase an SDV, get this, for use in his swimming pool. Amazingly, he reported the thing stolen just before the DEA agents murder."

"You said he was suspected in two robberies."

"Yeah, both were offshore bank accounts. Somehow, funds were transferred from one account to another. They finally end up somewhere in Eastern Europe and disappear. The information is mentioned in that file, a lot of technical jargon. But again, McBaine has this software company. He employed Eastern Europeans, among others. The odd thing is, after the second heist, his Eastern European employees, I think there were five, four guys and a woman, all suddenly disappeared. No sign of them. Their apartments were still in their names. No credit card activity. Their vehicles were left in the parking lot. It's like they were airlifted off the planet by Martians or…."

"If this was one incident, I'd be tempted to dismiss it as unfortunate. But all of this, he's gotta be involved in one way or another, and now he's washed up onshore here in Ireland. I don't know what to think."

"Well, you can see why a whole host of folks think he is one bad dude. But then you also have to admit he's damn smart. The bottom line is, whatever he's doing here, odds are it's not going to be good."

"Just a thought out of left field," Dillon said. "You mentioned the Eastern European people, four of them?"

"Five, four guys and a woman."

"What if, instead of being taken by Martians, they disappeared to Ireland?"

"But why? What can they do here that would make any sense? Yeah, there are Eastern Europeans working here, but first of all, they stick out. What would they do here that couldn't be done online somewhere else?"

"Maybe they're here to help take over the drug trade. Maybe they've got nine hundred kilos of cocaine to get started with, and they're going to get the two families, one in Costa del Sol and the other over here in Limerick, going after one another. What if they effectively eliminate all the competition and then simply take over? They use the existing Russian mob here as enforcers and protection. Working from here, they could become the biggest supplier in Europe."

Bergman got a quizzical look on his face. "You think? That's a hell of a lot of 'Ifs.'"

"Like anything that seems to be fluttering around this guy. I don't know," Dillon said.

"Me either, Jack. It sounds more than a little far-fetched."

"Just like the rest of this stuff. So, what about this? They execute two Gardai. Maybe tie it to one of the gangs. Now you've got the authorities coming after them with no holds barred. It could just work."

"Yeah, I suppose."

"Is it any crazier than saying he was up in the copilot's seat while a federal judge and his wife are being flown back to Allentown? By the way, you said the woman's mother was injured in a purse snatching. Could it have been a setup?"

"Maybe. We'll never know. She passed away in intensive care after five or six days, never regained consciousness. As a matter of fact, when the purse was recovered, it still had something like eighteen dollars cash and the woman's credit cards."

"Yeah, and Kevin McBaine comes off as the hero of the hour, and in case you have any doubts, there's a federal judge and his wife who'll back him up," Dillon said and shook his head.

"I thought you should know about the guy, but it still strikes me as a huge leap," Bergman said.

"Yeah, just like all this other stuff," Dillon said and nodded at the computer. "I think that—" His cellphone ringing interrupted him. He pulled it out and checked the screen, Paddy Suel.

"Sorry, gotta take this. Yeah, Paddy."

"They'll have the CCTV tapes at the Fitzgibbon Station in the next thirty minutes or so. I'm heading over there now."

"I'll meet you there," Dillon said and disconnected. "I gotta run, Eric. If you can email this to me, I'll go through it. Right now, these murders are our top priority."

"Just keep this McBaine in the back of your mind," Bergman said.

SEVEN

ergman escorted Dillon out to the main lobby, and Dillon hurried to his car. He took the Samuel Beckett Bridge across the Liffey River and onto Seville Place. From there, the road flowed into North Circular Road, and after a mile or so, he turned onto Fitzgibbon Street. The station was just two blocks ahead. He parked on the street and hurried up the steps and into the station. Thankfully, Sergeant Tierney was at the counter and recognized Dillon as he approached.

"Here to join DI Suel?" Tierney asked.

"Yes, he phoned me not more than fifteen minutes ago."

"I think you made it just in time. They're scheduled to review the footage in about ten minutes. Let me get someone down here to escort you up. Hang one of these around your neck, just to be on the safe side," he said, handing Dillon a lanyard with a visitors ID. He nodded toward an armed security officer sitting in one of the lobby chairs as he picked up the phone.

"It's a shame it's come to this, but can't say as I blame you," Dillon said.

"Dillon?" a uniformed officer called not three minutes later.

Dillon gave a quick wave and hurried out of the visitor's chair. "Hi, ya, Brian Dempsey, we're up on the third floor. Quite the crowd to view the tapes," Dempsey said.

They took the elevator up to the third floor with three other individuals. All five of them walked down the hall and into what appeared to be a large briefing room. The room reminded Dillon of one of his grade school classrooms. A row of bookcases was built in below the windows along the exterior wall. Yellowed window shades that looked fifty years old were drawn, and a large blackboard ran the length of the front wall.

There were maybe twenty or twenty-five white Formica topped desks and chairs, all occupied. Easily a dozen more officers were standing along the back wall. Dillon spotted Suel in the third row of desks. Suel turned at almost the same moment as Dillon spotted him and gave a little wave.

Two large flatscreens were resting on wheeled shelves at the front of the room. Next to the flatscreens was a podium. A man with a ginger-colored crewcut and a nose with a unique 'S' curve along the bridge was in the process of clipping a small microphone to his suit coat lapel. Other than the occasional whisper, the room was quiet. Almost everyone had a notebook and pen.

Dillon stepped over to the bookcase beneath the windows and moved up closer to one of the flatscreens.

He set his pocket notebook on the bookcase just as the ginger-haired man stepped behind the podium.

"Good morning. I'm DI Garret Kinch. I want to thank you all for being here. I only wish it wasn't under these circumstances. Our task is to determine who is responsible and arrest them. I will not only expect but insist that department procedures be followed at all times.

"At approximately 20:40 hours last evening, an anonymous phone call alerted the Fitzgibbon Station to what was suspected to be two shots having been fired in Mountjoy Square. Office Dermot Walsh was immediately deployed, and less than five minutes later, he radioed in the report that two uniformed officers had been discovered." Kinch pressed a button, and the flatscreens came to life with subtitles from the audio recording of the initial call.

"Oh my God. Oh my God."

"Officer seven four one state—"

"There's two, Jesus God. Liam, Kevin. There's blood. No. No. This can't—"

"Officer seven four one state your position and—"

"I'm in the bleeding square. Mountjoy Square. Officers down. Officers down. Officers down."

"So it begins," Kinch said. "Two officers murdered in cold blood. Murdered almost within sight of the station. We're expecting autopsy results later this afternoon. Thus far, we know they were murdered execution style. Shot in the back of their heads while on their knees. Both men were unarmed. Officer Jimmy Murphy was a two-year veteran. Officer Liam McCabe was thirty-seven days out of the academy."

Someone in the front row raised a hand.

"I'd ask that you hold your questions until after we view the CCTV footage. The footage, such as it is, represents the final twenty-eight minutes in the lives of our fellow officers. If there is something that raises a question, please note the digital time displayed in the upper right-hand corner, and we will review once we've seen the footage in its entirety. Thank you. Officer Dempsey, if you would dim the lights, please."

The room darkened, and the CCTV footage began to play. The footage began on Parnell Street. Some images were grainer than others, and at times, it was difficult to spot the two officers. The images were faster than normal time and skipped a second every three seconds. Other than that, nothing really unique appeared. Occasionally, one of the officers nodded or smiled at a passing individual.

At one point, they both seemed to stare, and it appeared McCabe made a comment to Murphy as they passed two attractive women in short skirts. Whatever the comment had been, it brought a smile to Murphy's face.

Once on Hill Street, the foot traffic thinned noticeably, but nothing stood out. They waited for a delivery truck to pass and then crossed over to Grenville Street. An elderly man with a cane and looking worse for the wear passed them, turned, and gave them the finger, not that they noticed. Two individuals, drinking from brown, liter-sized plastic bottles of Bulmers cider, sat next to a trash bin in front of the white-stucco two-story building covered with graffiti. They raised their bottles to the officers and got a friendly wave in return. That last image was twenty-three seconds before the footage ended, and the pair stepped across Grenville Street and into the square. They'd be murdered a minute or two later.

"Questions?" Kinch said a moment later.

"Your man giving them the finger on Hill street. I believe time was twenty-five-seventeen," a voice said from the back of the room.

"Yes, we've already spoken to him. If you're stationed here at Fitzgibbon, you'd undoubtedly recognize him as Arthur Dooley, resident in the council housing estate just at the corner of Hill and Grenville. We've interviewed him, and he's been confirmed as spending the evening in the Latchkey pub on Parnell. Any other questions?"

No one spoke. Kinch exhaled and said, "Very well. Lights, please." The lights came up, and Kinch said, "Obviously, every minute we waste allows the perpetrator to become that much more removed. Start twisting arms and asking questions. Someone out there knows something. For those of you not stationed at Fitzgibbon, please ensure Sergeant Dempsey has your name and contact information, so we can get information to you as quickly as possible. Anything you discover, no matter how slight, please contact us. One more thing before you go. No doubt, if you haven't been, almost all of us will be contacted by the media. No one, I repeat, no one is to correspond with the media. If you do, even if it is anonymous, we will find out who you are, and God help you, officially and unofficially. You will pay the price."

On that charming note, people began to push their chairs back and head out the door. Suel remained seated until the desks around him were vacated then headed over to Dillon.

"What was going on at the American Embassy?"

"Maybe some interesting information, maybe not. There's an American named Kevin McBaine who arrived in Dublin two days ago. He's suspected in three murders and two banking schemes, maybe."

"What do you mean, maybe?"

"Well, that's just it. The suspicion is tenuous at best, and yet, I don't know, maybe. Anyway, Bergman emailed the information to me. I haven't finished reading up on it, and we can both go over it when we get back to the office if we have time."

"What did you think of the CCTV footage?" Suel asked and gave a nod to someone on the far side of the room.

"Two things, first, at least from the footage, it doesn't appear they were followed. I'd like to chat with the two guys drinking the Bulmers, see if they recall anyone following at a distance."

Suel looked up at the clock on the wall. "It might be too early for the likes of those two to be out of bed, but we can check when we leave."

"A word, gentlemen," DI Kinch said, coming up behind them. "DI Suel, is it?"

"Yes, we've met once or twice," Suel said but didn't extend a hand.

"And you're the American?" Kinch asked.

"Yeah, Marshal Jack Dillon," Dillon said and smiled.

"Never ceases to amaze me what the powers that be are thinking," Kinch said and shook his head. "Just wanted to make it clear. Out of respect to DCI McCabe, I've agreed to have the two of you participate in our investigation. But I want to make it perfectly clear. Fitzgibbon Station is in charge of this operation. Any questions, concerns, or suggestions will be directed to us here. I receive the least bit of information you're operating in a manner contrary to that, and I'll have you removed and sanctioned immediately. Do I make myself clear?"

"Wouldn't think of doing otherwise," Suel said and smiled.

"And you?" Kinch said, looking at Dillon.

"Whatever he said," Dillon replied.

Kinch's eyes flared for a brief moment. "See that you remember that. There'll be nothing special about the two of you in this investigation."

"Of course," Dillon said and smiled.

Kinch looked like he was about to say something then maybe thought better of it and made his way out of the room.

"What'd I tell you?" Suel said.

EIGHT

They waited an extra couple of minutes before leaving the room, hoping they wouldn't run into Kinch. They took the elevator down to the main floor and walked into the lobby. Sergeant Tierney wasn't at the front desk. They gave friendly nods to the three officers working the desk and headed out the door.

"What do you say we see if the Bulmers mates have started their daily routine?" Suel said.

"One can only hope," Dillon replied.

They walked around the corner to Mountjoy Square and followed the brick path across the square. Other than footprints in the grass and along the edge of the path, no sign of yesterday's activity existed. The blue and white plastic tape that had been strung along the wrought iron fence and the brick path was gone with the exception of three or four-inch bits tied around the end of the fence. The street was no longer blocked, and the occasional car rolled down the street.

Dillon and Suel crossed over to Grenville Street and walked toward the two-story graffiti-covered structure. Dillon was thinking they were going to strike out when suddenly they saw a brown plastic bottle lifted on the far side of a metal trash bin and heard some laughter.

They walked to the far side of the bin. Suel smiled at the two men, each holding a nearly full plastic liter bottle of Bulmers cider. "Hi, ya's. How's it going?" Suel said.

Both men appeared to be in the same clothes they saw on the CCTV footage. Jeans and one in a light-blue, short-sleeved Dublin Jersey, the other a strappy white t-shirt often referred to as a wife beater.

"I ain't sharing," the man in the strappy white t-shirt said, but then grinned, displaying four missing front teeth.

"Not a problem," Suel said. "Did you hear about the business in the square the other night?"

They both nodded, and the one who said he wouldn't share said, "Sad news. We always waved at the lads. Friendly they were, never a bother. Saw them almost every day."

"Told us to stay safe," the man in the jersey said. "You have to wonder what the dirty old town is coming to."

Suel nodded and said, "Sure as hell the devil's work."

"Hope you catch the bastard. It doesn't serve any of us. The Guards will be extra cautious from now on, as well they should be, and it just runs everything amuck. Sorry to say."

"We watched some footage of you all giving a wave to the lads as they passed by last night. Wondered if you might have seen anyone following a bit behind them?" Suel asked.

The two looked at one another. The man in the strappy t-shirt unscrewed the cap from his bottle, took a swallow, and then screwed the cap back on. He shook his head and said, "No one behind them. Maybe ten minutes later, your wan on the corner went past, pulling her cart with groceries."

"Did you hear any shots?" Dillon asked.

They both shook their heads. The man in the jersey said, "Not that I can recall, but then maybe they weren't that loud. Not a lot of noise at that time of the night." He glanced over at his friend.

"We were out here for maybe, I don't know, another thirty minutes or so after they went by. Didn't hear any sirens until I was back inside."

"Yeah, best we're inside after dark. You never know around here. So, we're in right around 9:00 every night."

The man in the strappy t-shirt said, "I always like to catch the movie. I just settled onto the couch when it started. Vera was on. I catch the show every night at nine."

"Ahh, but you're a right boring plonker," his pal said and took another drink.

Suel took out two business cards and handed one to each man. "You hear anything, feel free to give me a call. Much appreciated, lads. Mind yourselves now."

The man in the Dublin jersey raised his plastic bottle in a toast, and Dillon and Suel headed back across the square.

"What do you think?" Suel asked.

"My first thought is, if they didn't hear the shots, maybe that was because it was a small-caliber weapon."

"What's your second thought?"

"My second thought is Kinch said the initial call that came through to Fitzgibbon Station was anonymous, and it said two shots."

"Which seems to be correct," Suel said.

"Yeah, this is off the mark a bit, but stay with me. The anonymous call says two shots. No one else reports that fact. Your two are out here drinking for another thirty minutes and never hear anything. Does that mean the lads are in the square, maybe held at gunpoint for over thirty minutes? Or does that mean they're maybe shot with a silencer, and the anonymous call came from the shooter himself?"

"That's not a bit off the mark, Dillon. That's way the hell off the mark."

"How about this? Your two lads are out there all day, every day, drinking down a liter of Bulmers, and by that time of night, they're both shit-faced. They heard the shots, but since they're on the piss, it doesn't register. They're home by 9:00, where they immediately fall sound asleep and have little or no recollection of a good portion of the previous day."

"Equally plausible," Dillon said. "There's one more thing I'm thinking of."

"Yeah?"

"We only saw CCTV footage of the lads walking toward the park. We've been told they take the same route at just about the same time every day. In other words, they've set a pattern. What if the shooter is aware of that and he's waiting for them in the park? What if he's been there for an hour or for ten minutes? What if he arrived from a different direction, and he times it so he passes them on the path, nods, says hello, and then has a gun at the back of their heads?"

"Yeah, interesting that. We should maybe get footage coming into the area from all directions and see if anyone turns up."

"You think?" Dillon said.

NINE

Dillon and Suel headed back to the Special Branch office at An Garda Síochána headquarters in Phoenix Park. Dillon collected three tea mugs, four plates, and a candy bar wrapper from his desk and took them into the break room. He dumped the plates and mugs into the sink. He poured the remnants of the coffee pot into his mug. He was joined by Suel.

"Did you get that email from Bergman?"

"I haven't checked yet. Just collected all the trash from my desk and dumped it in the sink." He took a sip of his coffee and followed up with a shudder. "Oh, God, that's awful," he said and dumped the rest of his mug into the sink. He set about making a fresh pot as Suel poured boiling water over his tea bag.

"With any luck, the email is here, and you can forward a copy to me," Suel said. "Let's chat once we've read up on it. Might not be a bad idea to go back through the recent history of the Linnehan family. At one time, they were the group in charge, but that was a few years ago. They got into it with the Doyles and ended up retreating to Costa del Sol."

They chatted on for a few more minutes. Suel tossed his tea bag in the trash, and Dillon filled his coffee mug from the fresh pot and took a sip.

"Is it any better?" Suel asked in response to the face Dillon made.

"Not really," Dillon said, and they headed back to their desks. The lights were still off in DCI McCabe's office. Dillon logged onto his computer, and there was the email from Eric Bergman. He sent a copy to Suel. He did a search of department records and brought up a number of files concerning the Linnehan family and what developed into a war with the Doyles out of Limerick.

The files listed a series of tit-for-tat killings starting back in 2010 and continuing for a number of years. The killings finally came to a tenuous halt in 2017 with the departure of Conor Linnehan and his two sons, Cillian and Padraig. Dillon glanced over at Suel, now in an animated phone conversation with someone.

Interestingly, DCI McCabe as a Detective Inspector, had been involved in a series of arrests of members of the Linnehan organization. McCabe was promoted to Detective Chief Inspector and placed in charge of Special Branch in 2016. No doubt due, in no small part, to his involvement in minimizing the control the Linnehan family was able to exert on a national level. Dillon wondered if that could have been a motive in the murder of McCabe's nephew, Liam?

A good two hours later, Suel walked out of the break room and pulled a chair alongside Dillon's desk. "Anything new?" he asked and took a sip of his tea.

"Yes and no. Or should I say more of the same. A number of interesting thoughts but nothing concrete. One thing that stood out. DCI McCabe was involved in a number of arrests and more than a couple of violent interactions with members of the Linnehan organization. Could that be one of, if not *the* reason, he was promoted to chief inspector and head of Special Branch?"

"Oh, yeah, without a doubt."

"Which leads me to yet another speculative theory."

"Oh, I can't wait."

"There are a number of reasons Conor Linnehan and his two sons, Padraig and Cillian, left for Costa del Sol. Obviously, the ongoing battle with the Doyle family. But also because of the nonstop pressure DCI McCabe put on them."

"That shouldn't come as a surprise. They were operating out of Dublin. McCabe was a cop here in Dublin. That's what he's supposed to do. He—"

"I get that, Paddy. I'm not questioning it. But I'm wondering if, because of McCabe's pressure, is it possible that, rather than two officers setting a convenient pattern, maybe Liam McCabe was specifically targeted because of his uncle's success in essentially chasing the Linnehans out of Dublin and the country?"

Suel looked like he was about to answer and stopped. He seemed to think for a long moment before he said, "We need to view the CCTV footage in all directions of Mountjoy Square. Another thought comes to mind, the so-called anonymous phone call about two shots being fired. Did they track the number? Or did they declare the call anonymous simply because the caller hung up?"

"I'll call Kinch on that question. Can you put in the requests on the CCTV footage?"

"Already done," Suel said and smiled.

Dillon's desk phone suddenly rang. He picked it up on the second ring. "Marshal Dillon."

"Yes, Marshal, this is Hugh Healy. We've finished the autopsies."

Dillon glanced at the time on his computer screen. It was almost 4:00. He raised his index finger, indicating Suel should hang on for a moment. "What did you learn?" he asked.

"Pretty much a confirmation of what we suspected. Death was caused by a small-caliber round. Both rounds appear to have been from the same weapon, but without shell casings, I can't confirm that. Death was instantaneous. Time of death was between 8:30 and 9:00pm. No indication of any physical assault prior to or after death."

"That pretty much confirms what we thought," Dillon said.

"There is something about the rounds that rings a bell. I'll be going through our records here. I've contacted DI Kinch and given him the same information and—"

"What did he have to say?"

"Nothing, really. Told me to send a copy of the report to him. I can email one to you if you'd like."

"Please do. Would you be able to provide a printed copy for me, too?"

"Print one? Yes, certainly, that won't be a problem."

"Good, I'll be over within the hour to pick it up. Anything else, Hugh?"

At the sound of Healy's name, Suel rolled his eyes.

"No sir, I wish I had more for you. I'll be searching our files looking for a similar round. I just can't seem to recall when it was exactly."

"Thanks for the call, Hugh. I'll see you in an hour," Dillon said and hung up.

"What did your boyfriend have to say?"

"What he had to say was it looks like they were killed with the same small-caliber weapon. Death between 8:30 and 9:00 last night. He can't be sure, but the rounds seemed similar to something he's seen, so he'll be going through their files trying to find it. No indication of any physical altercation. That makes me think whoever did this had them at gunpoint, got them down on their knees, and fired. It probably took longer to just say that than it did to commit the act."

Suel made an audible exhale and said, "Son of a bitch."

TEN

Dillon was in his car twenty minutes later, driving over to the Dublin City Morgue at the corner of Griffith Avenue and Drumcondra Road in Whitehall, Dublin. With the traffic at this time of day, it took him a good twenty minutes. He ended up parking on tree-lined Drumcondra Road just within sight of the morgue and walking for a couple of minutes to get to the building. Fortunately, it was a pleasant afternoon.

He entered the building and stepped up to the receptionist window. He recognized the woman behind the glass. She smiled as he approached and glanced at the Gardai ID hanging from Dillon's neck. "How are you, Marshal? Is it the two officers you're here to view? So very sad."

"Hi, Anne. Actually, I'm here to see Hugh Healy. He's expecting me."

"Of course," she said and nodded knowingly. "Have a seat while I phone him."

Dillon hadn't been seated for sixty seconds when Healy burst through the door. "Thank you for coming, Marshal. If you'll follow me," he said as he shook hands with Dillon. They walked down a long hallway with framed paintings of Dublin scenes hanging maybe every twenty feet. Dillon had been here a number of times and didn't pay any attention to the paintings. Just as they were about to step into the examination room, Healy took a right turn and opened the third door.

His office could be described as small, but it was at least twice as large as Eric Bergman's at the American Embassy. "Please have a seat, Marshal," Healy said as he settled in behind his desk.

As Dillon sat down, Healy handed him a manila envelope. "I'll email a copy to you. That's the printed copy you asked for. I've attached an image of the round to each report. Let me just bring up what I think I've found here," he said and began running his fingers over the keyboard. Three images suddenly appeared on the screen.

"This image on the left was recovered from Officer McCabe, the middle image from Officer Murphy. This image on the right was recovered from a gentleman by the name of Leonid Poletov in December of 2019. If you look just here in this lower area, you can see this small line. It's from a twenty-two short round, fired execution-style similar to our two instances last night, a six-to-nine-inch distance from the back of the head."

"I'm blanking on where this one occurred. You said the name was Poletov?" Dillon said.

"Yes, Leonid Poletov. A Russian gentleman. The scene was in Cabra, actually behind the Cabra House pub. Mr. Poletov had what might be described as a bit of a checkered career. I suspect our two officers may have been killed using the same weapon, but I can't be sure without the spent shell casings, unfortunately."

Dillon pulled out his pocket notebook and began to write.

"I've added that information to your copy of the report," Healy said.

"Did you give it to Kinch as well?"

"That was my intention. Unfortunately, he, umm, didn't seem to be interested and said that it had no bearing on the current case. The slugs from today's autopsies have been sent to forensics. They'll compare them, and hopefully, they'll be able to get Kinch's attention."

Dillon bit his tongue so as not to respond.

"In the Poletov murder, the shell casing…" Healy clicked the keyboard, and a new image appeared of a brass shell casing. "This casing was found at the scene. A twenty-two short. Note this mark at the end of the shell and…" He clicked a key, and the image of three rounds reappeared. "Note the hint of this indentation on all three rounds."

"So, you're telling me whoever murdered the officers last night was using the same weapon as this murder in 2019?"

Healy shook his head. "No, sir, I'm merely suggesting it's possible, but without the shell casings to compare, we'll never have confirmation."

"And they didn't find any shell casings?" Dillon asked.

"Unfortunately, not," Healy replied. "They could have been fired from a revolver, but based on the similarities of the three rounds, it seems more than likely all three rounds were fired from the same automatic pistol. Apparently, whoever the shooter was last night took the time to recover the shell casings."

"But he didn't do that behind the Cabra House pub?"

"Correct, of course, maybe it's not the same weapon. Or maybe it is the same weapon but a different shooter. Or maybe he learned his lesson and this time searched until he found the shell casings. Whatever the reason, they weren't recovered in Mountjoy Square."

"Not for lack of trying," Dillon said. "How soon were you there?"

"Our team? Oh, once we received word that the victims were An Garda Síochána, it couldn't have been more than fifteen or twenty minutes, and we were on site. Our technical van is all loaded and ready to go. If we received a call now, we would be able to depart within four or five minutes."

"That fast?"

Healy nodded. "In this business, the sooner, the better. In fact, when we arrived last night, the streets hadn't even been blocked off. There couldn't have been more than a dozen officers, if that, in the square. The first thing we did was set up the tent to protect the scene. It's not unheard of that some well-meaning individual would move the body, not realizing they're actually tampering with the scene. Especially in a situation like last night, the murder of two fellow officers, naturally, there's going to be a lot of emotion. But then, I guess I don't have to tell you."

"No, you don't. Okay, thanks. I'll get out of your hair, Hugh. If you would be so kind as to email me a copy of this report along with the images, I'll pass them on to DI Suel. And difficult as it will be, I'm sure DCI McCabe will want to see the report as well."

"Are you going back to the office yet tonight?"

"I am."

"I'll send it off in just a moment. It will be waiting for you when you arrive."

"Thanks for your help and your work. Much appreciated." Healy seemed to beam for a moment, and Dillon thought it was probably the rare time when the poor guy heard a positive response from others. "You hang in there," Dillon said and extended his hand. They shook hands, and Dillon said he could find his way out.

Healy nodded and sat down at his desk.

Dillon waved goodbye to Anne at the receptionist desk and headed out the door. By the time he got back to his car, he had decided a side trip would only take ten minutes. He took a right turn onto Drumcondra Road and took the next right onto Home Farm Road. He drove up Ballymun to the shops near his home and purchased a bottle of white wine from the cooler. He pulled up onto the footpath in front of his home and walked over to Tara's with the bottle of wine.

Her car was backed into the drive, and he rang the doorbell. He waited for what felt like an awfully long moment and rang the doorbell a second time. When there was no answer, he placed the paper bag with the bottle against her door and dropped a business card into the bag.

Lucifer met him at the door, and Dillon let him out into the front garden to do his business. Amazingly, nothing was scattered around the kitchen or the sitting room. He waited ten minutes then bribed the dog back in the house with a biscuit. He turned his car around and drove up the lane. He noticed the paper bag with the wine bottle was no longer leaning against Tara's front door. He drove back to the station and headed up to the Special Branch office.

At this hour, there were only four officers in the office, one of whom was Suel talking on the phone. He gave a nod as Dillon passed his desk. "Okay, thanks. Much appreciated. I'll be looking for it," Suel said and hung up.

"Good news?"

"We'll know in a couple of hours," Suel said. "You have plans for the evening?"

"I didn't a minute ago, other than reviewing the autopsy report."

"You sound about as exciting as me," Suel said.

"Why? What do you have in mind?"

"Three or four hours' worth of CCTV footage taken before and after the murders," Suel said.

"Okay, I'm willing to sit here and go through them."

"Perfect. I'm thinking of grabbing some takeout from the Aberdeen. You up for that?"

"I am. While you run and get that, I'll send you the autopsy report."

"You learn anything?"

"Yes and no. At no surprise, it would appear the same weapon was used on both our victims. Healy compared the slugs to a shooting that occurred behind the Cabra House pub back in December of 2019."

Suel seemed to think for a moment and said, "Was that some Russian? If I recall, the Times referred to it as the Christmas Eve Murder or something along those lines. I don't think the body was discovered until the following day."

"Okay, I don't know that, but I'll take your word for it," Dillon said. "Here's the interesting thing, Healy had images, and they've sent the slugs to forensics. He thinks there's a good chance the slugs match the one recovered from that victim back in 2019. Based on what he showed me, I'm inclined to agree."

"That could be interesting and might prove to be a lead, maybe the only one."

"Yeah, here's the other half of the story. He gave the same information to Kinch, and Kinch told him he wasn't interested and it didn't have any bearing on the case."

"What?"

ELEVEN

In between bites of fish and chips, Dillon and Suel reviewed the autopsy reports on Officers McCabe and Murphy. They compared the reports and the photographs of the two .22 short rounds to the case of the Russian murdered behind the Cabra House pub. There were definite similarities, and yet without the shell casings, they couldn't be 100% sure.

It was approaching 9:00 when Suel asked, "Do you feel like spending the next hour reviewing the CCTV footage? Even if we don't finish, we could get a good jump on it."

"Let's get started on it. I'm going to get another coffee. You want a tea?"

"Yeah, and I'll make it. You never seem to do it right," Suel said.

Five minutes later, they were both sitting at Suel's desk watching the CCTV footage. The images weren't that great, and the closer they got to the 20:30 mark, the images became darker on the footage. Still, it was better than nothing. They'd been watching for over an hour, and at the moment, they were both nibbling Yorkie chocolate bars. They were reviewing footage from Charles Street Great. The street was parallel and roughly one block east from Fitzgibbon Street. The digital time read 20:13. The images they were watching were from a CCTV camera just across the street from number 56 Charles Street Great. Number 56 was a three-story redbrick council housing structure. The camera was centered on a ground floor unit covered with spray-painted graffiti.

Panels of black painted chipboard hung over the door and the front window of the unit. The chipboard signified the unit was not only unoccupied but also deemed, for whatever reason, unfit for habitation. The individual suddenly crawling out of the lower portion of the chipboard covering the door caught their immediate attention.

"What the bloody hell?" Suel said and tapped a key on his keyboard, stopping the footage. "Did you get a look at this wanker?"

"The unit is supposed to be unoccupied," Dillon said.

"Well, apparently no one bothered to tell this worthless feck," Suel said and enlarged the image until it was completely unrecognizable. "Bloody hell," he growled as he returned the image to its normal size. He slowed the image speed down to once every fifteen seconds as the individual began to move toward Mountjoy Square. His blurry image appeared in two more cameras before he entered Mountjoy Square and disappeared. The digital time read 20:16.

Suel reversed the images until the individual was back on screen. "This camera is just on the corner, mounted on the side of Dorset College. He's about to cross Mountjoy Square East and enter the square. I think I know this lad, damn it. Give me a moment, and I'll come up with his name. Who the hell is he?"

"Run it forward and see if he comes back out of the Square," Dillon said.

At 20:42, the same individual came back out of the Square. He glanced over his shoulder twice and appeared to be moving substantially faster than his entrance a half-hour earlier. He was holding what appeared to be a cellphone phone up to his ear.

"You know what he's probably doing? He's phoning in the anonymous tip that he heard two gunshots. He's on the corner next to Dorset College again. That's where they identified the call originating from," Dillon said.

"God save us, but I know who in the hell this plonker is. What the feck is the bastard's name?"

"See if he heads back to that empty unit," Dillon said, and they proceeded to watch him over the next 90 seconds as he ran past the empty unit and disappeared from sight.

Suel was writing down the time and making a note on the street address. "I'll send in a request for more CCTV footage. Your man is associated, or at least was, with the Linnehans. I'm sure of it, but that was three or four years ago. Still, that's something."

"We should alert Kinch," Dillon said.

"I'll call him now," Suel said and clicked a number of keys until he had Kinch's contact information in front of him. He dialed the number, listened for no more than ten seconds, and shook his head. "Yes, DI Kinch, this is DI Suel, Special Branch. Time is 10:40 p.m. Marshal Dillon and I have been reviewing CCTV footage on Charles Street Great…" Suel went on to give a brief description of what they'd seen, the time on the footage, and left his cellphone number.

"I'm thinking we should go down there," Dillon said. "If for no other reason than to secure that unit in council housing. Maybe we can find something."

Suel nodded and said, "If you made that phone call wouldn't you want to get rid of that phone as fast as possible?"

"Yeah," Dillon said. "The smart move would be to take it apart and scatter the remains. Toss the battery someplace, maybe cut the sim card apart and scatter that to the four winds. That may be why they couldn't track it."

Suel nodded. "I'm going to head down there— no need for both of us to go. Drag your bum home and get some sleep. Let's touch base by phone tomorrow morning. Hopefully, I'll have the name of this plonker by then, and we can have a little chat with him. Call me at 6:30 tomorrow morning. You'll serve as my alarm."

"You sure you don't want me to go with you?"

Suel nodded. "I'm going to drop this in Kinch's lap. We start proceeding on this tonight, he's liable to lock us out of any future updates. They're bound to have a team working the night shift on this. I'll bring them up to date. Just remember to call me in the morning, half-past-six."

"All right. See if you can come up with that name."

"One can only hope," Suel said.

Tara's car was still backed into her drive, and the lights were off, which was a good sign. This way, Dillon didn't feel the urge to ring her doorbell and attempt to smooth things over. He could just go into his place and climb into bed with Lucifer.

He pulled into his drive, locked the car, and stepped into the house. He got the coffee ready for the morning and quietly climbed the stairs. Lucifer was sound asleep on the bed. Dillon quietly undressed, set the alarm for 6:00, and climbed into bed.

TWELVE

Lucifer woke him just a little after 5:00, anxious to go outside. Dillon was more than familiar with the unpleasant results of not letting the dog out under these circumstances. He groaned as he climbed out of bed, grabbed a biscuit on his way to Lucifer waiting at the front door, and tossed the biscuit out the door. He shaved, showered, dressed, let Lucifer back in, and made a breakfast of scrambled eggs and ham.

He was online for forty-five minutes before he phoned Suel then listened to him groan and clear his throat as he answered the phone.

"It can't be that time yet," Suel said, sounding only half-awake.

"Rise and shine sweetheart. We need to get down to Charles Street Great and that empty unit."

"They've got someone minding the place. I'll meet you there in thirty minutes," Suel said and hung up.

Dillon headed down to the empty unit. Sure enough, there was an officer leaning against the wall as he parked across the street.

"You're here to relieve me?" the officer asked, sounding hopeful.

"Afraid not. How long have you been here?"

The officer looked at his watch and said, "Going on nine hours, and I was on duty three hours before they called me here."

Dillon shook his head and clicked the fob on his keyring, unlocking his car doors. "I'll watch this place for a bit. Climb into the back of my car and grab some shut-eye before you fall asleep on your feet."

"You sure?"

"Yeah, very. You didn't hear anything from DI Kinch or his team?"

"You gotta be kidding me," the officer said and hurried to Dillon's car. He gave a wave as he opened the rear door and disappeared from view.

Dillon sent a text message to Suel, telling him to get someone to relieve the officer standing guard. He looked at the chipboard panel covering the front door. It appeared to have been one piece at the time it was installed, but someone had recently cut the bottom two feet from the upper section.

Dillon wedged his finger between the bottom portion of the panel and the doorframe and swung it open. The far side had been attached with a cheap hinge to the far side of the doorframe. Rather than step inside, he pushed the panel closed. He glanced up the street to the corner and Mountjoy Square just across the street. He recalled that the corner building had been labeled Dorset

College on a gray window shade that had been pulled down over the front window.

He had no idea if that was official, a joke, or perhaps a name from a hundred years ago. He could see the CCTV camera mounted on the side of the building that had recorded the individual entering and leaving the square. He glanced down Charles Street Great in the opposite direction, looking for a trash bin or even a sewer that might serve as a logical place to discard a cellphone. Unfortunately, nothing seemed to fit the bill.

Suel appeared around the corner maybe forty-five minutes later. He was carrying two cups of coffee. He raised one of the cups almost as a toast when he crossed the street.

"Where in God's name is the officer who's supposed to be standing guard?" Suel asked as he handed a coffee to Dillon.

"He's asleep in the back of my car," Dillon said and indicated his car with a nod of his head. "He's been out here since you contacted Fitzgibbon Station last night, and he'd already been on duty three or four hours. You hear anything from Kinch?"

Suel shook his head. "Supposedly up to his proverbial eyeballs micromanaging everything. I left another message for him with Declan Tierney at the front desk. He'll see Kinch gets it."

"Take a look at this," Dillon said and pushed open the lower panel on the door.

"Bloody hell, are you joking? Did you go in?"

Dillon shook his head. "No, I didn't want to risk contaminating the site. Although that said, if the word is already out about this, probably everything from parties to homeless housing has been going on in there."

"Did you contact the Fitzgibbon team about it?"

"No, why don't you give your man Tierney a call. Just to play it safe, so it doesn't seem like we're hiding information from them. I've got the sense your man Kinch would welcome the opportunity to lock us out of the investigation."

Suel nodded and pulled out his phone. Dillon took a sip of his coffee and quickly came to the conclusion it was much better than what he made in the Special Branch break room. Suel had just begun talking to Sergeant Tierney over at the front desk at Fitzgibbon Station when Dillon's phone rang. For the briefest of moments, he had hoped it might be Tara. He glanced at the screen and saw Hugh Healy's name.

"Marshal Dillon," he answered.

"Hi, Marshal. A bit of good news. After we talked about the shell casings last night, I got to thinking. You asked me how long it was before we had the tent set up in Mountjoy Square."

"Yeah, if I recall, you told me fifteen or twenty minutes."

"Yes, that was exactly what I said, and that got me to thinking last night, so I went back to Mountjoy Square after you left, and guess what I discovered?"

"You're kidding me. You found them?"

"Yes, sir. In an effort to protect the bodies, we erected the tent, and the frame of the tent hid both shell casings from everyone."

"Did you notify Kinch?"

"Not exactly. I left him a message and then notified forensics. They arrived almost immediately. I showed them where the shell casings were. They'd been stepped on and ground into the soil. They were actually covered by a boot print. I'd been using a flashlight, and I just happened to pick up the slightest reflection off a casing. I thought it was a wrapper of some sort at first. Anyway, forensics has them, and they're running tests as we speak. Hopefully, they'll have results later today."

"Did you happen to mention your suspicions about the Christmas murder behind the Cabra Club?"

"I did, and I sent them the images I took of the rounds. With any luck, they'll find a match."

"Hugh, that's damn good work. Thanks for going the extra mile on this. God forbid they'll be able to lift a partial print off of one of those casings."

"If I hear anything, I'll let you know," he said.

"Yeah, please do. Thanks for the call," Dillon said and hung up.

"You two seem to be getting close. What did he want, a date for tonight?"

"You know, Paddy, I think it's time for you to back off. The guy just went the extra mile and found something everyone missed. Despite the fact that everyone treats him like shit, he works his ass off. He found the shell casings."

"What do you mean, he found the shell casings?"

Dillon went on to tell him the story, finishing with, "So after everyone is sure they've searched the area, the man you refer to as a puff comes up with a thought and goes on his personal time, finds the shell casings, and calls forensics."

"He should have called Kinch."

"Yeah, as a matter of fact, he did that, and he's still waiting for a response. He also phoned forensics, and they got the casings last night. With any luck, they'll have results later today. The guy's good, Paddy, and if you keep treating him like shit, the force is going to lose him."

THIRTEEN

Dillon and Suel were seated in DCI McCabe's office two hours later, bringing him up to date. They hadn't really spoken to one another since Dillon told Suel about Hugh Healy finding the shell casings.

McCabe asked them the occasional question, but Dillon had the distinct impression he seemed to be focused elsewhere. No doubt on the murder of his nephew, Liam.

"So, you've seen footage of this individual entering and leaving the square. Did you recognize him? Did you inform the Fitzgibbon team?" McCabe asked.

"It took a while, but I did recall his name, Tully Moran," Suel said.

Since it was the first Dillon had heard the name, he shot a surprised look at Suel.

"I've informed the powers that be at Fitzgibbon Station. I sent a message along with the CCTV tape to DI Kinch."

"Good, very good. What was Kinch's response?"

"I haven't heard from him, but to be honest, I'm sure he's up to his proverbial eyeballs on a host of issues. He's got the information. I'm sure he'll deal with it and—"

McCabe shook his head and said, "Don't assume that. It would be just like him to set the information to the back of the line because he hadn't come up with it himself. Make sure they're looking for this individual."

"There's a BOLO out on him, sir," Suel said. "Everyone is looking for him."

McCabe nodded and seemed to think for a moment before he said, "Anything else?"

"That's about it for the moment, but things are changing by the minute," Suel said.

McCabe nodded. "The memorial service will be in seventy-two hours. I'd like you both to attend. I'm going to be in and out for the next few days, dealing with family."

"How's your brother and his wife doing?" Dillon asked.

"Not well. We can't imagine, but then how could we? Christ on a cross," McCabe said and shook his head.

"We'd better be getting back to work, sir. Any updates, we'll keep you informed," Suel said, rising out of his chair.

"Thank you, lads," McCabe said and stared off into space.

Once outside McCabe's office, Dillon asked, "So when did you remember your man's name?"

"It was thanks to you, actually. When you were on your high horse reading me the riot act about Healy, and before you say anything, okay, you were right… for a change. Anyway, you had me thinking you're a right moron, and that's when it flashed in my mind, moron, Tully Moran. See?"

"You gotta be kidding me?"

"Dillon, who the hell cares as long as we get the bastard?"

"Good point."

"By the way, come on over to my desk. I want to show you something." When they got to his desk, Suel said, "Check this out," as he brought up his computer screen. The screen came to life displaying the mugshot of a blonde-haired individual. The name Tully Moran was below the image, along with height and weight figures and a blood type. The image was dated December 2019.

"So, this is our man?" Dillon said, thinking the individual appeared to be the same person they'd watched coming and going on the CCTV footage.

"Yeah, notice anything?" Suel asked.

"He looks just like the guy we saw on CCTV footage. Well, and what I thought might have been a mole beneath his right eye is obviously a teardrop tattoo."

"Yeah, the other thing is that was a relatively new tattoo when this shot was taken. He'd been arrested for the Christmas Eve murder. The bastard has a brand-new tattoo signifying he'd murdered someone, and he still gets off. It turns out he had a solid alibi."

"Which was?"

"He was waiting in the Mater Hospital for his son to be born. He was on their security cameras from 7:00 in the evening until 9:00 the following morning. A good part of the time, he was sound asleep in a maternity waiting room chair."

"Waiting for the baby to be born?"

"Oh, it gets even better than that. After the child was born, it was determined through DNA that he wasn't the father. Probably good news for the mother and child, at least now they might have half a chance."

"And he's on camera?"

"Believe me. I've lost count of the people who've gone over the tape looking for a way, any way, to nail the bastard, but it's not happening."

"You have the woman's name?"

"It would be in the file. But it's been confirmed. He spent the entire evening and all through the night in the maternity waiting room. Then get this, once the baby was born, she didn't want to see him."

"Probably a good move. I'd still like to do some checking."

Suel handed a six-inch file to Dillon and said, "Her name is somewhere in here."

FOURTEEN

Ten minutes after opening the file, Dillon found her name, Shauna McNeese, along with a photo and a Dublin address beneath her name. She lived on Cleggan Avenue in Drumfinn, a section of Dublin. She was a reasonably attractive woman in a white blouse with a small gold crucifix dangling just above an ample cleavage. He picked up the file and set it back on Suel's desk. He wasn't sure where Suel was, so he left a short note and headed out the door.

The address was about an eighteen-minute drive from the Special Branch office, and that included waiting for two traffic lights. Cleggan Avenue was made up of a series of smaller, two-story attached houses. Most of them were gray or beige. The address listed to Shauna McNeese was pink. The only pink house on the road.

A yellow plastic car large enough to accommodate a small child was missing a front wheel and leaned at an odd angle just inside the front of the garden area. There wasn't any grass, just a patch of asphalt that looked like it could use some serious repair work. A faded red Hyundai with a cracked windshield and a dented passenger door was parked on the asphalt. A large stain from dripping oil was beneath the car.

What appeared to be a bedsheet was draped over the front window. The mail slot in the front door had three envelopes sticking out of it. One of the envelopes had a red stamp across the front that read, 'Past Due.'

Dillon looked at the hole in the doorframe where the doorbell used to be and knocked on the door. Maybe a half-minute later, the door opened, and a dark-haired woman with blue eyes opened the door. She looked similar to the photo he'd seen in the file, although her hair was shorter, and she'd clearly added some weight. Still, she appeared to be the same woman. Today she was in jeans and a t-shirt with what looked like a jelly stain on the front.

"Yeah," she said in a tone that would make one hope you were at the wrong house.

"Shauna McNeese?" Dillon asked.

"Yeah, and I can't help you," she said and began to close the door.

Dillon stopped the door from closing with his hand and pulled out his ID. "Dillon, An Garda Síochána," he said, holding out the ID just long enough for her to take note of An Garda Síochána in bold black letters before he tucked it back into his pocket.

"Oh, for the love of… Who is it now? I suppose the knackers about my TV license. They're actually sending the Garda to collect money. Sorry, I don't have any. You can tell them they'll just have to get in line behind everyone else."

A dark-haired little boy in a disposable diaper suddenly ran into the entry and wrapped his arms around one of her legs. What looked like chocolate or maybe Nutella circled his lips and was splattered across his stomach. As he wrapped his arms around her leg, he smeared the concoction on her jeans.

"Oh, no, I'm not here to try and collect money or anything like that. My name is Jack Dillon. I came across your name in one of our files from back in 2019, and I had a question is all."

"No one sent you to drain my bank account or collect my credit card?"

"No, nothing like that. First of all, if anyone shows up and says they're here to drain your bank account or collect your credit card, call us because they're lying. We don't do that sort of thing."

She seemed to relax, maybe. "So, what are you here for. An eviction, is it?"

"No, nothing like that. I just had a question. As I said, we're looking over a file from 2019. I believe you were at the National Maternity Hospital delivering maybe…" Dillon pointed to the little guy now apparently surgically attached to her left leg.

"Yes, Rowen. Born December 26th."

"Yeah, at the time, there was a gentleman in the waiting room. Blonde, he was—"

"He was and is a major pain in the bum. He's not Rowen's father. Believe me, I would never let him—"

"But he did spend the evening in the waiting room."

"Of course he did. His no account brother gave me a hundred euros so he could sleep there."

"You were paid a hundred euros so Tully Moran could sleep in the waiting room?"

She rolled her eyes and said, "Honest to God. Do you lot ever talk to one another? That wasn't Tully in the waiting room. Tully was the knacker what paid me. That was his twin brother, Fergus. Drunker than the proverbial skunk, I might add. I'm going there to deliver a baby, and your man is so shite-faced I've to help him into the building because he could barely walk. He passed out in the bleedin' waiting room. Tully told me Fergus needed a place to sleep that night. Thought it would be funny when Fergus woke up and found himself in the maternity wing. He paid me a hundred euros. So, what did I care? Plus, they took a blood sample from him, told me he wasn't the father. Hello? I sure as hell already knew that."

"You're telling me that was Fergus on the camera."

"The camera?" she asked.

"Yeah, a security camera in the waiting room. They've film of him sleeping through the night."

"Who in God's name would want to watch Fergus sleeping? That knacker was snoring his bleeding arse off."

"You told this to the Gardai?"

"Yeah, they came around. Oh, must have been a week or two after Rowen was born. Said they'd seen film of Moran sleeping in the waiting room and wanted to know if he was the father. I told them no, he wasn't, and that was the end of it."

"When they asked you, did they mention Tully Moran?"

"No, were you listening? I just told you, they asked, was Moran in the waiting room. I told them yeah, he was. Never asked me if it was Tully or Fergus. They're the Gardai. Don't they fecking know?"

"Good point," Dillon said. "You wouldn't happen to know where I might get in touch with Tully or Fergus, would you?"

"Haven't seen Tully in at least a year, and I consider myself lucky. If you want to see Fergus, you could catch him over at Glasnevin Cemetery. He's been residing there for the better part of a year. Drunk driving and a bridge abutment, not a good mix. Is that it? It's almost time for my show to come on."

"Oh, yeah, of course. Don't let me hold you up. Thanks for your time and for setting me straight."

"Jaysus," she groaned and closed the door.

FIFTEEN

Dillon had just climbed back into his car and hadn't driven more than a hundred feet when his phone rang. He pulled to the curb, hoping it might be Tara. He checked the screen and answered, "Hi Paddy, I was just about to head back to the office."

"Don't bother. I'm heading over to Charles Street Great. Kinch finally received permission to search that unit. In fact, they're in there now. I want to see what they find."

"I'll see you over there," Dillon said, and Suel hung up.

It was a twenty-minute drive. He parked across the street from the square and walked around the corner. The chipboard panels that had covered the door and the front window had been removed. The door and the front window were open, no doubt for light since the power was probably turned off.

Dillon hung his ID around his neck. He raised it as he walked past the officer standing outside for security. Three guys were standing out in front of the corner unit, drinking cans of beer. Two women were up on the second floor leaning over the railing in an attempt to see what was going on.

As he stepped inside, he was hit with a dreadful odor. Clearly, the toilet facilities hadn't been functioning. The only furniture in the front room was the remnant of a green faux-leather two-seater couch. The seat cushions were missing, and both back cushions featured slits running across from the upper left to the lower right corners.

Someone had apparently thrown up in the opposite corner of the room. The kitchen area, such as it was, looked like a bomb had gone off, literally. All but one of the six cabinet doors had been pulled off their hinges. Three of the doors were completely missing. Two empty white Styrofoam food trays rested in what was the kitchen sink. The chrome faucet was broken off. The bathroom, opposite the kitchen area, was completely destroyed. Broken chunks of porcelain on the floor were all that was left of the sink and toilet. Dillon stepped into the rear room, at one time a bedroom. A full-length mirror was still attached to the ceiling.

Suel was in there talking to two uniformed officers. The officers wore face masks and latex gloves. Dillon figured they were probably more for protection against the germs and God only knew what else festered in the place. At least he found the three missing kitchen cabinet doors or what was left of them. They'd been set on fire, he guessed in an effort to provide some heat. Now, they were mostly a pile of ash with the exception of the three metal handles.

Suel waved him over and then pointed to a bra and what looked like a leather skirt crumpled up in the corner. "You weren't down here last night, were you Dillon?"

"No, and I won't be until my shot record gets up to date," he said. "You guys find anything?"

All three of them shook their heads. "You're looking at pretty much exactly what we found. There was an empty bottle in the front room. It's on the way to be fingerprinted," Suel said.

"I can only imagine," Dillon said.

"Not what you think. An empty bottle of Redbreast, Small Batch."

"I don't think I've ever heard of it," Dillon said.

"Same with us. Well, I mean, I've heard of it but never tasted it. A bottle goes for about three hundred and twenty euros. If you can ever find one," one of the uniformed officers said.

"What in the hell was Moran doing in here?" Dillon asked.

"Maybe he just stopped to use the toilet," Suel said, which brought another set of laughs.

"I would guess just cooling his heels. The unit's been empty for at least a year," one of the uniformed officers said.

"More like two years, Mack," the other officer said. "Bunch of gobshites broke in here, partied every night for a couple of weeks. The station was getting calls twenty-four seven. Finally, the residents had enough, and they're the ones who destroyed the kitchen and the toilet and sink. Just to keep the eejit party animals away."

"I can't say as I blame them," Suel said.

"Anything else to see?" Dillon asked.

"No, I recommend we step into the fresh air," Suel said, and they quickly exited the unit.

The three guys were still at the far end of the building drinking beer, but they didn't appear to be the least bit interested in whatever the Gardai were involved in.

"Where'd you park?" Suel asked.

"Across the street from the square," Dillon replied.

"See you, lads. Keep us posted on the fingerprints," Suel said.

"Stay safe," Dillon said as he and Suel headed toward the park.

"You learn anything from your woman?"

"Are you referring to the always charming Shauna McNeese?"

"She didn't look all that bad in the picture."

"Pictures can be deceiving, Paddy. Besides, it was two years ago. Yeah, now that you mention it, I learned quite a bit from her."

"Oh?" Suel said and shot a look at Dillon.

"Yeah. For starters, that isn't Tully Moran sleeping in the waiting room at the National Maternity Hospital."

"What do you mean, it's not him? She told the interviewing officer it was Tully Moran. She identified the picture of him."

"That's right. She did, sort of. But what the dumb shit asked her is, 'Was that Moran?' and—"

"And she said it was. I've read the transcript."

"So have I. Listen to me. They asked was it Moran but never mentioned his first name, Paddy. Just the surname. And your man in the photo and on the tape sleeping through the night isn't Tully Moran. It's his twin brother, Fergus Moran."

"What?"

"Yeah and get this. Tully Moran paid her a hundred euros to bring his drunken twin brother Fergus to the National Maternity Hospital. He was so drunk she had to help him into the waiting room, where he promptly passed out and slept the night away. Your man Tully is actually using the image of his twin brother Fergus as his alibi."

"Tell me you're pulling my leg, Dillon."

"That's what she told me. It would seem to make sense. By the way, she hasn't seen nor heard from either one of them in over a year and hopes it stays that way."

"You believe her?"

"Yeah, I do. She had a collection notice hanging from the mail slot in the door. She lives in a rundown little place over in Drumfinn. She's got no money. She has a two-year-old running around. Just about the last thing she needs is a problem with the likes of us. I have no reason to doubt her. Oh, and by the way, Fergus Moran? He was killed in a car crash last year. The ever-charming Miss McNeese told me drunk driving and a bridge abutment. I guess he's buried in Glasnevin Cemetery. Does Kinch or anyone have any current information on Tully Moran?"

Suel shook his head. He kicked his foot at a small stone on the footpath, missed, and said, "We've got shit, Dillon."

SIXTEEN

Dillon and Suel returned to their respective desks and began going through what little information there was on Tully Moran. The lights were off in DCI McCabe's office, so they set up in the break room. They pushed two tables together and began painstakingly going through the handful of files. They made a note of the addresses and the few contacts that were listed. Unfortunately, further investigation determined that the handful of contacts who weren't already dead had apparently taken up residence in Costa del Sol, Spain.

"Bear with me here," Suel said. "What if it wasn't Tully Moran we saw on that tape but his twin brother Fergus? You know, maybe your woman wasn't telling the truth, and your man Fergus is alive and well?"

"Perfect, except for the part where I don't think she was lying to me. Let me just Google the obituaries for the past year."

"Oh God save us, this is nothing but one dead end after another," Suel said.

Dillon brought up Fergus Moran's obituary three minutes later. He turned his computer screen toward Suel. "Here's the final update on your man, Fergus," Dillon said.

Suel just shook his head. They knocked off just before 9:00, no wiser than when they started. Dillon headed home and drove down the lane to his place. A car was partially pulled up onto the footpath in front of Tara's house.

So much for going over and knocking on the door, he thought and then wondered who was visiting. No doubt she was serving the wine he had left at the door. He thought for just a half-second about letting the air out of one of the tires on the car but then remembered the disastrous results when he slit a tire on her father's car. Fortunately, he'd come out the hero on that one, ultimately. But why press his luck?

Lucifer met him at the door and hurried outside to relieve himself. Dillon cleaned up the shredded trash bag and its former contents in the kitchen. He checked the sitting room and his bedroom, and surprisingly, there wasn't any mess. He took a chicken breast out of the refrigerator, turned on the oven, and set the table for one.

He sprinkled lemon pepper on the chicken breast, placed it in the oven, and grabbed Lucifer's leash. He stepped out of the house, locked the door, and attached the leash to Lucifer's collar. They hadn't been out for more than ten minutes when Dillon's cellphone rang. Paddy Suel calling.

"Yeah, Paddy. What's up?" was how he answered.

"Just heard from Kinch. They've got the bastard."

SEVENTEEN

Dillon met Paddy Suel at the Special Branch office just before 7:00 the following morning. Dillon arrived with two cups of fresh coffee, and Suel brought two scones.

"A celebration and we sure as hell have earned it," Suel said and raised his coffee in a toast.

Dillon touched his paper cup against Suel's and then took a bite of his scone. "I'll be glad to put this to bed. I had visions of this going on for weeks or even months. Where did they find him?"

"Get this," Suel said. "They caught him yesterday morning waiting to board a ferry to Cherbourg."

"Cherbourg, France?"

"Yeah. He had a flight scheduled from Paris to Seville, and from there, it's maybe a two-hour drive to Costa del Sol. They're thinking someone was probably going to meet him in Seville and drive him down to Costa del Sol."

"Have they interviewed him yet?"

Suel grinned. "That begins at precisely 10:00 this morning, and we have reserved front row seats. He spent the night at Mountjoy locked in solitary. No telling what the Linnehans are liable to do once they find out he didn't make it to France. His flight to Seville wasn't due to land until late this afternoon, so with any luck, we've got the better part of at least today before he's missed. Plenty of time to put on some pressure."

"Will they offer him some kind of deal?"

"Not exactly. My sense is the only deal they'll offer is to not place him in the general population. Good lord, he wouldn't last the day. No, I could see him being shipped over to the UK or maybe even Canada or the US."

"Wherever they send him, word will get out sooner or later."

"Yeah, but just now, he'll be desperate," Suel said and took another sip of coffee. "All they have to do is put the word out he's talking, and his days will be numbered."

"Does DCI McCabe know?"

"Not that I'm aware of, but if someone gave him a personal call, it wouldn't surprise me."

"That was fast, going from no idea where Moran is to having him locked up. That's damn good work," Dillon said.

Suel shook his head and said, "That's damn good luck."

They arrived at Mountjoy Prison just before 9:30. Suel drove, which gave Dillon the rare opportunity to view the various shops and foot traffic and not have to pay attention to the road. Once inside Mountjoy Prison, they met in a conference room with eight other officers. Although Dillon recognized a number of individuals, DI Kinch was the only one whose name he could recall.

There was more than one pat on the back and a lot of smiles. Eventually, DI Kinch addressed everyone. He thanked them for their work, congratulated them, and then said, "I'm sure I don't have to mention this, but I'm going to anyway. The interrogation will begin in a few minutes. Our suspect has been seated in the room for the past two hours. The individuals conducting this interrogation are from Fitzgibbon Station. You are invited to watch. Quietly. Should something develop where you think a subject should be addressed, write it down and give the note to me."

There seemed to be a collective exhale from the assembled group.

"If anyone makes a comment, a suggestion, or asks a question, you will be removed from the viewing room. There is seating available for everyone. You will be seated. We now have ten minutes to use the restroom. I suggest everyone avails themselves of this opportunity."

With that, everyone, including Dillon and Suel, left the conference room and headed down the hall to the restroom.

They entered the viewing room as a group. The lights were dimmed. The seating consisted of three rows of eight seats. Each seat was stationary, upholstered, and on a raised platform, making it slightly higher than the seat in front of it, much like a theatre. Dillon and Suel took seats next to one another in the second row.

Seated on the other side of the tinted window and facing them was Tully Moran. He was in an orange jumpsuit and shackled. A chain, maybe twelve inches long, ran between his ankles. His hands were cuffed and attached to the edge of the steel table by a chain. Dillon figured there was probably a chain around Moran's waist that the handcuffs would be attached to while walking to and from his solitary confinement cell.

Suel elbowed Dillon and then pointed to his right cheekbone and flashed three fingers.

Dillon glanced at Moran and made a mental note of the fact that he now had three teardrops tattooed beneath his right eye.

A large clock was mounted on the wall behind Moran and up near the ceiling. The clock reminded Dillon of a classroom. At exactly 10:00, the door to the interview room opened. Three officers entered and sat down opposite Moran.

Dillon watched the clock. No one said anything for thirty seconds, and then one of the officers asked, "Mr. Moran, would you like a water or perhaps a tea?"

Moran shook his head.

"Would you respond, please? Would you like a water or—"

"No, damn it."

"For the record, your name is Tullian Brian Moran?"

Moran smiled and said, "I ain't saying shit to you."

More than one head shook in the viewing room.

"Mr. Moran, you do realize that you are a prime suspect in the murder of two An Garda Síochána officers in Mountjoy Square and that—"

"I guess you weren't listening. I'm not going to say shit to the likes of you."

That went on for the next ninety minutes. Moran occasionally responded, but always with the same line. "I ain't saying shit to you."

Dillon didn't pick up on it, but the lead officer had given some kind of signal, and suddenly, all three men stood in unison. "Perhaps some time to consider would help, Mr. Moran," the lead officer said, and they all walked out of the room. A minute later, Kinch left the viewing room. He stepped back into the room and signaled everyone to follow him out into the hall. They walked back to the conference room where they had originally gathered, and only then did people start to talk.

After a minute, Kinch asked for quiet and then said, "Suggestions, anyone? Obviously, Mr. Moran does not appear to be in a cooperative frame of mind."

"Legal representation?" someone asked.

Kinch nodded and said, "We've another eighteen hours before that is mandated. That said, I take your point, and he may not respond until representation is provided. Still, we've eighteen hours left."

Suel said, "The three teardrops below the right eye. I was aware he had only one. Are the additional two recent?"

Kinch nodded, "They are quite recent, maybe 48 hours old. They have been photographed repeatedly. Again, no response from Mr. Moran. In fact, as unfortunate as it may be, his responses this morning were the most he's said since he was brought into custody. Any other questions or comments?"

The room was quiet for a long moment before someone asked, "Lunch?"

"Yes, thank you. Out on circular drive, there's Two Boys Brew, with coffee and sandwiches. Doyle's pub on the corner, nice menu, no alcohol, please. Around the corner is a McDonald's for anyone not faint of heart and just beyond that is the Bald Eagle, with a lovely menu and fast service. Any other questions?"

No one said anything.

"Very well, gentlemen, ninety minutes, and we'll meet back here. Thank you."

Dillon and Suel hurried over to the Two Boys Brew coffee shop. They both ordered a coffee, a Reuben Toastie, and grabbed a table in the back.

"What do you think?" Suel said.

"I think the toastie looked good and—"

"Not the lunch, you nob. Moran, what do you think about that knacker?" Suel asked.

"I think he's hanging on for his life. You know, as well as I do, once word gets out he's been arrested, there's an automatic price on his head. Right now, he's praying that the fact he's not talking will somehow get back to the Linnehans, but let's face it, he's screwed. I'd guess by sunrise this morning, word was filtering through The Joy that he was in there somewhere. I don't see how he's going to make it to the end of the month."

"He's damned if he does and damned if he doesn't. Serves the bastard right."

"No argument from me, but it would be nice to know who set this up to begin with," Dillon said.

"I would guess, at the end of the day, they'll have a little 'Come to Jesus' chat with him. Explain the simple facts that he's a dead man if he thinks he can remain quiet. Just the fact he's in that interview room all day. Word is already out that he's been spilling his guts, and nothing he can say is going to change that."

"Where do you think he's been for the last two days? He obviously wasn't staying in that council housing."

"I don't know," Suel said and shook his head.

"What about this? Suppose he was paid to make the hit. Maybe half upfront, half on completion, or maybe he just got a wad of cash. You think he might have stayed in a fancy hotel or spent a couple of nights with some hot number? Maybe he partied at a bunch of pubs. Maybe he ran up a credit card bill. Who made the arrest?"

"I don't know," Suel said.

"You think it was Kinch?"

"No, if it was Kinch, he would have told everyone that he made the arrest. But I have an idea who might know," Suel said and pulled out his cellphone. He smiled at Dillon and punched in a number.

"Who you calling?"

"Yeah, Declan. It's Paddy Suel. Give me a call when you've got a minute. We're at The Joy watching the interrogation of Tully Moran. I'm curious who brought him in initially. If you call this afternoon, I won't be able to answer, so just leave a message."

"Declan Tierney?" Dillon asked.

"Yeah, there's a pretty good chance he'll know, or if he doesn't, he'll know who will."

"Make sure you got that thing back on silent, or Kinch will have you locked up."

EIGHTEEN

They'd been back in the viewing room for a good two hours. Only about half of the people who'd been watching this morning returned for the afternoon. The other thing that had changed was that the three men conducting the interrogation were now taking turns asking questions. It didn't really matter. Tully Moran's response was the same one he'd given that morning. "I ain't saying shit to you."

Suel elbowed Dillon and pointed to his trouser pocket, signaling a call coming through. Wisely, he decided not to pull his cellphone out of his pocket.

At 4:40, the questioning stopped, and the lead officer said, "Let me explain some simple facts to you, Tully. We understand you're hoping to get the word out somehow that you're not talking to us. Here's the problem. Even though up till now it's true, no one is going to believe you. You've been in this room since 8:00 this morning. Everyone is convinced you've been spilling your guts to us. About the only way you are going to make it through this is to cooperate. If you cooperate, we can move you somewhere safe. By safe, I, or rather we, mean somewhere out of the country. Maybe the UK, maybe Canada, or even the US. But until you decide to cooperate, I'm afraid you're on a limited timeframe, and if you decide not to cooperate, we can't move you. I'm not lying, Tully. I'm not threatening. Hard as it is to hear, those are just the facts. Please think about this carefully while you still can."

Tully grinned and said, "I still ain't telling shit to the likes of yous."

"Suit yourself, son. Legal counsel will be appointed tomorrow." With that, the three men stood and walked out of the interrogation room. Kinch opened the door, and the five individuals made their way down the hall. Dillon and Suel, along with two other officers, followed Kinch into the conference room.

"Questions?" Kinch asked. When no one said anything, he said, "Thanks for your patience. We'll be back at it 9:30 tomorrow morning."

With that, Dillon and Suel headed out of the conference room and through the various security stations until they were finally out of Mountjoy Prison. As soon as they climbed into the car, Suel pulled out his phone.

"Let me give Declan a call. Hopefully, he's got a name." He tapped the screen and placed the phone against his ear. A moment later, he said, "Good, Declan. Were you able to get a name? Do you know his schedule? I see. Okay, yeah, if you would. Thanks. Dillon owes you one. Yeah, you too. Thanks again."

"That was quick," Dillon said.

"Yeah, an officer by the name of Mickey Ryan made the arrest. He's out of Store Street Station. They're a good bunch. Ryan spotted your man at Ferry Quay 18, waiting for the ferry to France. He's sending me the— Oh, here it is now. Ryan's phone number," Suel said as his phone vibrated.

Suel tapped the number displayed on the screen and then turned on the speaker. The phone rang four times, and then a voice answered, "Ryan."

"Hello, Officer Ryan, this is DI Paddy Suel with Special Branch. I'd like to buy you a pint once you're off duty. Want to thank you for spotting your man Tully Moran before he got onto that ferry for France."

"DI Suel, is it? How'd you get my name and number?"

"Ryan, I'm in Special Branch. Look, my partner and I have been chasing dead-end leads for the past forty-eight hours and getting absolutely nowhere. We're just out after watching your man's interrogation at The Joy today. Wanted to thank you."

"You learn anything?"

"Yeah, he's a right pain in the ass," Suel said.

Ryan laughed and said, "Who's your partner?"

"An American, Marshal—"

"Dillon, is it? Marshal Dillon? He the American that took out that bunch at Dublin airport a few years back?"

"Yeah, that's him. He'd like to meet you," Suel said and shot a look at Dillon.

"Yeah, I guess I can do that. I can only stay for one. Can't make a night of it."

"That would work for us. You just tell us where and when," Suel said.

"Mmm, you know where Grainger's is?" Ryan asked.

"Across from Connolly station?"

"Yeah, that's it. I'll see you there in about forty-five minutes. I'll be wearing a Six Nations jersey."

"Looking forward to meeting you, Mickey."

"Likewise, see you shortly."

NINETEEN

Grainger's was a triangular-shaped, three-story building on the corner. The exterior of the first floor, Grainger's Pub, was painted black with gold lettering that read 'Cafe Grainger's Bar.' The second and third stories of the pub were brick and painted white. Inside, the place was nicely appointed with a similar black and gold motif. Taps for over twenty different beers plus another three for Guinness ran along the length of the bar. Five other people, a table of four and a solo guy, were in the pub when Dillon and Suel entered. Dillon looked at the bartender and pointed to an empty table in the corner.

The bartender nodded and said, "What'll it be, lads?"

"Two pints," Dillon said.

"I'll bring 'em over to ya's." Maybe five minutes later, he brought two pint glasses of Guinness over to their table.

"We'll run a tab," Dillon said and handed him a credit card.

They hadn't taken more than two sips when a red-haired guy about six-foot-two stepped inside. He was wearing a jersey with light-blue, red, white, green, and dark-blue three-inch wide stripes. As if that wasn't enough, the logo for the Six Nations Rugby tournament was over his left breast.

Dillon and Suel gave simultaneous waves. As Ryan approached their table, he said, "I'll have the usual, Jerry. DI Suel?" he asked as he pulled out a stool and looked back and forth from Suel to Dillon and back again to Suel.

"That's me, Officer Ryan. You mind if I call you Mickey? Call me Paddy, and this is the famous Marshal Dillon," Suel said and waved a hand at Dillon.

"Call me Jack. Nice to meet you," Dillon said.

"So, you lot were looking for your man Moran?"

"Not just us. You must have seen the BOLO on him if you grabbed him down at Quay 18. Were you down there on a tip?"

"A tip? No, in fact, we were down there just making our presence known. There's been a problem with pick-pockets of late. We were just making an appearance, and I caught sight of him climbing out of a car. The teardrop tattoos are what gave him away. Good thing too. They were beginning to board the ferry. Another few minutes, and he would have been on board and headed for France."

"He put up a fight? Try to resist?" Suel asked.

Ryan shook his head just as his pint of Guinness arrived. "Oh, thanks, Jerry," he said to the bartender. He raised his pint to Dillon and Suel and said, "Sláinte." Everyone clinked glasses and took a sip. "Your man was too busy staring at the women in line in front of him to pay any attention to us. We just calmly approached from either side, and by the time he took his eyes off your woman's bum, it was too late."

"What about the car he climbed out of? Was it a taxi?"

"No, an old faded red thing. Had a crack in the windscreen, and the passenger door was dented. He said something to your woman behind the wheel. She gave him two fingers and drove off. Didn't look very happy."

"An old faded red thing. You think it might have been a Hyundai?" Dillon asked.

"It could have been. But once he climbed out, we were so focused on him I can't be sure."

"Was the woman dark-haired? A bit on the heavy side?"

Ryan shook his head. "Sorry, we just saw her and the car for half a second, and then we were following your man. Wanted to get to him before he got on board."

"Well, thanks to you and your partner, he's locked up in The Joy."

"You learn anything listening to the interrogation?"

They both shook their heads. "He thinks he's in a movie and is going to get credit for not talking," Dillon said. "What's going to happen is, after spending an entire day telling the interrogation team he wasn't going to talk, the general population at The Joy will think that's exactly what he was doing, talking."

"Unfortunately for Moran, they're going to think the worst, and unless he cooperates, his time is limited, and we can't do anything to protect him," Suel said.

"Why don't they place him in isolation?"

"That's where he is now, but it only takes one mistake. They leave his cell door open, or he's escorted somewhere and they overpower the escort. He's what you might call a marked man. At some point, he has to eat or be escorted to the shower. They've got nothing to do but sit and wait for an opportunity," Dillon said.

"They explained things to Moran this afternoon. Tried to tell him the way things were going to work, but he acted like he knew everything. I'd say right now he's his own worst enemy, and he has no idea," Suel said and took a sip.

"Any thoughts on who was behind the killings?" Ryan asked.

"Nothing definite yet, but Moran is obviously fingered for pulling the trigger. We feel pretty confident he was acting on the behest of someone higher up," Dillon said.

"You know, when we were bringing him in, he kept telling us he'd be out in twenty-four hours. Told us we had no idea the heat we were going to get for arresting him."

"He didn't happen to mention a name, did he?"

"Afraid not. To be honest, he didn't appear to be the least bit concerned. It was like he thought he was in charge, despite his hands being cuffed behind his back. Nothing short of delusional if you ask me."

They chatted on for a bit. Suel offered to order another round, but Ryan begged off and said he had a wife and a one-year-old at home. He shook hands and headed out the door.

"Seemed like a nice enough lad," Suel said and drained his glass. "What are you thinking?"

"I'm thinking the car he described dropping off Moran sounded an awful lot like the one I saw parked at Shauna McNeese's over in Drumfinn."

"McNeese?" Suel asked

"She's the one who was delivering the baby while Moran's brother was passed out in the waiting room."

Suel seemed to think for a moment and said, "So what you're telling me is we're not going to be ordering another pint."

"Yeah, it's such a lovely drive over to Drumfinn and Cleggan Avenue; I know you wouldn't want to miss it."

"Settle up with your man, Jerry, and we'll be off."

The drive over to Shauna McNeese's home took the better part of a half-hour. Each time they were forced to stop for a traffic light, Suel swore just a little longer. "Is it any wonder we've people moving out of the city? These bleeding lights, for the love of God. I'm tempted to put the siren on and just get everyone to pull over."

"And then I'd have to report you," Dillon said.

"All I can say is it's your turn to buy the next round."

"I just bought the last round," Dillon said.

"Perfect, then you'll know how to do it."

Eventually, Suel made it to the Drumfinn district and turned onto Cleggan Avenue.

"That's her place up ahead on the left. The pink place."

"Oh, what the bloody hell. Can you imagine living across the street from that and having to look at it all day long? Lord love a duck, it probably glows in the dark," Suel said as he pulled up onto the sidewalk. He parked in front of the driveway, effectively blocking it.

TWENTY

The faded red Hyundai was parked exactly where it was the last time Dillon had seen it. He suddenly wondered if Tully Moran had been there the other day when he spoke with Shauna McNeese at the front door. Maybe Tully had even been listening to their conversation.

The yellow plastic car was still missing a wheel and appeared to be in the exact same place as the last time he saw it. An empty cardboard box for a new flatscreen TV was wedged between the recycle bin and the house. Based on the late payment notices he'd seen in the mail slot, he thought the flatscreen box was interesting. He knocked on the door, and they waited.

"What a dump," Suel said a second before the door opened.

Shauna McNeese focused on Dillon and said, "For God's sake. Now, what do you want?"

She appeared to be dressed in the same clothes as before. The chocolate stains remained on her jeans around her knee. Her t-shirt now had what appeared to be two additional jelly stains and maybe one of tomato sauce.

"Nice to see you again, Shauna. Care to invite us in?"

"No, not unless you have a warrant."

"We can get one if you'd like. Of course, that's going to involve a number of people coming in and going through everything, no doubt leaving a mess. Might be better just to invite us in for a little chat."

She seemed to think about that for a moment and then said, "Okay, but I don't know anything I haven't already told you."

She stepped back as they entered and then closed the door behind them. Dillon immediately detected a faint smell, not pleasant. They were in the front room with a worn couch against the wall and a large, seventy-inch flatscreen resting on a coffee table opposite the couch. A number of unopened envelopes were piled on the floor beneath the coffee table. More than a few of the envelopes had red writing on the front, signifying past due notices. Toys, dirty plates, bowls, and three wine glasses were scattered around the room.

McNeese walked through the room and into the kitchen, where the smell grew stronger. A cat was stretched out on the kitchen counter, licking its paws. The little dark-haired boy, Rowen, was seated in a highchair. The tray on the highchair had a pile of what looked like macaroni. Rowen had a good deal of it smeared across his face and in his hair.

"How's Rowen doing?" Dillon asked.

"His usual self," McNeese said, sounding like she wasn't giving a compliment. She took a cigarette from a pack on the kitchen table, lit it, and blew smoke up toward the ceiling. "So, what is it you want?"

"Wondering if you've heard anything from Tully Moran," Dillon said.

"I told you before. I haven't heard from him in over a year."

"Yeah, that is what you told me… before," Dillon said, letting that last word hang out there.

"We're just interested in some information. No one needs to know we talked," Suel said.

"I might have had a word or two on the phone. The plonker called me just out of the blue. I was telling you the truth. I hadn't heard from him in over a year and then all of a sudden, he calls. We only talked for maybe a minute."

"And what did he have to say?"

"He said he was leaving the country, and he didn't know if he'd ever be back. Honest, I ain't lying to ya's. That's what he said. I just thought, good riddance."

"Did you see him?" Dillon asked.

"He said he was leaving the country."

"Yeah, I heard that. So, did you see him? Did he come over for dinner? Meet you in a pub? Did you give him a ride somewhere?"

At the mention of a ride, she got a look on her face suggesting she knew she was caught.

"Did you give him a ride, Shauna?" Dillon asked again after a long moment.

"Oh God, all right, yes, I did, I did. He was leaving the country and never going to come back. I thought it would help to get his worthless ass out of Ireland for good. You know, he's nothing but trouble, always has been."

"Nice, you're doing your civic duty," Suel said.

"How's that new flatscreen working out?" Dillon asked.

"Now you wait just a minute. I didn't ask for that. He just showed up with it. Made me take it even after I told him I didn't want it."

"I'm sure that's the case. How'd he get here?"

"Get here?"

"Yeah, did he walk carrying that flatscreen all the way from a shop or—"

"No, he had it delivered, and his friend dropped him off."

"Did you meet his friend?"

"No, he just waved from the car and disappeared around the corner. He's American."

"Oh, yeah, that sounds like Kevin McBaine. He's actually a pretty nice guy."

McNeese nodded and said, "Yeah, he's the one what paid for the flatscreen, not Tully. Told me it was because I did him a favor and promised to give Tully a ride in the morning."

"Did he call you on the phone?"

"Yeah, Kevin did. That's how I got the flatscreen. Told him if Moran wanted a ride, he'd have to get me a new flatscreen. Rowen broke the one I had, knocked it over the little—"

"Show me the number on your phone, Shauna."

"The number?" she asked, suddenly sounding more than a little nervous.

"Yeah, the number McBaine called you from, let me see your phone."

She pulled her phone from the front pocket on her jeans, turned it to recent calls, and clicked on the link. "Here it is. Ain't going to tell you much." The screen read 'Number Unknown.'

Suel reached over and took the phone from her hand. "We're going to borrow this for just a bit and then get it back to you."

"My phone? But you can't do that. What if someone calls me?"

"I guess they'll have to leave a message," Suel said. "Anything else?" he asked Dillon.

"No, I think that about wraps it up. Really wish you would have called me when you heard from Tully, Shauna. It would have helped."

"I umm, tried to, but you didn't answer. Yeah, I—"

"Should I check for your message, or you want to think about that?"

She seemed to do just that, think about it. "You know, now that I remember, Rowen was crying, and I probably forgot to leave the message. You know, minding the little one and all."

"Yeah, sure. I know."

They let themselves out of the house and heard her lock the door a second later. "God, the term dump doesn't do the place justice. I feel sorry for that wee one. Poor little fella doesn't have a snowball's chance in hell with a mother like that," Suel said.

"And the courts will do everything in their power to make sure he stays with her," Dillon said.

They drove back to the station and, once inside, immediately headed for the tech department. At no surprise, it was locked. They took the elevator up to Special Branch. No one was in the office and, based on the files stacked on DCI McCabe's desk, it appeared he had been out all day. Dillon left a phone message for Emily in the tech department. He mentioned the cellphone and asked her to contact him in the morning. "What do you think?" Dillon called over to Suel.

"I think we may have a very busy day tomorrow, and the wise move would be to head home."

Dillon nodded, and they went their separate ways. As he drove down his lane, the lights were on in Tara's house, but he didn't feel the urge to try to smooth things over tonight. Instead, he took Lucifer for a long walk beneath the full moon, then settled in front of the TV with a chicken sandwich and watched the news. He was in bed just after eleven and slept through the night.

TWENTY-ONE

Dillon turned off the alarm clock fifteen minutes before it was set to go off. He got the coffee going then went back upstairs to shave and shower. He'd eaten breakfast and was just getting on his computer when Lucifer came down the stairs. He let him outside, filled his food and water dishes, and enticed him back in with a biscuit. He was back in the office a little before 7:00. Amazingly, there were no dirty dishes left on his desk. Suel entered about twenty minutes later, and just as Dillon was about to say something, his cellphone sounded.

"Hi Emily, thanks for returning my call."

"I'm just in the door and got your message. What's up?"

Dillon gave a quick explanation of Shauna McNeese's cellphone and said he'd bring it down in a minute. He hung up and headed to Suel's desk. "I'm taking the phone down to the Tech department. You planning on going back to The Joy?"

"Yes, depending on Tully Moran's response, I may not be there very long."

"Keeping my fingers crossed he's had time to think things over, and he'll cooperate," Dillon said.

"Yeah, well, don't hold your breath."

"We'll leave here about nine. I'll drive," Dillon said.

"Fine with me," Suel replied and headed to the break room.

Dillon hurried down to the first floor and pressed the buzzer at the Tech Lab. "Yes?" Emily's voice replied a moment later.

"Jack Dillon, Emily."

"Be there in a minute," she said.

They were standing at a counter in the Tech Lab. Emily had Shauna McNeese's cellphone connected to a device that was displaying the calls on a larger screen. There were actually three calls from an unknown number.

"It's going to take a while," Emily said. "I may be able to get the location where the calls originated from but not much more than that. If the phone is still live, we may be able to identify a call being made, but don't hold your breath. The longest of those three calls was just one minute, which suggests whoever is making the call immediately gets to the point and disconnects. There's a pretty good chance they may have already disposed of the phone and purchased a new one. You said you think it's an American?"

"That's what we hope. We're thinking it may be an individual named Kevin McBaine, but that's just an educated guess at this stage."

"It's going to take a couple of hours. I should have something by the end of the morning."

"I'm going to be watching an interrogation at The Joy this morning. If you send me a text message, I may not be able to answer for an hour or two."

"Not a problem," Emily said, and Dillon went back up to Special Branch. The lights were on in DCI McCabe's office. Dillon and Suel knocked on the doorframe. McCabe waved them in.

"Thank you, lads," McCabe said as they entered. "Take a few minutes and bring me up to date."

"It's short and sweet," Dillon said and went on to tell him of Tully Moran's arrest and the suspected interaction between Moran and Kevin McBaine. After that, he filled McCabe in on the phone down in the Tech Lab.

"How you keeping, sir?" Suel asked when Dillon had finished.

"Humf, to be honest, I'm not sure. It seems like a bad dream I can't quite wake up from. Liam's folks are distraught. Same with the Murphy family. It's something no parent wants to experience. A dark, bottomless hole," he said, shaking his head.

"Well, we'd better get over to The Joy," Dillon said. "Hopefully, things will be a little more productive today."

"Yes, yes, by all means. Keep me posted," McCabe said. He pulled the top file from the stack on his desk and opened it.

"Oh, for lord's sake. The poor bastard," Suel said once they were out of the office. They were about to head down to the parking area when Suel's phone rang. "This might be the call I've been waiting for," Suel said. "You better go. I'll meet you at The Joy."

Dillon climbed behind the wheel. It was a twenty-minute drive over to Mountjoy Prison. He parked on the far side of North Circular Road and walked over to Mountjoy Prison. He went through the various security stations and was escorted into the conference room. This morning, there were a total of seven officers, including Dillon, waiting to go into the viewing room. Kinch wasn't around. Nine thirty, the time the interview was supposed to begin, came and went, and still no Kinch or anyone else for that matter. No one seemed to know what was going on.

"You think your man saw the wisdom of making a deal?" someone asked.

"I don't see it happening. Moran in solitary confine-ment with only himself to listen to. He thinks he's doing a bang-up job and doesn't have the slightest clue what the rest of the population is thinking. Right now, he's his own worst enemy," another replied.

Kinch entered the room five minutes later. He did not look happy as he walked to the front of the room. "Everyone take a seat. This will only be a minute."

Everyone quickly sat down. Kinch looked over the group and took a deep breath. "Tully Moran was found dead in his cell this morning at 6:15 a.m. Quiet, please,"

Kinch said as comments started. "Cause of death is being ruled as a suicide pending further investigation. It appears he hung himself using his jumpsuit. That's all the information I have at the moment. As we learn more, I'll update. Obviously, it's early in the investigation process."

"He was in solitary confinement?" someone asked.

"That's my understanding. His body was found in his cell by the officer bringing breakfast. I want to thank you for your time. As things develop, you will be informed. Thank you," Kinch said and headed out of the room.

The room was quiet for a long moment. Someone eventually mumbled, "Justice is served," and everyone began to head out.

Dillon headed toward his car with another officer. Neither one said anything until the other officer pressed the fob and the lights on his car flashed. "What do you think?" Dillon asked.

The officer shook his head. "About Moran? No surprise. I doubt it was suicide, but we may never know, damn it. I think there's a pretty good chance Moran was the bastard that pulled the trigger, but there's no way that idiot planned those killings. Someone higher up got Moran to do the deed."

Dillon headed back to the station. When he entered Special Branch, the door to McCabe's office was open, and the lights were on.

He knocked on McCabe's doorframe. McCabe was on the phone. He waved Dillon in and pointed at the chairs on the opposite side of his desk. "I see. Yes. I would appreciate that, and thank you for the call," he said and hung up. "Back early, I see."

"Yes, sir. Apparently, Tully Moran took his life last night," Dillon said. "Supposedly hung himself with his jumpsuit."

"That was the phone call I was on. What do you think?"

Dillon thought for a moment. "What I think is we'll never know if Moran took his own life. That said, he may have been the man who pulled the trigger, but he wasn't the brains behind this. That was someone higher up the ladder, a lot higher up, and that individual is still out there."

McCabe stared off into the distance for a long moment then said, "Any idea who it might be?"

"We think that American, Kevin McBaine," Dillon said. "He arrived in Dublin four days ago. He was instrumental in getting Moran a ride down to the ferry. It was only a matter of luck that two officers happened to be there and spotted Moran. A few minutes later and he would have been on board, and they never would have seen him."

"Make it your top priority. Where's the Kinch team on this?"

Dillon shook his head. "We're not aware they know about McBaine. We can keep them informed and—"

McCabe held up his hand. "Maybe think about informing them on a need-to-know basis. Work your case, find this bastard McBaine. If you need anything, let me know. I want whoever is responsible for this. Anything else?"

"No, sir."

"Then don't let me hold you up."

TWENTY-TWO

Dillon left McCabe's office thinking the first thing he would do was check with Emily down in tech. His desk phone rang just as he was about to reach for it. "Marshal Dillon," he answered.

"Yeah, Marshal, Hugh Healy."

"Hugh, nice to hear from you. What's up?"

"I just got off the phone with forensics. Call over there and ask for Niall Reid. He did the exams on the shell casings, and he picked up a partial fingerprint."

"Niall Reid, okay, thanks, Hugh, I'm on it." Dillon hung up. He called forensics and asked for Reid. The phone rang a half-dozen times before it was answered.

"Reid."

"Niall Reid?" Dillon asked.

"Yeah, what do you need?" he asked, sounding rushed.

"This is Marshal Dillon up in Special Branch. I just received a call from Hugh Healy regarding a partial fingerprint you recovered on some shell casings."

"The double homicide, Officers McCabe and Murphy."

"Yeah, that's it. We're working on that case. A few things have recently changed. Are you in the lab now?"

"Yeah, and I'll be here eternally. We're really backed up, although that case took priority."

"I'd like to stop down," Dillon said.

"Ask for me when you get here. Oh, and I like my coffee black," he said and hung up.

Dillon headed out of the office and hurried over to the Coffee Cafe truck parked just outside the gate. "Medium coffee, black, and better give me a scone, too," he said. He paid and hurried back into the Garda area. Forensics was different from Emily's Tech Lab. He walked into the lobby, showed his ID, and asked for Niall Reid. When he said Reid's name, the receptionist gave him a look suggesting, 'Are you sure that's who you want?' Then placed the call.

"He'll be out in just a moment," she said as she hung up her phone.

Dillon had no sooner settled into a chair than the door opened and a heavy-set man with salt and pepper hair and wearing a white lab coat over a shirt and tie stepped halfway out. "Dillon?" he asked.

Dillon pegged him for fifty. He rose from the chair and handed Reid the coffee and the scone.

"I'm liking your style," Reid said and took a sip of coffee. "Mmm, much better than the dredge we have here. Come on back."

They walked through a series of halls to Reid's office, which was one of a half-dozen lined up along a wall in a lab. Reid set the coffee and the scone on his desk and said, "Come on back out to the lab."

Dillon followed him out to a counter with a computer screen mounted on the wall. Reid ran his fingers over the keyboard, and three images of the actual rounds and shell casings appeared.

"I've already forwarded this to Kinch at Fitzgibbon Station. But Healy mentioned he'd been working with you."

"Yeah, quite the guy. After they've given up the search, he goes out on his own time and finds the casings. Apparently, they'd been beneath the frame on the tent or something."

Reid nodded. "We were able to match them to the casing left at the scene of the Christmas Eve murder behind the Cabra Club back in 2019."

"And that's a definite match?" Dillon asked.

"Absolutely, .22 short rounds from an automatic pistol. You can see this line on each one of the casings. As the round was fired and the casing ejected, it was scratched. This round on the right," Reid said, pointing at the screen. "is an exact match to the two from the Mountjoy Square murders. If you could locate the weapon, I could give a one hundred percent confirmation. Otherwise, I'm at ninety-nine-point-nine percent."

"I'm thinking the weapon is probably somewhere at the bottom of the Liffey," Dillon said.

"Possibly, although whoever was responsible for the Christmas Eve murder didn't think to dispose of it back then, so it might still be around."

"Hugh Healy mentioned you recovered a partial fingerprint as well."

"Yes, actually two," Reid said and ran his fingers over the keyboard. "We've identified one as belonging to your suspect." The screen brought up a set of fingerprints along with an older mugshot of Tully Moran sporting just one teardrop tattoo.

"Yeah, Tully Moran. No surprise there," Dillon said. "How accurate is the identification?"

"Positive it's his left index finger."

"You just said you found two fingerprints?"

"Right, unfortunately, no match on the second. Whoever it was isn't in our database. I'm thinking possibly a merchant or an arms dealer. Perhaps someone who sold the ammunition."

"Can you access US sites?"

"We can. The largest one would be the Integrated Automated Fingerprint Identification System, IAFIS. That's the largest but not their only one, US Department of Defense and some other sites as well. Are you thinking of someone in particular?"

"Yes, an American by the name of Kevin McBaine."

"Spell that surname for me," Reid said then typed McBaine's name on a separate screen as Dillon spelled it out.

"He arrived in Ireland a few days ago. He's a person of interest, although we haven't been able to locate him. He's rumored to have links to the Linnehan gang."

"Interesting. It's going to take a while, but I'll get going on that. Has he been connected to Moran?"

"Loosely but nothing definitive. That said, his name keeps popping up as a possibility."

"It's going to take a bit to get clearance and then run the print through. Possibly later today but more likely tomorrow," Reid said.

Dillon pulled out a card and handed it to Reid. "Call me if you get a hit."

"Will do, and thanks for the coffee and that scone."

"The least I could do. I don't know if you heard, but apparently, Moran was found dead in his cell at The Joy this morning."

"No, I hadn't heard that. They had him in the general population?"

"My understanding is he was being kept in solitary confinement. I watched him all day yesterday while he was in interrogation. He certainly appeared to think he was in control. He never once answered a question other than to say he had no comment."

"Hmmm, amazing he was that polite."

"Actually, he wasn't."

Reid smiled at that and said, "Let me show you out. As soon as we get anything on that print, I'll call you."

"Thank you," Dillon said as Reid opened the door to the lobby. "A pleasure meeting you."

"The pleasure was all mine. I'm off to enjoy that scone and coffee. Thanks again."

Dillon headed back to Special Branch. He was in the process of gathering two empty tea mugs from his desk and placing them in the break room when his phone rang. "Dillon," he answered.

"Hi, Jack," Emily said. "I've got something off that cellphone on those unknown numbers. Are you able to come down and have a look?"

"I'll be down in just a minute. Thanks for the call," he said and disconnected.

He dumped the tea mugs in the break room sink. Suel wasn't in the office, so he hurried down to Tech Lab. He rang the buzzer, and Emily opened the door a moment later.

"Well, that was fast," she said by way of greeting.

"I don't suppose it came up with a picture of the guy and the license number of his car?" Dillon said as they headed back to a large computer screen.

"Funny you should say that. Umm, unfortunately, nothing like that came up, but there are a couple of items." She moved a mouse across a pad and brought up an image on the screen, actually, a Dublin map. She enlarged it a number of times until it was focused on Stephen's Green, a large park in the center of Dublin. There were three red dots placed in the corner of the park that was labeled Edward Delaney's Famine Memorial. Emily looked over at Dillon and smiled.

"So, what does this mean? Someone was calling Shauna McNeese while she was looking at the Famine Memorial?"

"Just the opposite. Whoever phoned her was standing there in the park when they called. The phone calls were hours apart. I have a hunch. You want to hear it?"

"Yeah, please."

"You're thinking or hoping that these calls were from the American, right?"

"Yeah, Kevin McBaine."

"So he's calling her from the park, and it's probably a safe bet he didn't stay right there for eight hours and occasionally make a phone call."

"Okay."

"Well, directly across the street is a five-star hotel."

"The Shelbourne?" Dillon asked.

"Right. Maybe that's where he's staying or was staying, and he went across the street just in case she or someone, you, for instance, traced where the call came from."

"Emily, that's great. Hang onto that phone just in case he tries to call her again. Any activity, let me know."

"You got it."

"Oh, and thanks, maybe we just might have a chance," he said and hurried out of the lab. He ran up to his desk and printed off a half-dozen photos of Kevin McBaine from the file Eric Bergman had sent him. Suel

was still out of the office, so he left him a note and hurried down to his car.

TWENTY-THREE

Dillon parked two blocks from Stephen's Green and considered himself lucky to find a parking place. He walked past the Shelbourne Hotel, crossed the street, and headed into Stephen's Green. It was a large park with benches along the paths, swans in the ponds, fountains, and a few thousand people taking photos or just walking around.

Dillon sat down on a bench opposite the Famine Memorial, four abstract figures set on the northeastern corner of the green. He glanced at the image of Kevin McBaine that he'd printed off and watched the people passing by. No one appeared to be on their cellphone, let alone look like McBaine.

He crossed the street and entered the Shelbourne Hotel. The Shelbourne is a five-story brick structure billed as a renaissance hotel and a National Irish Treasure. Dillon figured it would be the rare occasion he'd ever think of staying there. It was for the high and mighty, the Kevin McBaine's of the world.

As he entered, a uniformed man at the front door said, "Good afternoon, sir," and held the door for him. A

long marble hallway led to the front desk. Areas with tables and cushioned chairs were on either side of the hallway. Dillon decided to take a seat and watch the foot
traffic. He settled into a chair and waited.

Half an hour later, a balding gentleman in a gray suit
approached and said, "Excuse me, sir. Would you happen to be a guest?"

"No," Dillon said.

"I'm sorry, but this area is for hotel guests. Perhaps
you'd find yourself a bit more comfortable in one of our
bars or restaurants."

"No, this is just fine. I'm actually waiting for one of
your guests," Dillon said and flashed a smile.

"Very well, sir," the man said. He nodded gracefully
and left.

Dillon decided, if he'd caught the guy's attention,
he'd better either leave or go to the front desk and ask
for a manager. He rose from the chair, stretched, and
headed toward the front desk.

A younger gentleman in a gray suit and red tie
smiled and said, "Good afternoon, sir."

"Good afternoon. I'd like to see a manager, please."

"Is there a problem, sir?"

Dillon shook his head and pulled out his ID. "An
Garda Síochána."

The gray suit seemed to study the ID for a bit. He
glanced up at Dillon twice before he said, "One moment,
please." He stepped through a door and returned a half-

minute later. "It will be just a minute, sir, and someone will be with you," the gray suit said and flashed a smile.

A moment later, the door opened, and the same guy who'd asked Dillon if he was a guest stepped out and got a surprised look on his face. "An Garda Síochána?"

"Yes, Marshal Dillon. I wonder if we might talk privately."

"But of course, please," he said and extended his hand toward the open door. Dillon stepped in. The man closed the door behind them and said, "I'm Owen Kelly. What seems to be the problem?"

"Not really a problem. Wondering if you may have a gentleman staying here," Dillon said.

"Follow me, please," Kelly said and led the way down the hall to an office. The desk was stacked with files and had a large computer screen on one side. A black nameplate with white letters read Owen Kelly. "Please have a seat. If you don't mind, I would like to see some identification. You're American?"

"Yes," Dillon said and handed his ID card across the desk. "I'm assigned to An Garda Síochána. I work in the Special Branch."

"I see," Kelly said, handing the ID card back to Dillon. "And what exactly do you need from the Shelbourne?"

Dillon pulled out a copy of Kevin McBaine's picture and handed it across the desk. "This gentleman's name is Kevin McBaine. He's an American. We think he may be staying here."

"And is there a problem?"

Dillon thought for a moment and decided he didn't want to hear how the hotel could neither confirm nor deny without a court order of some sort. "There might be, potentially. I hope to avoid any problems. We don't have definite proof, but we suspect he may have been involved in the recent murder of two Garda officers. He is associated with the Linnehan gang. They're drug—"

"I'm familiar with the Linnehan crowd. We had an incident four years ago, dreadful, absolutely dreadful. This gentleman's name, again?" he asked, clicking some keys on the keyboard.

"Kevin McBaine, M-c-B-a-i-n-e," Dillon said, spelling out the last name.

"Yes, we do have someone by that name registered here. What exactly are you planning? We really don't need—"

"How long is he staying here?"

Kelly glanced at the screen. "Two more days, and then he's set to check out on Saturday."

"I would like to avoid any situation here in the hotel. We'd simply follow him. Does he have a vehicle registered?"

"Yes, he does. The ahh, license number is 211-D-2305. It's listed as a black BMW-5. Here," Kelly said and wrote down the license number on a notepad. He tore off the sheet and handed it to Dillon. "I've added his suite number at the bottom."He reached into a drawer and handed Dillon a business card.

"Thank you," Dillon said and handed one of his cards to Kelly.

"Please call me if I can be of any assistance. If you can eliminate any involvement here, on the premises, it would be greatly appreciated. With all our guests, it could quickly become a real disaster."

"Exactly what I would like to avoid. It would help if you didn't mention this to anyone, especially staff," Dillon said. He stood, they shook hands, and Kelly walked him out to the front desk.

Dillon headed back to his car, thinking about what his next move was going to be. He climbed into his car, pulled out his cellphone, and called Suel.

"What is it?" Suel said by way of answering.

"Some potentially good news. Are you in the office?"

"Not at the moment. I got a line on the place where your man Moran appears to have been living. I've a warrant, and we're here now going through the place. So far, we've come up empty-handed."

"Give me the address, and I'll meet you there," Dillon said. He wrote down the address in his notebook and then input it into the GPS on his phone. The place was located in an area of Dublin called East Wall, on Ravensdale Road.

TWENTY-FOUR

The units were old, attached, two-story brick units with slate roofs. Each unit was no more than twelve feet wide with a narrow first-floor window. A single same-size window on the second floor was centered above the front door and first-floor window. Fifteen units were attached to one another. There were no front gardens or a parking area for a car, which meant all the cars had to be parked on the narrow street and pulled halfway up onto the sidewalks. Dillon guessed the block of units had to be at least a hundred and twenty years old. He saw Suel's car parked halfway on the sidewalk, a half-dozen units ahead. He pulled onto the sidewalk at the end of the line of cars and parked.

A uniformed officer stood just outside the door of number thirty-one. He nodded as Dillon approached and said, "Hope there's room for you inside."

He wasn't joking. Dillon stepped into a narrow hallway with a staircase. A small front room with a fireplace was off to the left. He had been in bathrooms that were larger than the front room. A half-empty bag of coal leaned against the wall next to the fireplace. The coal-burning fireplace would be the source of heat for the room and confirmed the lack of a radiator. Opposite the fireplace was a ratty-looking couch with a worn gray blanket crumpled up on one end. The back wall, eight feet away, had a doorway that led into a small kitchen.

Dillon popped his head into the kitchen. There was a two-burner stove, a small refrigerator, another coal-burning fireplace, and a small cabinet. Two uniformed officers were going through the cabinet, stacking the contents on the floor. Mismatched plates and saucers, a half-dozen pieces of silverware, and glasses that looked like they'd been stolen from pubs eliminated any room for a third individual.

"Is DI Suel around?" Dillon asked.

"Think he's upstairs," one of the officers said without looking up.

"Probably taking a nap," the other added, and they both laughed.

Dillon headed out to the small hallway. The staircase wasn't carpeted, and the steps were worn from over a century of traffic. He grabbed onto the railing as he started to climb the stairs and it wobbled back and forth. The stairs creaked and groaned as he climbed up to the second floor.

There were two doors. One led into a bathroom and the other, straight ahead, led into the only bedroom. Suel was in the bedroom going through dresser drawers. Sean Donnelly, the photographer Dillon had met in Mountjoy

Square, was leaning against a wall and looking at something on his cellphone. The bed was unmade, and based on the condition of the sheets, probably hadn't been changed in at least a year. One thin pillow embellished with sweat stains was on the bed. Another small coal-burning fireplace was about three feet from the end of the bed. A large saucepan filled with chunks of coal rested on the floor next to the fireplace.

Donnelly looked up and gave a nod as Dillon peeked into the bedroom.

"Nice digs, don't you think?" Suel said. He tossed a box of latex gloves to Dillon and said, "Better put these on for your own protection. The state of this place, good Lord. No telling what you're liable to catch."

Dillon quickly pulled on the gloves. "You find anything?"

"Some pills he shouldn't have but not much else."

"Hugh Healy called and put me in touch with Niall Reid in forensics."

"Reid? A bit heavy-set, salt and pepper hair?"

"Yeah, that's the guy. They matched the two shell casings to the one from the Christmas Eve murder at the Cabra Club."

Suel stopped rummaging through a pile of clothes and looked up. "You're kidding me. Really?"

"Yeah, and that isn't all. A definite fingerprint match on one of the shell casings to Tully Moran."

"On the shell casing from the Cabra Club?"

"No, a casing from Mountjoy Square. There was also another fingerprint they couldn't match. I gave Reid Kevin McBaine's name. He's going to be in touch with the FBI and run the print through their system."

"You've been busy."

"That's not all. Turns out McBaine is staying at the Shelbourne. He's scheduled to check out on Saturday."

"Is he going somewhere over here or heading back to the States?"

"I don't know. I'll check with the airlines and Bergman at the embassy. Who knows, maybe McBaine is heading to Spain."

"Costa del Sol?" Suel asked.

"No idea."

"Anything on Moran's death? Did someone get to him?"

Dillon shook his head. "I haven't heard anything. I have a tough time thinking he committed suicide."

"If McBaine is at the Shelbourne, are you thinking of bringing him in?"

"We don't have enough to go on right now," Dillon said. "I told the manager at the Shelbourne I didn't want to try anything in the hotel. I'm thinking we find out where the car came from. It's probably a rental. Hopefully, we can track it and see what he's up to."

"Well, we're not finding anything here, and it's turning out to be a waste of time, unfortunately," Suel said.

"Is there a shed or anything in the back?" Dillon asked.

"No, nothing."

"You check the floorboards yet?"

"That's next on the list," Suel said.

"I'll go downstairs and start in the front room."

"Yeah, I'll be finished up here in fifteen minutes or so and join you."

Dillon peeked into the bathroom before heading down the stairs. The sink and the tub looked as though they hadn't been cleaned in at least a year. The mirror above the sink was cracked, and the bottom right-hand corner had been broken off, leaving a jagged edge. A soiled, light-blue towel hung from a towel rack. He decided he really didn't need to examine the toilet.

He went back down the stairs. There was a grimy streak on the stairway wall, about six inches wide, from years of hands running along the wall. Dillon ran a gloved hand along the wall rather than risk holding on to the wobbling stair rail. He stepped into the small front room and looked around. The ratty, worn couch was the only piece of furniture. Two empty beer bottles were on the floor at the end of the couch.

He felt the few tiles around the fireplace, all securely attached to the wall. He bent down, looked up the chimney but couldn't see anything. He moved the ashes using his foot and found nothing. He pulled the worn gray blanket from the couch and tossed it on the floor.

There was a stain on the blanket, possibly grape juice but more likely wine.

The two bottom cushions on the couch were threadbare. Dillon pulled them off, examined them, and set them on top of the blanket. A one-euro coin rested on the frame of the couch along with what appeared to be petrified french fries. Dillon left the coin and the fries where they were.

He walked into the kitchen. The two officers that had been emptying the cabinet had just pulled the two-burner stove away from the wall and were examining a pair of dead mice.

"Probably died after eating something your man cooked," one of them said.

"Or maybe they just sucked on the gas line so they wouldn't have to deal with this place anymore," the other replied.

"You find anything?" Dillon asked.

"Yeah, two bodies," one of them said as he pointed at the dead mice, and they both laughed.

Dillon picked up one of the table knives from the silverware piled on a plate. "Just going to check the floorboards," he said.

The worn floorboards in the front room were pine. They were six inches wide and approximately a half-inch thick. They ran the length of the ten-foot room. There was a small space, maybe an eighth of an inch, between each board. Dillon started at the back wall, inserting the table knife in an attempt to raise the board. It didn't move. He worked his way across the room and then moved maybe four feet down toward the front wall and repeated the process. He continued all the way to the front wall and got the same result. He pushed the worn couch away from the wall just as he heard Suel and Donnelly making their way down from the second floor.

"Any luck?" Suel asked as he stepped into the room.

"You tell me," Dillon said and pointed toward the floor.

The couch had been positioned on top of five floorboards. A two-foot length on the three boards closest to the wall had been cut from the ten-foot board. Dillon inserted the table knife, raised one of the boards, and lifted it off the floor joists, revealing a space. He stacked the other two boards, one on top of the other, and slid them out of the way. Three plastic containers with lids sat on the clay soil beneath the floor.

"You win," Suel said and then called the other two officers. "Hey, something you lot should see."

The two uniformed men from the kitchen stepped into the front room and stopped. "We should have started looking there, under that germ-infested couch," one of them said.

"Let me take some photos and document this, lads," Donnelly said and began taking pictures. He photographed the couch, the open area, the stacked floorboards, and finally, a half-dozen shots of the plastic containers.

The containers were larger than what you'd store food in. Once Donnelly had finished taking photos, Suel said, "Okay to take them out?"

"Yeah. Line them up in front of the window. I'll take some more shots, and then we can open them."

Dillon and Suel lifted the plastic containers up onto the wooden floor. Suel pulled out a flashlight and shined it down in the open space. He lowered his head into the area and moved the flashlight all around. "Nothing else down there," he said and brushed the dust and some of the grime from his shoulders.

Donnelly lined up the three containers and photographed them a number of times. "Best you lads with the gloves place them in front of the window," he said.

Suel grabbed the largest of the containers, and Dillon picked up the other two. They set them in front of the window, and Donnelly took a few more photos.

"Okay, open one of them," Donnelly said as he placed a different lens on the camera. Suel pulled the lid off of the largest container, looked down, and said, "Feck me."

"What is it?" Donnelly asked.

"A Beretta pistol." Suel bent down and then looked over at Dillon. "It says .22 short right there on the hand-grip."

"Paddy, we should have forensics here to take possession," Dillon said.

Suel seemed to think for a moment and nodded. "Yeah, I'll make the call. Damn it. I should have had them here, to begin with."

TWENTY-FIVE

Dillon and one of the uniformed officers had to move their cars when the forensics van pulled up. The vehicle was a white paneled van with Forensic Services written in blue letters on the side and then the word GARDA with an image of the logo.

Dillon recognized the two officers dressed in blue hazmat suits.

One of the officers was carrying a clipboard. As they entered the front room, Suel said, "Thanks for coming so quickly, Tommy. We pulled these out from underneath the floorboards. We moved them here to photograph, took the lid off the one, and stopped. Should have had you lads here. Haven't touched them since, and we were gloved throughout."

One of the team glanced in the open container and said, "A pistol?"

"Yeah, short rounds. The plonker living here is suspected in the murder of the two officers in Mountjoy Square. The rounds used in those murders were .22 shorts, just like that pistol."

"Did anyone touch the weapon?"

Suel shook his head and said, "No. Soon as we saw it, we stopped."

It took no more than a half-hour. Suel introduced the Forensics team, Tommy McKenzie and Cully McCormack. They placed each container in a large, white plastic bag, made notes on the clipboard, had Suel sign transfer documents, and left. Sean Donnelly, the two uniformed officers, along with the officer standing guard at the front door, left within fifteen minutes of the Forensics team.

"Anything else you can think of?" Suel asked.

Dillon shook his head. "This may be one of the advantages of having a suspect at the bottom of the social scale. It doesn't take much time to search his residence."

"I was so anxious to get in here I sort of skipped the forensics team. I just wanted to get this guy and—"

"And you did, Paddy. If they can tie that weapon to the shell casings and the rounds fired. Hopefully, his prints are on the weapon. There's a damn good chance we got him. We—"

Dillon's cellphone suddenly rang. Emily from the Tech Lab.

"Yeah, Emily."

"I've got activity on that unknown number."

"You mean he's making a call?"

"The number made a call to the phone you gave me. The caller's location was Stephen's Green again, roughly the same corner by the Famine Memorial."

"Did you check voicemail on the phone?"

"Yeah, no message left."

"Have any other calls come in on that phone?"

"There's been a total of five, well, plus the unknown number a couple of minutes ago."

"So that call was automatically sent to voicemail?"

"Yes, probably after two or three rings whatever number the woman had it set at."

"Can you go in there and adjust it, so he has to stay on the line for maybe ten rings?"

"I suppose I could…"

"I'll take full responsibility. I'll send you an email requesting it and follow up with a signed document. I'm hoping, if he got dumped into voicemail, he might call back. I'm going to cool my heels in Stephen's Green and see if I can spot him. I'll call you once I'm there."

"Okay. Don't forget that paperwork."

"I promise," Dillon said and disconnected.

"You off somewhere?" Suel asked.

"Back to Stephen's Green. McBaine placed a call to Shauna McNeese. It would seem he may be a little closer involved with her than simply giving a wave as he drove off."

"What do you plan on doing if you spot him?"

"I haven't thought that far ahead."

While Suel locked up Tully Moran's place, Dillon left and headed back toward Stephen's Green. Along the way, he tried to come up with a plan. By the time he found a parking place, he still hadn't arrived on a plan of what he'd do if he spotted McBaine. He pulled into a parking area just off Baggot Street and then walked as fast as prudently possible without attracting attention along the four blocks to Stephen's Green.

He settled in on the same park bench as his last visit and waited, then he waited some more. While waiting, he thought of something and phoned Emily. She answered on the third ring.

"Dillon?"

"Yeah, Emily. A question for you. If we got a burner phone, could you transfer that unknown number so I could call it?"

"Yes, that wouldn't be a problem. The problem lies more within the department. You're talking paperwork, two levels of approval, not counting the requisition to purchase the phone. If it was rushed through, it might take three days but plan on a week. That's if it's approved."

"And if I just purchased a burner and brought it to you?"

"That would take about three minutes."

"Got it. I'm in Stephen's Green now. Could you place a call to that unknown number, let it ring three times, and hang up? I'm curious to see what happens."

"I'll do it now and call you back," Emily said. She called back a minute later. "I placed that call. I'll let you know if a reply comes through. I had a thought."

"Tell me," Dillon said.

"Get that burner phone and text message this person. Tell him you don't want to talk on the phone. Come up with some excuse, and maybe you could start some text conversation."

"Do you know if there's been any news report on Tully Moran's death?" Dillon asked.

"I'm not aware of any, but that doesn't mean it hasn't happened. Hang on and let me Google his name."

Dillon thought he could hear her on the keyboard. A moment later, she was back on the phone. "Nothing from what I'm seeing. He's listed as having been arrested as a suspect but nothing about hanging himself this morning."

"Strange, the media would normally be on that right away unless we're attempting to keep it quiet, but that's not going to work."

They disconnected. Dillon waited another twenty minutes and called Emily again. "Anything on the phone?"

"Nothing."

"Strange. Okay. I'm going to head home. You should do the same. I'll get a burner tonight and drop it off first thing in the morning."

"You sure you don't want me to wait here?"

"Thanks but no. It will be at least another hour before I can get back there. I'll see you in the morning," he said, and they disconnected. He phoned Suel.

"Dillon, where are you? Are you coming back into the office?"

He gave Suel an update on the failure of phone activity with McBaine.

"Sounds like he's maybe caught on to you. I've got a piece of news from Forensics," Suel said

"Tell me they found McBaine's fingerprints on that pistol."

"If only. No, unfortunately, nothing like that. They did find a bundle of cash. Two grand in hundred-euro notes."

"That could be payment for Mountjoy Square," Dillon said.

"Yes, it could be. Quite possibly is, and we've no way to prove it. They've put a rush on the Beretta. I phoned your man Reid, and he's seeing to it. We should hear something hopefully tomorrow."

"I just have the sense we're running out of time. McBaine is scheduled to check out of the Shelbourne on Saturday, which reminds me, I need to phone Bergman at the Embassy."

"Well, don't forget we've the funeral, double funeral actually. Liam McCabe and Jimmy Murphy tomorrow morning at Christ Church Cathedral, dress uniform, ten o'clock," Suel said.

"Thanks for reminding me. I completely forgot. I'll be in early tomorrow morning. Any update on Moran's death?"

"Update?"

"If he was in solitary confinement, it's not making sense to me. Emily just checked a few minutes ago, and there's nothing on the news about his death. Does that strike you as strange?"

"Now that you mention it, yeah."

"You think Kinch is withholding information from the press?"

"I don't think Kinch has anything to do with it. But it still doesn't seem right. Let me make a couple of calls. If I learn anything, I'll get back to you," Suel said.

As Dillon headed back to his car, he kept thinking, more questions and no answers. He drove to a Euro store and purchased a cellphone for thirty euros with a fee of twenty euros per month. It was more than he wanted to pay, but if it somehow landed Kevin McBaine, it was worth it. He drove home, noticed the lights were on at Tara's as he passed by, and parked in his drive.

TWENTY-SIX

Lucifer met him at the door. He set his cellphone on the kitchen counter, clipped the leash onto Lucifer, and they headed out for a walk. They walked toward the shops, crossed Ballymun Road, and went into Albert Park. The route around the park was just a little over a mile, and they walked the route three times. Each time the foot traffic was just a little less than before until, on their third pass, they only saw two other people, both walking dogs.

They headed home, and along the way, Dillon placed a call to Eric Bergman. He didn't expect him to be in, and he left a message. "Hi Eric, Jack Dillon. Kevin McBaine is due to check out of the Shelbourne Hotel on Saturday morning. Do you have or could you get flight information? Give me a call when you're able. I've an update on the murder of the two Garda officers. I suspect McBaine is involved, but we have no proof at this stage. Thanks in advance."

The moon was just beginning to rise as he walked Lucifer down the lane past Tara's house. The curtains on the front window were partially open, and he saw her curled up on a chair in her sitting room. Based on where she was sitting, she was probably watching TV.

He brought Lucifer into the house and tossed him a biscuit. Lucifer settled onto his pillow next to the fireplace in the sitting room and inhaled the biscuit in three bites. He snuggled deeper into the pillow, gave a loud sigh, and closed his eyes.

Dillon took some sliced ham from the refrigerator, made a sandwich, and devoured it in about three minutes. He slipped into a comfortable pair of jeans and a casual shirt. There were two bottles of wine in the rack, a red and a white. He pulled the red from the rack, checked himself in the mirror opposite the staircase, and stepped outside.

He walked across the lane to Tara's and rang the doorbell. She answered a moment later, and his first thought was she was unaware it was him at the door.

"Oh, Dillon, hi," she said but didn't invite him in.

"Hi, Tara. Look, I umm, just wanted to drop off a bottle of wine. Sorry about the other night, but we had two officers murdered, and I've been working that case ever since. Anyway, my apologies," he said and held out the bottle.

She glanced at the bottle for a moment and then shook her head. "Sorry I was so bitchy. I didn't realize what had happened. Look, you want to come in for a glass?"

It was exactly what he was looking for, but instead, he heard himself saying, "Thanks, but I'd better not. I'm at work early. We've got the funeral tomorrow, and things are really crazy as you can imagine. Just wanted to give you this and hopefully get back in your good graces."

"You sure you don't want to come in?"

"Thanks, but I'd better not. Could I take a rain check?"

She laughed at that and nodded. "Yes, when things settle down, I would love to see you."

"Okay, thanks. Well, umm, I'll get out of your hair. Thanks for understanding," he said and took a couple of steps back.

"Thank you for the wine, Dillon. I'll save it until you can join me."

"Fair enough," he said then turned and headed back to his house. He didn't hear the door close until he'd crossed the lane. He wasn't sure if he should pat himself on the back or bang his head against the wall. Either way, what's done was done.

He stepped into the house, locked the door, then urged Lucifer upstairs, turning off the lights as they went.

TWENTY-SEVEN

illon was up at five the following morning. He made a quick breakfast, checked his computer for messages, showered, and shaved. He woke Lucifer just after six and coaxed him outside with a biscuit. He filled the food and water dishes, pulled on his dress uniform, let Lucifer back in, and headed off to work.

He arrived in Special Branch thinking he might be the only one there at this hour. There were already six other officers, all in dress uniforms. Amazingly, there were no dirty dishes on his desk. What looked like a fresh pot of coffee was on in the break room. Dillon took a sip, expecting the worst, and was pleasantly surprised. He responded to a couple of emails, left another message for Eric Bergman, and walked down to Emily's lab.

He pressed the buzzer next to the door, and a moment later, a male voice answered, "Yes?"

"Hi, I'm Marshal Dillon from up in Special Branch. I'd like to drop off something for Emily."

"She's not in yet."

Dillon shook his head and said, "Yeah, I know that, but I would like to leave this on her desk. She's expecting it first thing this morning, and I'm going to be out of the office."

There was a long pause and then a sigh. "Alright, if you'll wait just a moment, I'll be there."

Dillon waited a couple of minutes. Eventually, a heavy-set guy with bifocals and crumbs in his goatee opened the door. He was wearing a lab coat and chewing something. He got a surprised look on his face when he saw Dillon in his dress uniform. "You have something for Emily?"

Dillon handed him the box with the cellphone. "She was going to run some tests for me on this. I've left a voicemail message for her. If you would just leave this on her desk, please."

He finished whatever he'd been chewing and swallowed. "Okay, yeah. I'll leave it on her desk."

"Thanks, much appreciated. What's your name?"

"O'Neal, Quinn O'Neal."

"Thanks for your help, Quinn. Please see that she gets that phone."

"Of course," he said and closed the door.

"Prick," Dillon said, but he whispered it, just in case O'Neal was still on the other side of the door.

He hurried back up to Special Branch. Suel was just stepping out of the break room with a steaming mug of tea. "Well, Dillon, nice and early, or are you just stopping in after last night?"

"Very funny, no, just dropped off something for Emily down in the lab. Are you familiar with someone named Quinn O'Neal down there?"

"Oh, yeah. A rather large character, glasses as thick as a Coke bottle, and very impressed with himself."

"Yeah, that sounds about right."

"Yeah, he's a bit of a character. He also does the work of two and is damn good. Stay on his good side, and it'll pay off. By the way, he loves pastries, all kinds."

"Well, that explains the crumbs in his beard."

"That sounds like him," Suel said and laughed.

"I suppose it's too early to hear anything from forensics on the Beretta," Dillon said.

"It is, but they've put it at the top of the list. Anything on McBaine?"

Dillon shook his head. "Niall Reid was going to check with the FBI on that second fingerprint they found on the shell casing. Hopefully, that won't take too long. I know it's a slim chance, but if it would come up as McBaine, that would be the answer to my prayers."

"Let's keep our fingers crossed, which reminds me, I want to make a call to the lads looking at the Beretta. Tell them to connect with Reid if he gets access to McBaine's American file."

"Wouldn't that happen automatically?"

Suel shook his head and said, "Why take the chance?"

Dillon's desk phone rang, and he hurried over to answer it. "Marshal Dillon."

"Hi Jack, Eric Bergman. I just got your message. It sounds like you might have something on McBaine."

"Not quite. Bits and pieces, but I feel like there's a lot more. We just need to catch a break. He's staying at the Shelbourne. I checked with the manager there yesterday. McBaine is due to check out on Saturday. I don't know if he's headed back to the States or somewhere else."

"We've got his passport number here. I should have an answer on his schedule later this morning."

"I'll be at the funeral for our two officers this morning until probably the noon hour. Leave me a message if you get something."

"You got it," Bergman said and hung up.

TWENTY-EIGHT

Dillon and Suel left a little after nine for Christ Church Cathedral. They drove separately. The way things were going, there was a good chance they would have to head off in opposite directions following the service. The church was filled to overflowing, and uniformed officers from all over Ireland lined both sides of the street for blocks.

The hearses approached slowly, followed by the families on foot. DCI McCabe was there with his arm linked to a woman, most likely his sister-in-law, Liam's mother. Liam's father carried a small child next to a tear-stained young woman who looked as though she hadn't slept for days. The Murphy family followed; two children, a boy and a girl, maybe six or seven, held the hands of their mother. A number of siblings followed with families.

There simply wasn't room in the cathedral for everyone. Dillon and Suel waited outside with hundreds of officers. The service was broadcast on speakers mounted outside the church. No one said much, but then, what could you say? Two young men, young fathers, husbands, sons, murdered.

It seemed to go on forever, and then suddenly, it was over. The caskets were carried out to the hearse as bagpipers played mournful tunes. More vehicles appeared, and the families climbed in and drove out the way they'd come, on their way to Glasnevin Cemetery. They drove past uniformed officers with arms held in a salute and tears in their eyes.

TWENTY-NINE

illon's phone rang as he walked back to his car, Niall Reid. "Hi Niall, please tell me you've got something."

"Hi Marshal, this must be your lucky day. We've got a hit on that second fingerprint on the shell casing. You were right, Kevin McBaine. A perfect match."

"Oh, that's great news, Niall. We had a team take three plastic bins from the home of Tully Moran late yesterday. There was a Beretta pistol in one of the bins. It fired .22 shorts. Did they happen to get in touch with you?"

"That would be Tommy McKenzie and Cully McCormack. Yeah, we talked. They were interested in the McBaine fingerprints. They're working on that now. Once they're finished running the prints, we'll do some tests on the Beretta. If I had to guess, I'd say the odds might be better than seventy-five percent that we'll find a match."

"That would be great. Don't let me hold you up," Dillon said and disconnected. He phoned Suel.

"What?" is how Suel answered.

"I just heard from Niall Reid. They got a fingerprint match from Kevin McBaine on one of the shell casings."

"Oh, God bless, that's fantastic. We'll apply for a warrant and—"

"Hold on. Let's give them a couple more hours. The team from yesterday—"

"Tommy and Cully?"

"Yeah. Reid said they're running prints on the pistol, and they'll be looking for McBaine along with Moran. They're going through FBI files now. Once they're finished, they'll run the ballistics test. That's going to take the better part of the day."

"Let me get things rolling now. We're going to need McCabe's signature. He's with family all day, but I know where they'll be. I'll take the paperwork to him and get him to sign off."

"You want to wait for the test results? We won't have them until later today at the earliest."

"No, let's get things moving now. If the test results prove inconclusive, we're not going to get the warrant, so let's move ahead like we have the results. That way, if and when the results come through, we're further ahead. You said McBaine is leaving in a couple of days?"

"Well, that's when he's scheduled to check out of the Shelbourne. Don't know where he's going, and I've got Bergman at the embassy working that line."

"Okay. I'll get the warrant. Can you keep an eye on McBaine?"

"I'll have to find him first, but I think I've got a way to do that."

"Keep me posted," Suel said and disconnected.

Dillon thought it just might be a good idea to go home and change rather than trying to track McBaine while wearing a dress uniform. He let Lucifer out the front door then hurried upstairs and changed. He bribed Lucifer back in the house with a biscuit and headed out to his car.

Deitora, the permanently unhappy woman who lived next door, was out in her front garden trimming her roses. "Oh, if it isn't Mr. Dillon. Don't tell me you're planning to pick up the dog droppings we've all been forced to look at for the past week."

"Nice to see you, Deitora. Enjoy your day," Dillon said and quickly climbed behind the wheel and backed into the street. He tooted his horn three times and drove up the street as Deitora glared. He watched her in the rearview mirror as she stared until he turned at the corner. It was probably a good thing he was too far away to read her lips.

He stopped in the shops, ordered a takeout sandwich, and then ate it as he drove back to the station. Once he pulled into the parking area, he took out his cell and called Emily.

"Well, Dillon, I was just thinking of you."

"Hopefully, on a positive note."

"Let's not go there," she said but then laughed.

"Did your close personal friend Quinn O'Neal happen to leave a cellphone on your desk?"

"Oh please, he's not a close personal friend. Yes, he did leave it. I've loaded it with the unknown number and took the liberty to check the text messages the woman sends."

"Shauna McNeese."

"Yes, but she signs off on her text messages using the letters SMC, all caps."

"Interesting. Did you see any texts that she sent to the unknown number?" He was out of his car now and inputting the entry code on the keypad next to the rear door of the station.

"Not that I could find. Hello, are you still there?"

"Sorry, I was multi-tasking, inputting the code on the door as we talked."

"How did that work?" Emily asked and laughed.

"I want to send a text message to McBaine. I'm heading to your office now."

"I'll be waiting at the door."

Actually, she was waiting at the door. She stood with the door half-open and watched Dillon approach down the hall. "I thought you were at the funeral," she said.

"I was, but figured I'd maybe have a better chance of following McBaine if I wasn't wearing my dress uniform."

"Good point. Come on in," she said, holding the door for him. "I've got your burner phone all set up." As

Dillon followed, he looked around for Quinn O'Neal, the fat guy with the crumbs in his beard he'd left the phone with.

"Where's your boyfriend, Quinn?"

"Watch it, Dillon, or you'll end up at the bottom of my list."

"Okay, sorry, it won't happen again," he said as they entered her office.

"It better not. Okay, here's your burner. It has one number saved, the same unknown number that goes to Kevin McBaine. Now you're going to send him a text so you can follow him?"

"I'm going to text him as Shauna McNeese. I'll say something like she wants to talk but not on the phone and can he meet her, maybe suggest she has information. You said you looked at text messages she's sent?"

"Yeah, there's a bunch of them. You want to take a look?"

"Maybe just a couple. Was there anything that stood out, abbreviations, nicknames, or a phrase?"

Emily shook her head. "No, other than the three letters at the end, SMC. All capital letters."

"And you didn't find any texts sent to McBaine?"

"I didn't find any sent to the unknown number. I did go through probably the preceding four weeks of text messages. Most looked like they were to friends, just standard things, meet at a pub or maybe some gossip."

"Okay, let's give it a try. Keep your fingers crossed."

Dillon began inputting the text message to McBaine on the burner:

Urgent. Need to talk in person. Can you meet me? SMC

"I'm wondering where I should ask him to meet."

"Some public place," Emily said.

"Yeah, but someplace where he can't disappear. How about under the Broom Bridge along the Royal Canal? It's public, but there are only two directions he can really run."

Dillon nodded and pressed send.

"What are you doing? You didn't tell him where?"

"Yeah, I want to see how he responds. Or, even if he responds."

They waited for a good ten minutes. Dillon was beginning to think it didn't work when suddenly Shauna McNeese's phone signaled a text message coming through. He swiped his finger across the screen and pressed the image for messages. There was just a question mark from the unknown number.

"Thank God," Dillon said. He picked up the burner and input another message.

Yes. Gardai asking questions don't want them tracking phone.

Can we meet 2 hrs

An immediate reply came back,

Where

Dillon replied,

Royal Canal, Broom Bridge, Cabra, path under bridge. 2hrs SMC

They waited a good twenty minutes before McBaine replied.

OK

"It's about time," Dillon said. "I better get going if this is going to work." He stuffed both phones in his pocket and hurried out of the Tech Lab.

"Good luck," Emily called after him.

He took the elevator up to Special Branch. Suel was in civilian clothes and just settling in at his desk. "Paddy, you got plans for this afternoon?"

"What do you have in mind?"

Dillon took out the burner phone and turned it on. "Text messages with McBaine. I convinced him I was Shauna McNeese, said we have to talk."

Suel scrolled through the short exchange of messages and looked up at Dillon when he reached McBaine's ***OK***. "He fell for it?"

"Looks that way. I'm thinking you and me, maybe two other guys, someone doing back-up, and we'll get him."

"Shauna McNeese going to be there?"

"No, she doesn't know a thing about this. I've got her phone, so he can't contact her. He bought into the burner, so with a little luck, we'll get him," Dillon said.

"So that's how you got him to fall for this. Good thinking. I've got a thought. Let's dress you up like McNeese and—"

"What?"

"Jack, a wig with those lousy clothes you're wearing will work. We'll position you under the bridge. Look, he's bound to do something like ask her to show herself, and he'll still be in his car ready to take off." Suel spun his chair around and looked at the various officers seated at their desks. "Let me get a group together. Hey Kate," he called, and a woman looked up from her computer screen. "You still got that Halloween wig?"

"Don't tell me you're thinking of switching sides, Paddy," she said then leaned over and pulled out a long black wig. "You'd better learn how to walk properly."

A number of people laughed.

Dillon walked back to her desk, picked up the wig, and pulled it on.

"Oh, Jesus wept," she said, then stood and adjusted the wig on his head. She reached into her purse and pulled out a small mirror. "Here, see what you think."

"Mmm-mmm maybe if he doesn't get too close. I don't know."

"A little lipstick and some makeup might go a long way in convincing him," Kate said.

"Great idea. We'd better get some pictures," Suel said.

"Now, just hold on a minute here," Dillon said.

THIRTY

Dillon was standing beneath the Broom Bridge an hour later, fully forty minutes before Kevin McBaine was due to show. Built in the 1840s, the bridge crosses over the Royal Canal. The footpath along the canal runs beneath the bridge. Dillon wore the wig along with a protective vest beneath a pink sweater. A black leather purse was draped over his shoulder.

Three women in Special Branch had insisted on applying makeup. His cheeks were rouged, he wore red lipstick, and they'd done work on his eyebrows, now covered by the pink framed sunglasses. He had a nine-millimeter pistol just beneath the pink sweater and red nail polish on both hands.

Suel was standing fifty feet off to the left with another woman, both armed. They were pretending to feed the swans and ducks. Another couple was an equal distance on the right. The woman was seated in a wheelchair with a blanket on her lap. A semiautomatic Heckler & Koch HK416 rested beneath the blanket, and the officer pushing the wheelchair was armed as well.

Everything appeared to go off without a hitch until the moment McBaine was to arrive. At that exact moment, two guys walked along the path and headed beneath the bridge toward Dillon. "You're looking well, Missus. Care to take a sip?" One of them said to Dillon and held up a brown plastic one-liter bottle of Bulmers cider.

Dillon shook his head no and looked the other way.

"Aw, come on now, darling. A pretty thing like you shouldn't be alone on a gorgeous late afternoon. What do you say to a bit of a tipple and see where we end up?"

Dillon indicated with a wave of his head that they should keep moving.

"Ahh, but you're about to miss out on the best night you've had in a long time. What do you say if… Hey, wait a minute here. Are you some kind of puff? Dressed up and trying to look all sexy-like? What the bleedin' hell?"

"Get your ass out of here before you find yourself in real trouble," Dillon said just as the burner phone signaled a text message coming through.

"You're a fecking American? You are really off the deep end. Ya know what? You think you can come over here and be some pervert walking around trying to fool the likes of us?"

"Get the hell out of here," Dillon said.

"What are you going to do, you puff?" one of them said and pushed Dillon hard.

Dillon chopped him in the throat. As he reached for his neck, Dillon gave him a solid knee between the legs. He collapsed onto the asphalt path and vomited. His pal grabbed a handful of hair and pulled off Dillon's wig. He got a surprised look on his face just as Dillon punched him three times in the face, and he fell backward into the canal. Dillon reached in the water and grabbed the wig. He attempted to place it on his head while at the same time pulling the cellphone out of his pocket.

Suel and the female officer, the woman in the wheelchair, and her partner were all running to Dillon's aid.

Dillon looked at the text message.

U w/2 guys?

He sent a response, *No*, and texted *Where are you*, but never got a response.

"Bloody hell. Do you have any idea what the hell you've done? Damn it! Cuff 'em and lock 'em up," Suel shouted. "We almost had him. We could've got the bastard, but you two eejits had to get involved."

The guy with the bloody nose was just pulling himself out of the canal. Suel placed his foot on the man's shoulder and pushed him back in. "Pull that bastard out of there and cuff the both of them. We'll see how they like being charged with assaulting an officer, interfering with an arrest, and anything else I can think of. Bloody hell." He looked over at Dillon, attempting to straighten his wig. "How you doing, princess?"

"We had him, Paddy. We almost had him. Damn it."

The officer who'd been pushing the wheelchair and the woman who'd been with Suel had cuffed the men's hands behind their back. The woman carrying the rifle was on the phone talking to someone. Ten or twelve people had begun gathering on either side of the bridge. The scene was so strange no one was saying anything.

Five minutes later, a van arrived and parked just off the bridge where the road widened. The two men were placed in the back of the van, and the collective team headed for their vehicles.

Dillon was still wearing the wet wig as he climbed into the car. Suel slid behind the wheel and said, "For the love of God, will you ever take that damn thing off?"

"So close, Paddy. We could have had him."

"I want to draw and quarter those two bastards."

"Dumb asses," Dillon said and shook his head.

Once back in Special Branch, Dillon laid the wet wig on a corner of Kate's desk. He folded the pink sweater and left it on her chair. He headed for the restroom and spent the next fifteen minutes washing off the makeup and lipstick.

Suel was nowhere to be found when Dillon returned to the office. Kate and the other woman were in the break room regaling a half-dozen people with their tale of the botched plan.

As Dillon walked in with his empty coffee mug, Kate said, "Oh, here he/she is now. The favorite of all the knackers along the canal."

Dillon smiled, took a bow, and everyone applauded. He filled his coffee mug, took a sip, and grimaced. It was dreadful, and he thought, just now, he could really use something a lot stronger.

"I like what you've done with those fingernails," one of the guys said, and even Dillon had to laugh.

THIRTY-ONE

Dillon's phone was blinking when he arrived at his desk. He had two messages. The first one was from Eric Bergman at the US Embassy. He phoned Bergman, who picked up after the second ring.

"Hi Eric, Jack Dillon."

"Jack, how's it going?"

"You don't want to know," Dillon said then forced a more positive tone. "I had a message you called."

"Yes, I checked on flights. Kevin McBaine is scheduled to fly to Spain on a three o'clock flight this Saturday. He's flying KLM, Dublin to Seville." He went on to give Dillon the flight information.

"Okay. Anything else I should know?"

"No, that's about it. Anything I can do to help?"

"Yeah, if you've got a way to add a couple more days to the week, that would be great."

"I'm afraid that's out of my league. Listen, if you think of something I can do, just let me know."

"Thanks, Eric, much appreciated," Dillon said and disconnected.

The second message was from Niall Reid in forensics. Dillon ended up leaving a message and was about to go online when his phone rang. "Marshal Dillon," he answered.

"Hi Marshal, Niall Reid, sorry, I was on another line and missed your call."

"I was returning your call, Niall," Dillon said.

"Oh, yeah, silly me, it's been one of those days. I have a couple of items for you. First, the Beretta pistol that I believe was discovered at the home of Tully Moran."

"Yeah, along with a number of other items."

"Right, the three plastic containers," Reid said. "The pistol has four partials belonging to Kevin McBaine, none of which are on the handgrip and, more importantly, none are on the trigger. Just a guess, but it would seem to suggest he may have handed the pistol to someone, possibly Moran."

"Not exactly what I was hoping for, but not all bad," Dillon said.

"Yeah, I get that. This might brighten things a little. The hundred-euro notes, twenty of them to be exact, amounting to two thousand euros, have McBaine's fingerprints."

"Really, how many have his fingerprints?" Dillon asked.

"Oh, each and every one. If I had to hazard a guess, I would say he may have counted them out to ensure there were exactly two thousand euros."

"Wonderful," Dillon said. "We didn't look in the other two containers, and as a matter of fact, once we saw the pistol lying in the open container, we stopped and called your team in. We should have done that initially, but, well, it was just crazy."

"There was a box of twenty-two caliber short rounds. Six of the rounds were missing. A few pieces of jewelry, no way to establish this, but most likely stolen. There was a digital camera, no images, odd bits of female clothing, a couple of knives, a jar full of one and two-euro coins. That's pretty much it."

"Have they test-fired the Beretta for comparison yet?" Dillon asked.

"I believe they have, but I've not received any results yet."

"Please call me when you hear something. Thanks, Niall. Sorry if I'm sounding down. This is probably the best news I've received all day."

"We all have days like that. Hang in there. I'll be back to you as soon as I learn something."

"Thank you," Dillon said and hung up.

He went online and entered the license number of McBaine's BMW-5, kicking himself for not doing it earlier. Eventually, the license number came up, a 2021 BMW-5 listed to Enterprise Car Rental out at Dublin Airport.

He phoned Enterprise, listened to a recording, and was placed on hold. After ten minutes, he disconnected and drove out to the airport. He followed the directions for the return of a rental car and eventually pulled into the Enterprise lot. As he climbed out of his car, a young man approached, maybe nineteen or twenty.

"I'm sorry, sir, but this area is reserved for Enterprise vehicles being returned. You must have taken a wrong turn. If you follow the exit directions on the sign at the end of the parking—"

"An Garda Síochána," Dillon interrupted and held out the ID draped around his neck.

The young man glanced at the ID, stared at Dillon's red fingernails for a moment, then looked at Dillon and apparently decided he didn't need any trouble. "Yeah, sure," he said and hurried toward a line of a half-dozen returned vehicles.

Dillon headed into the Enterprise office.

"Good afternoon, sir. Returning a vehicle?" the woman behind the counter asked.

"An Garda Síochána," Dillon said and held out his ID card, which, once again exposed the red nail polish on his fingers.

It clearly got the woman's attention, but ever the professional, she asked, "How may I help you?"

"I've got the license number of a vehicle registered to Enterprise. I'm wondering if you can track it."

"Track one of our cars? Yeah, sure, we do it all the time. Is there a problem?"

Dillon shook his head and said, "We believe the gentleman renting the vehicle is an American, Kevin McBaine. We've received notification of a death in the family, and they've been unable to reach him. We've been asked to help."

She seemed to think about that for a moment then nodded and said, "We should be able to do that. Do you have the license number?"

"I do," he said and handed her a sheet with the license number and McBaine's name.

"This shouldn't take long," she said as she typed the information into her computer. Maybe thirty seconds later, she said, "Here we are." As she spoke, she turned the computer more toward Dillon, and a map of Dublin appeared with a red dot down in the lower right-hand corner. She clicked on the plus sign, enlarging the map each time she clicked until it focused on the red dot. Street names appeared and then the names of various buildings and retail outlets.

"It looks like the vehicle is parked at the Shelbourne hotel," she said.

"Would there be any way to get this uploaded onto my phone? I'm afraid he might leave between now and when I arrive at the Shelbourne."

"I'm not sure we can do that. Wouldn't it be against the law?"

"I don't think it would be against the law because we're trying to reach him to give him family information. If we were trying to arrest him, that might be against the law. Of course, if you didn't want to give us the information and we couldn't reach him, he wouldn't know his parents had been killed in a car crash. I'm just thinking that could result in an awful lot of very bad publicity. I don't even want to think of the headlines."

Her eyes grew wide at the suggestion of headlines.

"What if you gave me the URL to track just this vehicle? That way, you'd just be helping with this particular circumstance, but it's not like I'd have access to all the different cars you have out there."

She seemed to think about that for a minute and then said, "I suppose we could do that. Can I burn a copy of your ID? That way, you know, if there was a problem, I could…"

"That's not a problem," Dillon said as he pulled the lanyard over his head and handed his ID to her. Once again, she focused on his red fingernails but didn't comment.

She stepped back, lifted the lid on the copy machine and positioned his ID, then printed off two copies. She handed the ID back to him.

"If you could just copy that URL and email it to me, I can take it from there," he said and handed her a business card.

She seemed to relax a bit once she saw the email address with An Garda Síochána. A moment later, his phone identified an email arriving from Enterprise.

"Oh great, there it is. Can't thank you enough for taking the time, Shannon," he said, reading her name tag.

She nodded and said, "Enjoy your day." The way she said it sounded more like an encouragement to get out of the Enterprise office as quickly as possible.

Dillon smiled, thanked her again, and then left before she came to her senses and realized she shouldn't have given him the URL to track McBaine. He was just leaving the airport when his phone rang. He pulled over onto the shoulder of the road and took out his phone, Suel. "Yeah, Paddy. What's up?"

"Got a call from Declan Tierney. Word is Tully Moran wasn't in a solitary unit when he was murdered."

"Not in a solitary unit? Where was he?"

"Apparently, a holding cell. Left there for fifteen minutes while they transferred someone out of a solitary unit to make room for Moran. Sometime during those fifteen minutes, he was murdered."

"But they said he hung himself using his jumpsuit."

"Partially correct. He was strangled using the sleeve on a jumpsuit, not necessarily his sleeve."

"What the hell? Do they have anyone?"

"Get this, a gentleman by the name of Cormac Doyle."

"Doyle? Like the gang out of Limerick that drove the Linnehan's to Costa del Sol?"

"One and the same," Suel said.

"And they've got this guy?"

"Where's he going to go?" Suel said. "He's locked up in The Joy."

"But apparently still free to kill someone."

"Thought you should know."

"Thanks for the call, Paddy. I'm heading back. I should be there shortly."

"Thanks for the warning. I'll see you when you get here."

Dillon pulled into a Tesco on Drumcondra Road. He purchased a bottle of nail polish remover then hurried back to the office. Once back in the Garda Headquarters, he went into the restroom and proceeded to spend the next twenty minutes removing the red nail polish from his fingernails. It wasn't completely gone, but he'd used up all the paper towels in the restroom, so he headed up to Special Branch.

He input the access code, and once the door buzzed, he stepped inside and headed for his desk. As he passed Kate's desk, she wrinkled her nose and, in a voice that carried throughout the room, asked, "Does anyone smell nail polish remover? Dillon, could that be you?"

THIRTY-TWO

Dillon ignored the two plates and the cereal bowl stacked on his desk as he fired up his laptop. He copied the URL from the Enterprise email and brought up the Dublin map. McBaine's car appeared to still be at the Shelbourne. He phoned Emily down in Tech.

"Yeah, Dillon," was how she answered.

"Just checking in, Emily. Anything happening on Shauna McNeese's phone?"

"Let me check. I looked maybe an hour ago, and there were two calls. Nothing from the unknown number. The two callers left voicemail messages, but I haven't listened to them."

"Probably either girlfriends or places she owes money," Dillon said. "Check on them just to be sure, and if anything turns up, let me know."

Suel entered the office twenty minutes later and made his way to Dillon's desk. "Anything happening with your man McBaine?" he asked as he approached.

"No. I talked a woman out at the car rental agency into giving me a link to trace his car. I just checked. It's still parked at the Shelbourne."

"That strike you as strange?"

"A little, but that said, I don't know what else he'd be doing— going to a museum? Sightseeing? He doesn't strike me as the type. You get any more news on this Cormac Doyle person that killed Tully Moran?"

"Only that he's already in for life. Apparently lifts weights all day, every day. He's probably thinking, what's one more murder on his record? Pretty soon, he'll have a court date to look forward to."

"He had to have some kind of recent information. What the hell was Moran doing within reach of someone like that? I thought he was supposed to be isolated."

"Declan Tierney seemed to think they were exchanging words. You know, giving one another a hard time. Moran probably got close to get in the last word, and Doyle reached through the bars and grabbed him."

"You think McBaine could have had something to do with this?"

Suel shook his head. "I don't see how. Currently, Doyle isn't allowed visitors. We can check, but I doubt he got a phone call. Maybe there was some previous history. We'll probably never know. They've got Doyle on videotape strangling Moran, but by the time the guards got there, it was too late. Moran wasn't going to tell us anything. I'm thinking his death just makes the world a little bit better."

DCI McCabe suddenly stepped out of his office. "Dillon, Suel, a moment of your time, please."

"Shit," Suel said under his breath, and they headed into McCabe's office.

"Have a seat, gentlemen," McCabe said as he settled into his desk chair. "I'm just off the phone. Apparently, Cillian and Padraig Linnehan arrived in Dublin two hours ago. Given the murder of Tully Moran, I find it, mmm, troubling."

"You think they're back to even the score?" Suel asked.

"I don't know. Both were instrumental in the activity two years ago, and clearly, their departure to Spain had a gradual calming effect. I'm unaware of any close connection to Moran. Have you picked up on anything?"

Both Dillon and Suel shook their heads.

"A number of possibilities but nothing concrete," Dillon said.

"Any idea where they are?" Suel asked.

"The information they left with passport control was an address on the south side of Dublin on Torca Road." McCabe touched a couple of keys on his keyboard and brought up the address. Suel pulled out a notebook and wrote it down. "And the individual who murdered Tully Moran, Cormac Doyle, is serving a life sentence. No possibility of parole," McCabe said.

"He's in The Joy until he's dead, and even then, they may wait another day or two just to be sure," Suel said.

McCabe seemed to think for a moment. "Just remain aware, gentleman. Something's up. God knows what, but something's in the wind. Anything on the American, McBaine?"

"I was able to obtain a tracking app from Enterprise Car Rental. His car is currently parked at the Shelbourne. It's been there for most of the day," Dillon said.

"How on earth did you manage to get that?"

"Good manners and a pleasant smile," Dillon said.

"Well, mind yourselves, something is out there. That's all. I'll let you get back to it."

"Thank you for the update," Dillon said.

"What do you think?" Suel asked once they were out of McCabe's office.

"I think, unfortunately, he's probably right, some-things brewing, and it can't be good."

"The Linnehans coming back to town, and Tully Moran murdered. It could be the start of something."

"I think I'll pay Shauna McNeese a visit."

"Dillon, she's not a player. She was a one-night stand for Moran, and according to her, your American—"

"McBaine."

"Yeah, he bought her that flatscreen. She doesn't know anything," Suel said.

"So, who does? You think you're going to get any-thing out of Cormac Doyle?"

"I'm sure she doesn't even know Moran's been killed and, if she does, she doesn't care."

"I have to return her phone at some point. I might as well do it tonight on my way home."

"Suit yourself. I'll check that address the Linnehans gave," Suel said.

THIRTY-THREE

Dillon phoned Emily. The phone rang a half-dozen times, and just as he was about to hang up, she answered. "Dillon?"

"Oh, hi, Emily. I wasn't sure you were still there."

"Actually, I was just about to head out."

"Glad I caught you. I wanted to return that phone to its owner. You want to meet me at the door? I'll head down right now."

"I'll be waiting," she said and hung up.

Suel was on the phone. He nodded as Dillon hurried past. Dillon took the elevator down to the main floor and wound his way through the back halls until he came to the Tech Lab. True to her word, Emily was waiting for him just outside the door.

"Oh, thanks for waiting. Sorry to hold you up, Emily. Hot date with Quinn O'Neal?"

"Don't even go there, and you're not the least bit funny," she said and then laughed. She handed him a plastic evidence bag with Shauna McNeese's phone.

"Anything on here that shouldn't be?" he asked.

"No, we just monitored the calls coming in. Nothing from the unknown number since your incident at Broom Bridge."

"God, I wanted to kill those two idiots. We almost had McBaine, and then they had to show up, wrong place, wrong time."

"Good luck, sorry, but I've got to run."

"Enjoy your evening," Dillon said and watched until she disappeared around the corner. He went out the back door and climbed into his car. He pulled the McNeese phone out of the evidence bag and set it on the passenger seat. He headed out of the parking lot to Drumfinn and Shauna McNeese's home.

Amazingly, he didn't have to wait for a single stoplight along the way, and in no time, he was turning onto Cleggan Street. McNeese's pink house stood out like a sore thumb on the street. At this hour, there were a number of cars parked along the street, all parked halfway up on the sidewalk. Dillon pulled onto the sidewalk blocking McNeese's driveway and climbed out of the car. Her faded red Hyundai looked like it hadn't moved since the last time he was here. The yellow plastic car missing the front wheel was in the same spot. Two envelopes were stuck in the door's mail slot. Dillon pulled them out of the slot and knocked on the door.

He turned his head to listen better and thought he could hear Rowen, the little boy, crying inside. He knocked on the door again, this time just a little harder.

She still didn't answer. He waited half a minute then pounded on the door hard, and still, she didn't answer.

On a whim, he tried the doorknob, and the door opened. "Hello? Hello? Shauna, it's Jack Dillon with An Garda Síochána," he called and stepped inside. "I'm returning your phone. Shauna?" he called a bit louder this time, thinking, for God's sake, do something with the little guy crying.

"Shauna, Jack Dillon," he called again and headed in the direction of the crying child. He saw Rowen first, red-faced with a runny nose and bloodshot eyes. He was sitting in his highchair. The child focused on Dillon, and the volume of his crying increased as he raised his arms toward Dillon.

Dillon saw a pair of bare feet on the kitchen floor, and he automatically said, "Shauna," as he stepped around the cabinet. She was stretched out on the floor with a baby bottle lying next to her. The bullet hole was centered on her forehead. Her eyes had that glassy stare Dillon had seen far too often.

He stepped over and lifted the little boy out of the highchair. The child wrapped his arms around Dillon's neck and sobbed into his shoulder. Dillon stepped out of the kitchen and pulled out his cellphone. Paddy Suel answered on the second ring as little Rowen continued to cry.

"Now what do you— Dillon? Dillon, are you there? Dillon? What's—"

"Paddy, someone shot her. She's dead in the kitchen."

"Shot who? Who the hell is making all—"

"Shauna McNeese, she's been murdered. Get a team over here, Paddy. Can you hear me?" He half-shouted and then said, "It's okay, Rowen. It's okay. Shhhh, shhh. It's okay. You're all right. You're gonna be all right."

THIRTY-FOUR

Dillon was seated on the couch in the small sitting room. He'd given Rowen a bottle, and the little boy was covered with a blanket, fast asleep in Dillon's arms. The forensic medical teams were in the kitchen. Suel and other officers were in the process of going through the upstairs rooms.

Two female officers entered the sitting room. One was a brunette. The other appeared older with gray hair. "Marshal Dillon?"

Dillon looked up and nodded.

"How's he doing?"

"He's been asleep for a good while. I changed him and gave him a bottle. Not sure when he last had some solid food. There was something on the tray of the highchair, but I just wanted to get him out of there. He shouldn't have to…" but his voice trailed off.

The women glanced at one another. "You did the right thing, Marshal," the gray-haired woman said. "He needs sleep right now, and the bottle helped to calm him, the poor little thing."

"You're going to take him?"

"In a bit. We've social services standing by," the brunette said.

"Could I hold him for a bit longer?"

They seemed to consider that for a moment before the gray-haired woman said, "I think that would be a good idea. We've to pack some clothes and nappies for the little one. If you'd hold him for a bit more, we'll be back."

Dillon nodded, and they stepped out of the room and climbed the stairs. He could hear their voices upstairs but couldn't make out what was being said. They were back down maybe fifteen minutes later. Suel followed them into the sitting room.

"Marshal?" the gray-haired woman said in a soft voice.

"Yeah, I know," Dillon said and handed Rowen to her.

"Oh, my, he's big. Hasn't missed too many meals," she said and carefully lifted him onto her shoulder. Rowen made some noise but never opened his eyes.

Dillon stood and pulled the blanket up over Rowen's back. "Take good care of him. He didn't deserve this."

"He'll be in good hands, Marshal. Thank you, you've no idea the long-term effect your kindness will have on this child."

"His name is Rowen," Dillon said and kissed the little boy on the back of his head.

"Thank you, Marshal," they said in unison and headed out the door.

Dillon watched them through the front window for a moment, then cleared his throat and looked at Suel. "Okay, where are we, Paddy?"

"Jack, we've plenty here to do the job. Maybe think about going home. Take it easy. We can get on it tomorrow and—"

Dillon shook his head. "No, let's get on it now. As first on the scene, I'll have to make a statement. Is someone back at the office who can do the interview?"

"Yeah, I can set it up. You sure you don't want to—"

"No, let's get it done. I really don't want to wait until tomorrow."

"Okay, let me make a call. Most likely Burke and O'Keefe. Head back. You sure you're okay?"

"Let's just say I'm eager to find whoever did this."

"Okay, I'll see you tomorrow, and Jack, good job. If you hadn't been here, there's no telling what would have happened to the little boy."

"Yeah, thanks," Dillon said and headed out the door. Once he climbed into his car, he pulled out his cellphone and brought up the search on McBaine's rental car. It was still parked at the Shelbourne Hotel.

He headed back to the headquarters building and took the elevator up to Special Branch. As he stepped into the office, Jim Burke spun around in his desk chair and said, "Dillon, we got the call from DI Suel. You still want to do this?"

"Yeah, let's get it done."

"Okay, we're all set up in interview room two. You want to grab a coffee or something before we get started?"

Dillon thought about a coffee but, based on the hour, decided against it. "No, I'm good to go. Let's get it over with."

The interview lasted the better part of two hours. There was a veritable laundry list of standard questions that had to be asked, plus ones specific to the particular case. When they eventually finished, Dillon thanked Burke and O'Keefe. They chatted for a half-minute, and he headed home.

He pulled into his drive and parked. Lucifer met him at the door and hurried into the front garden. Dillon grabbed a biscuit along with Lucifer's leash and stepped back outside. Given the hour, the park had already been closed for a while, so they walked along a number of neighborhood streets in the moonlight. All the while, Dillon was thinking of little Rowen and Shauna McNeese. It was close to midnight when they returned home.

Lucifer slowly headed upstairs. Dillon doubled checked the locks on the doors and windows. He got the coffee ready for the morning and then headed upstairs to his bedroom. Lucifer was already asleep.

Dillon crawled into bed and eventually drifted off to sleep. He dreamt of little Rowen, fortunately, not crying but sleeping soundly in his arms.

THIRTY-FIVE

Dillon woke the following morning before the alarm went off. He slipped into jeans and a sweatshirt and went downstairs. He turned on the coffee and then stepped outside into the front garden. He grabbed the small shovel, cleaned up a week's worth of deposits left by Lucifer, and headed back into the house. He showered, shaved, was dressed and on his second coffee when Lucifer came down the stairs. He let him outside, tossed him a biscuit then filled his food and water dishes.

He let Lucifer back inside and climbed into his car. He pulled out his cellphone. McBaine's rental car was still parked in the Shelbourne parking ramp. He headed off to the office, arriving before 7:00. He was at his desk going over a file on Cormac Doyle when Suel arrived.

"How's it going, Dillon? Can I get you a coffee?"

"Thanks, Paddy, but I'm okay."

Suel opened a white paper bag and pulled out a chocolate doughnut that he proceeded to place on the stack of files sitting on Dillon's desk. "Brought you a little something. Figured you'd need the sweetening."

Dillon chuckled. "Thanks, Paddy. That's very kind. You don't have to worry. I'm fine."

"Yeah, you're better than fine, but that doesn't mean you can't use a little sweetening. For God's sake, we all can. I ate mine in the car."

Dillon smiled at that. "Okay, yes, I could use a coffee. Thank you."

"How'd your statement go last night?"

"Pretty much by the book, which was just fine. Not a bother."

"Let me get you a coffee," Suel said and headed for the break room. He returned a couple of minutes later and set Dillon's mug on the desk. "You check in on your man McBaine this morning?"

"Car is still parked in the Shelbourne ramp. I'm hoping his fingerprints or DNA show up in the McNeese evidence. We need more than we've got now to make an arrest."

"Is it today he's scheduled to fly to Spain?" Suel asked.

"Yes, on a KLM flight at three this afternoon. We need something to happen, and pretty soon, or he's going to be able to board that flight and leave the country."

"Damn it. I just checked. It's early, but there is nothing connecting him to the McNeese murder yet," Suel said.

"We need something. Cormac Doyle was not allowed visitors, so McBaine wasn't stopping at Mountjoy. No phone calls to Doyle for the past month. You think he knew Tully Moran from before and just grabbed the opportunity? Maybe he didn't know anything about him murdering the two officers," Dillon said.

"Yeah, maybe. I just want to stop McBaine from leaving the country. We need to interview that bastard."

Dillon nodded and said, "Let me attend to my sweetening." He took a bite from the chocolate doughnut. "Mmm, I left a message with Eric Bergman to check on McBaine's flight and see if he's still scheduled. I—" Dillon's phone rang, and he said, "Oh, this may be him now. Marshal Dillon," he answered.

"Yes, Marshal, thank God, I reached you. This is Owen Kelly at the Shelbourne."

Dillon signaled Suel with a wave of his finger. "What seems to be the problem, Owen?"

"I'm afraid it's the gentleman you were inquiring about."

"Kevin McBaine?"

"Yes. He's dead."

"Dead?"

"The cleaning staff entered his room this morning and found him dead in bed."

"You're sure he was dead. Did you—"

"Absolutely sure. I went in there myself. This was not a natural passing."

"Okay, we'll be down there immediately. I think—"

"I'm hoping you can do this quietly. I've not contacted anyone else. Not the sort of publicity we need.
Would it be possible not to use the main entrance?"

"I think we can do that. Is there a service entrance
somewhere in the building and maybe a service elevator?
If we could park in back and use a service elevator, we
could get to the room without the majority of your guests
learning of this. Unfortunately, our van is labeled Forensic Services with a logo on either side."

"The rear is fairly private. In fact, I'll arrange for
private parking. Can you spread the word not to arrive
with sirens blaring?"

"I'll get on that right away. I'll be there in twenty
minutes," Dillon said.

"I'll meet you in the rear, at our service entrance.
Thank you, Marshal," Kelly said and hung up.

"Don't tell me McBaine is dead," Suel said as Dillon shut down his computer and stood.

"That's what he said. He wants us to enter through
the service entrance at the rear of the building. We can
park back there. No sirens or flashing lights. The scene
is secure, but I'm going to head down there now. Can
you alert forensics and the medical examiner?"

"I'll give you a five-minute head start. See you
down there," Suel said as Dillon headed for the door and
hurried out to his car. He climbed in behind the wheel,
pulled out his phone, and clicked on the link tracking
McBaine's vehicle. It was still in the Shelbourne parking
ramp, which got Dillon wondering just how long

McBaine had been dead. There was a good chance he could have been murdered sometime yesterday and only discovered this morning.

He headed out of the parking lot and drove down to the Liffey River. He drove along the River to the O'Connell Street Bridge, crossed the Liffey, and eventually turned onto Kildare Street. He drove up the street, and just before the top of the street, he pulled into a narrow alley behind the Shelbourne Hotel. He was just about ready to think this wasn't going to work as he drove maybe fifty feet down a narrow entrance when suddenly he pulled into a larger area with a loading dock and plenty of spaces to park.

THIRTY-SIX

As Dillon pulled up against the Shelbourne Hotel, Owen Kelly, the manager at the Shelbourne, stepped out onto the loading dock. He was dressed in another gray suit, or maybe it was the same one. Dillon climbed out of his car, gave a nod, and pressed the fob on his keys, locking the car door.

He climbed up the stairs alongside the loading dock and shook hands with Kelly.

"Thank you for coming, Marshal. Good lord, I can't believe this has happened."

"You were in the room?" Dillon asked.

"Yes, security called me immediately. Staff had just entered to clean. It couldn't have been more than thirty seconds when they spotted the body. Our policy is they check the bedroom and bathroom before beginning their work. They left the room and phoned security. Security phoned me, and we entered the room together. Couldn't have been in the room for more than a minute. We confirmed what had been reported, left the room, and stationed an individual in the hallway so no one would enter."

"As our team arrives, they'll want to interview you, security, the cleaning staff, anyone who was in the room."

"Of course."

"If you can show me where the service elevator is, our teams should be arriving in the next twenty minutes or so. We'd like to keep this as quiet as possible for you."

"Please follow me. The elevator is just down the hall and around the corner. The gentleman's suite is up on the fifth floor, number 504, a lovely suite overlooking Stephen's Green," Kelly said as if he was selling the view.

They walked down a short hallway, around the corner, and there was the elevator. Across the hall from the elevator through a pair of swinging doors was the laundry facility. The light above the elevator doors suddenly chimed and lit up. The elevator doors slid open, and a moment later, two women pushing four-wheeled carts filled with bed linens stepped out of the elevator. Both women smiled and nodded at Kelly as they pushed the carts across the hall and through the swinging doors.

"Any security codes or anything necessary to use the elevator?" Dillon asked.

Kelly shook his head. "No. It will open up on the fifth floor in a hallway labeled 'Staff Only.' There's a simple four-digit code to open those doors, 1824, the year the hotel was established."

Dillon took out a notebook and wrote down the code. "Just in case I forget. We'll be looking at a lot of things up there. Would it be possible to have someone stationed down here to show the officers the way?"

Kelly nodded and said, "Let me alert someone this instant."

"Good, I'll wait out on the dock. I expect the forensics and medical teams to be the first," Dillon said. While he waited on the dock, he phoned Suel, who was following the forensics van at that moment. They were just about to cross the O'Connell Street Bridge, having taken the same route as Dillon.

"Yeah, Paddy, plenty of room to park behind the hotel. Take Kildare Street up to the Shelbourne."

"Yeah, that's what I need, street directions in my hometown from an American. That's the route we're taking. See you in a few minutes," Suel said and disconnected.

The forensics van turned into the alley a few minutes later. Dillon gave a wave as it headed toward him and then pulled next to the loading dock. Suel pulled his car in and parked behind Dillon's car.

Suel climbed up the loading dock stairs and said, "Oh, me mam would be so proud of me coming into the Shelbourne."

"Yeah, the service entrance," Dillon said, and they both laughed.

Another vehicle, the medical team, pulled into the alley and headed toward them. Dillon recognized Hugh Healy behind the wheel and gave a wave. Healy nodded back.

"Be on your best behavior, now, Paddy. If it wasn't for Healy going the extra mile, we wouldn't have the shell casings linking the killings to the Christmas Eve murder at the Cabra Club."

"Yeah, yeah, I know. You don't have to remind me."

Owen Kelly stepped out onto the loading dock with a young man he introduced as Paulo.

"Nice to meet you, Paulo. Thanks for helping us. How's it going?" Dillon said and extended his hand.

"Is going good," Paulo said and shook hands. He had a heavy accent but obviously understood Dillon's question. "Does he have the code for the fifth-floor doors?" Dillon asked Kelly.

"Yes, he's more than able to direct anyone coming in."

"Have him ask for an ID just to play it safe," Dillon said then looked at Paulo and said, "Comprendo?"

"Don't worry about it," Paulo said, suggesting he was more than capable.

Everyone laughed. The three people in the forensics team were climbing the stairs. Dillon recognized Niall Reid and behind him, Sean Donnelly carrying two cameras and a briefcase. Hugh Healy was stacking what appeared to be four medical cases on the end of the loading dock. Dillon and Suel each picked up a case, and everyone but Paulo followed Owen Kelly to the service elevator.

Kelly pushed the elevator button, and the doors immediately opened. Once everyone was in the elevator, Kelly pushed the button for the fifth floor. As the doors opened on the fifth floor, Kelly said, "If you need restroom facilities, there is a men's and lady's room back here." He pointed in the opposite direction from where they were heading. "The code to open these hallway doors is 1-8-2-4," he said, inputting the code. It made a soft buzz, and he pushed one of the swinging doors open. They headed down the hall toward a man in a gray suit standing in front of the suite.

"Here we are, suite 504," Kelly said. "I'll leave you to your task. Please feel free to contact me should you need anything. Thank you again for keeping this matter private."

"Thank you, Owen," Dillon said, and the man standing guard opened the door to the suite. They stepped into an elegant front room with twelve-foot ceilings, a crystal chandelier, and a fireplace. Above the fireplace was a beveled glass mirror with an elaborate gold frame. Massive draperies hung over the two windows overlooking Stephen's Green. An antique coffee table with a glass top was positioned in front of the fireplace. A burnt orange upholstered chair was positioned on either end of the coffee table, and a pink patterned couch faced the coffee table and fireplace. Elegant lamps sat on end tables. A carved antique wooden sideboard with a white marble top rested against the back wall. Four crystal glasses and a bottle of Midleton Irish whiskey rested on the marble top.

Everyone on the forensic and medical teams pulled out sealed plastic bags with white hazmat suits and boots. They stepped into the suits, slipped on the boots, latex gloves, and donned medical masks. Niall Reid glanced around then gave a nod, and they walked toward the bedroom. Dillon and Suel slipped on latex gloves and watched from the front room.

THIRTY-SEVEN

illon and Suel remained in the front room with the fireplace. They would enter the bedroom once the initial examination was completed. They could see Kevin McBaine, or what was left of him, from where they stood. It was not a pretty sight. His face was blooded, swollen, and black and blue. He was arranged in the center of the four-poster bed, leaning against the headboard with his arms outstretched, looking not unlike a modern version of the crucifixion. His wrists were bound to the posts on the left and right side of the headboard with black zip ties. At first, Dillon thought he must have wiped some of the blood from his face because both hands were bloody, but then he realized all the fingers on McBaine's hands were missing and scattered over the bedsheet. One of the fingers still had a gold ring with a black stone.

McBaine's head hung down at an angle, and from what they could see, he had obviously been beaten severely. Dillon's first thought was that someone, somewhere on the fifth floor, must have heard the screaming or the racket, but as he glanced around, everything appeared in place. Nothing, in fact, appeared to be out of order with the exception of McBaine, well, and the bloodied bed.

Sean Donnelly was busy taking photographs from either side and then from the foot of the bed. He eventually gave a nod, and one of the forensics team began to gather the fingers scattered on the bed and place them in individual evidence bags.

It was more than an hour before Dillon and Suel were allowed into the bedroom. Hugh Healy was in the process of obtaining body temperature and having a discussion with Niall Reid about the cause of death. Reid suggested heart failure due to the unpleasant activity. Healy suggested asphyxiation.

Dillon noticed a suit coat and trousers in the bedroom neatly draped over an upholstered chair in front of an antique desk. The desk had a notepad resting on it, a time of '7:00' written on it.

He pointed to the notepad and said, "What do you think, Paddy?"

"A dinner reservation? Meeting someone? Yesterday? The day before? It might mean something, then again, who knows?"

"Let's try and be a little more positive," Dillon said and felt the pockets on the suit coat. He pulled out a set of car keys with an Enterprise Car Rental tag from the right-hand pocket. He pulled a cellphone from the left-hand pocket. The phone was a flip phone with a screen that folded over the keypad. "I'm guessing this is a burner," Dillon said and set the phone on the desk. He pulled a breast wallet and passport from an inside pocket and set them next to the burner phone. He took a much more expensive-looking, dark blue iPhone from the other inside pocket and set it next to the wallet and passport.

"That damn phone runs close to fifteen hundred euros," Suel said.

"Yeah, so he carries that top-of-the-line item along with one that goes for maybe thirty euros. What do you think?"

"I think the thirty-euro phone might be the more interesting," Suel said and picked up the burner. He flipped open the screen and pushed a couple of buttons. "Hmmm, a total of three incoming phone calls, all from the same number. Not a busy guy. Most recent was yesterday, just after four."

"And that's a call, not a text?"

Suel pushed a couple more keys. "No record of any text messages."

"Give me that number," Dillon said and entered the number on his phone as Suel read it off to him.

"Got it?" Suel asked

Dillon nodded and said, "So he gets that call around four and maybe writes down 7:00 on the note pad. Could be he's meeting someone for dinner here. It's a high-buck place. That could be impressive to someone. His car never left the parking ramp. You want to check and see if there might be security footage from the dining room?"

"Yeah, I'll do it now. What's your man's name again, the manager?"

"Kelly, Owen Kelly. His office is behind the front desk down on the main floor."

Suel nodded and headed out of the room.

Dillon grabbed some evidence bags from a box resting near the door to the bedroom. He placed the two phones and the passport in separate evidence bags and labeled them. He went through McBaine's wallet, four credit cards, a New York state driver's license, two insurance cards, a library card, and twelve hundred and forty euros cash; twelve hundred-euro notes, and two twenty-euro notes. That reminded Dillon of the twenty euro notes with McBaine's fingerprints that Tully Moran had hidden in the plastic container beneath the floor.

Behind all the cash was a receipt from the Saddle Room restaurant in the Shelbourne. Apparently, dinner for three to the tune of six-hundred-and-forty euros. The receipt was dated just last night at 9:07. Dillon phoned Suel.

"Yeah, Dillon?" Suel answered.

"Just found a receipt in McBaine's wallet from last night at the Saddle Club Restaurant here in the hotel. Dinner for three that ran six-hundred-and-forty euros. Paid last night at 9:07. If they've got security cameras, he should be on there."

"Perfect, gotta go," Suel said. Dillon heard him say, "Mr. Kelly, my name is DI Suel, and we…"

"I think I've got it," Hugh Healy said, causing Dillon to look over just as Healy cautiously pulled back a large pair of tweezers from McBaine's mouth on the end of which hung something large and black.

As Dillon walked over, he said, "What in the hell is that?"

"It's what caused his asphyxiation. Someone crammed this sock in his mouth. No doubt to muffle any scream. At some point, he swallowed the sock. It lodged in his throat, and that's what ultimately caused his death. Based on what we've found thus far, I would call it somewhat of a blessing for him. Obviously, whoever did this wasn't about to let him live."

"So if they stuffed that sock in his mouth, that means he wouldn't be able to answer anything they asked him."

"Yeah, that's correct," Healy said.

"Have you been able to determine the time of death?"

"Not officially, but if I had to hazard a guess, I would say somewhere between 9:00 last night and midnight."

"Okay, Hugh, thanks. Please keep me posted once you determine an official time of death."

"Will do," Healy said just as Dillon's phone rang, DI Suel. "Yeah, Paddy, what do you have?"

"I'm in the security office just beginning to view your man McBaine at the dinner table. Care to guess who he's having dinner with?"

"Let me guess, Cillian and Padraig Linnehan?"

"You win the prize," Suel said.

"I'll be down in just a moment. You're in the security office?"

"Right, it's down on the lower level. Same side of the hall as the elevator and three doors beyond it."

"I'm on my way," Dillon said. He disconnected and said, "Niall, they've got something on the security tapes downstairs. I'll be back in maybe a half-hour or so." Reid nodded, gave a quick wave of his hand, and went back to examining the zip ties that had been used to secure McBaine's wrists to the bedposts.

"I'll be back," Dillon said to the security man standing in the hallway. He input the 1824 code at the end of the hall, pushed the door open, and waited for the elevator. The elevator stopped on the third floor, and a woman pushed in another four-wheel cart full of bed linens. She smiled and nodded at Dillon then pushed the illuminated lower-level button on the control panel.

Once the door opened on the lower level, Dillon let the woman with the laundry cart go first then stepped out of the elevator and walked up the hall. The third door was marked 'Security,' and he entered. As he stepped inside, he could see Suel seated at a distant counter in front of a computer screen. He was one of three people watching the screen.

"Hi, can I help you?" a man at the desk just inside the door asked.

"Got a call to join those folks," he said and nodded toward Suel and the other two men.

"Go ahead," the man said.

Dillon made his way around a half-dozen desks. He stood behind the three men focused on the somewhat blurry black and white image on the screen and said, "Thanks for the call, Paddy."

"This is my partner, Marshal Dillon," Suel said, not taking his eyes off the screen.

"Hi, ya's," both men said in unison and remained focused on the screen. One was ginger-haired and the other dark-haired. The ginger-haired man was the larger of the two.

"He's American, but don't hold that against him. Dillon, this is definitely Cillian and Padraig Linnehan. No idea what they're discussing, but things seem to be on an even keel."

"If they went up to your man's room, we'll have tape on that," the ginger-haired guy said.

"I brought the receipt from the dinner last night," Dillon said and handed an evidence bag with the dinner receipt to the ginger-haired guy.

He looked at it, shook his head, and chuckled. "Oh, God, will you look at this? None of us can afford to eat here."

"Or stay here for a night," the dark-haired guy said.

"You gotta be kidding me. Six hundred and forty euros? That's an awful lot of pints," Suel said and passed the receipt to the dark-haired guy.

"You mind if we fast forward to maybe the last few minutes?" Suel said.

"No, in fact, I was just going to suggest that," the ginger-haired guy said. "We've already sent a copy of this to your email address."

They watched the final four minutes of the tape. All three individuals stood. One of the Linnehans said something that apparently was funny. They all laughed, and the one man gave McBaine a friendly pat on the shoulder.

"Let me just get to the security camera at the elevators," the ginger-haired guy said and typed something on the keyboard. A moment later, an image of the two elevators appeared. He fast-forwarded through the next couple of minutes. He slowed for a moment as two figures appeared, but it was a couple stepping onto an elevator, and he sped up for three more minutes, and suddenly, there were the two Linnehans indicating with a grand wave of the hand that McBaine should enter the elevator first.

"I doubt they just walked him to the door," Suel said. "Can you send this to me also, and if you could find tape of those two leaving, that would really help."

"But of course," the ginger-haired guy said.

Suel and Dillon thanked both men and left the security office. "What do you think?" Suel said once they were back on the elevator.

"I think we have enough to bring them in," Dillon said. "Now we just have to find them. It would be a good idea to get a BOLO out on the two of them. We've been running around like chickens with our heads cut off. It's time to start putting some heat on these two."

THIRTY-EIGHT

When they returned to room 504, there was a gurney with a folded black bodybag parked behind the pink patterned couch. Dillon noticed that the bottle of Midleton whiskey and the four crystal glasses on the sideboard were now in separate evidence bags resting on top of the sideboard.

Healy stepped out of the bedroom, nodded at Suel, and smiled at Dillon.

"How's it going, Hugh?" Dillon asked.

"We're just about finished here. We've a bit more accurate time of death. Somewhere between 10:15 and 10:45 last night. Cause of death will officially be listed as asphyxiation barring something appearing on the toxicology reports."

"The fingers?" Dillon said. "Any idea how they were removed?"

"It appears to be some sort of shears. Possibly a hand-held pruner of some sort. I'm thinking something that could be easily concealed in a jacket or a coat. He was also beaten before the fingers were removed. I'll know more after the autopsy, but I suspect some broken ribs, possibly three. Clearly, his nose was broken, I believe the jaw as well. We'll confirm tomorrow, but I suspect a fairly serious skull fracture. Bruising on the right forearm suggests an attempt at a defensive move, but that's about it. Most likely, the attack came as a complete surprise. Just a guess, but I think either the broken nose or the blow to the back of the head represents the initial attack. He never really had a chance to fight back."

"We'll talk tomorrow, Hugh. Please leave me a message as to when the autopsy is scheduled."

"Sure thing," Healy said. He nodded at Dillon and Suel then wheeled the gurney into the bedroom.

Niall Reid stepped into the front room and said, "We're going to be a few more hours."

"Anything unique?" Suel asked.

"You mean like a business card from the murderer? No, sorry to say. One thing might be interesting. The whiskey bottle and the four glasses. We found fingerprints. You said the victim had been staying here for a week?"

"Not quite a week," Suel said.

"Different sets of prints on all four glasses. We'll see if we can get a name. It could just as well be previous people staying in the room. We should have a better handle on it tomorrow. You found that set of car keys?" Reid asked.

Dillon nodded. "They were in the pocket of his suit coat."

"You have any idea what he was driving?"

"I do," Dillon said and took out his phone. He clicked a couple of keys and brought up the information. "The vehicle is a rental from Enterprise out at the airport. It's a black BMW-5, License number 211-D-2305. I've had the tracking link on it for the past day and a half. The car has been in the Shelbourne ramp that entire time. You could check with Owen Kelly for the exact location. You haven't recovered a weapon of any sort?"

Reid shook his head. "If you're referring to a firearm, no, nothing like that thus far."

"Strange. Well, okay. Thanks, Niall. Soon as you have something, let us know."

"But of course," Reid said and went back into the bedroom. He stepped aside for Hugh Healy and another man wheeling the gurney. McBaine was now enclosed in the body bag and strapped down on the gurney.

"We'll be back up to grab our cases," Healy said. "I want to get the victim secured in the van and to the lab as quickly as possible."

"We can grab those cases, Hugh. We'll meet you down on the loading dock," Dillon said and held the door for Healy and his partner as they wheeled the gurney with McBaine's body out into the hall.

"Paddy, give me a hand with these cases, okay? We'll get Healy out of here. You going back to the office?"

Suel shook his head for a half-second, bringing himself back to the here and now. "Oh, sorry, yeah, I'm heading back to the office. I want to check on that address McCabe gave us."

"I'm going to touch base with Owen Kelly before I go back to the office. Try and keep us on his good side," Dillon said. They walked into the bedroom. Other than the blood-stained sheets and the zip ties hanging from the bedposts, the room appeared ready for the next guest. They rode the elevator down to the lower level and carried the medical cases out to the loading dock. Healy was just closing the double doors on the back of the medical van. He and his partner headed over to the loading dock, and each grabbed two cases.

"Thanks, Hugh. Keep us posted," Dillon said.

"Yeah, umm, thanks, Hugh. You need anything, just call," Suel said.

"Yeah, thanks, lads. I'll do that," Healy said and gave a friendly nod to Suel.

Dillon and Suel watched as they placed the cases behind the front seats of the medical van then climbed in and backed up. Healy was behind the wheel, and as he pulled away, he gave a quick toot on the horn and a wave.

"Thanks, Paddy, that was nice of you to say."

"Aw, I guess you're right. He ain't that bad. You touching base with Kelly?"

"Yeah, then heading back to the office. I'll see you there?"

"You will," Suel said and headed down the stairs to his car.

Dillon headed up to the front lobby and asked to see Owen Kelly. A moment later, Kelly opened the door leading to his office and motioned Dillon to join him. As Dillon approached, Kelly led the way to his office.

"Please have a seat, Marshal. Any news?"

"Yes and no. First, I want to thank you for your assistance and help. Without you and your staff, things would not have gone as smoothly as they did."

"With all due respect, thank you. You could have barged in the main entrance with sirens blaring, and five minutes later, we'd have the media all lined up out front. Any ideas of who, what, or why?"

"Not much to say at this point," Dillon said, keeping what little they'd learned close to the vest. "Our forensics team is still up there processing the scene and will be for the next few hours. That's pretty standard. It will probably be a couple of days before I have any information for you. I'll try and keep this as quiet as possible. I know the less publicity, the better for the Shelbourne."

"Much appreciated. If I can be of any help, don't hesitate to get in touch," Kelly said as he stood. He extended his hand, signaling, unless Dillon had something else, the conversation was over.

Dillon smiled, shook hands, said, "Thank you," and left.

THIRTY-NINE

Dillon phoned Emily in the Tech Lab once he was seated in his car. She answered on the third ring. "Dillon?"

"Hi Emily, I don't know if you've heard, but our latest main suspect in the murder of the two officers was found dead this morning."

"Are you talking about Mc-what's-his-name?"

"Yeah, Kevin McBaine. It's an ongoing investigation, murdered last night, found this morning."

"Oh. My. God."

"Yeah, well, I did get a phone number off a burner phone in his possession. He received three calls from the number, the most recent coming in at 4:00 yesterday afternoon. I'm hoping you can trace the number for me."

"Possibly, I won't know until I try. What's the number?"

"I'll text it to you in just a moment. Anything you can find on this would help. I'm heading back to the office shortly. I should be there in twenty minutes or so."

"Come to the lab when you arrive. If I'm able to get anything, I'll hopefully have it by then."

"Okay, sending you the text now. Thanks, Emily."

"Not a bother," she said and disconnected.

Dillon logged onto text messages, brought up Emily's cell, and sent her the phone number from McBaine's burner phone. Once that was done, he left the Shelbourne Hotel and drove back to the office. He made his way to the Tech Lab and pressed the buzzer.

Emily answered almost immediately, "Tech Lab."

"Hi Emily, it's Dillon."

"Be right there," she said. A moment later, she opened the door.

"Were you able to track the number?"

"I was," she said, not sounding all that positive.

"You make it sound like there's a problem."

"As long as the phone is on the system, we should be able to locate it within a hundred centimeters."

"So that's about thirty inches?"

"Closer to thirty-nine. One inch is equal to two point five four centimeters, so it's really just a simple matter of basic mathematics to—"

"So, you know where it is?" Dillon interrupted.

"It's on Grafton street, in front of the McDonald's, actually."

"McDonald's? Does that mean someone is in there eating lunch?"

"Not really. It's showing up as being just outside the McDonald's."

"Maybe they're seated outside?"

"I don't think they have seating outside. It's Grafton Street, after all."

Dillon nodded, pulled out his cellphone, and called Suel. The line was busy.

"Okay. Keep an eye on it. I'll call you back in a minute. Oh, and thanks, Emily," he said and hurried to the elevator. When he stepped into Special Branch, Suel's desk was empty. He hurried through the office and into the break room. Fortunately, Suel was there. He was in the process of dipping a tea bag up and down in a mug of boiling water.

"Paddy, I think I've got something on the Lennihans."

Suel looked up and said, "What?"

"Emily is tracking the number that was on McBaine's burner phone. It's on Grafton Street."

"What are they doing there? Shopping?"

"It's just outside the McDonald's."

"They ate at the Shelbourne last night, and now they're eating at McDonald's?"

"I'm heading over there. You want to come or not?"

"Okay, I'm coming," Suel said and took a quick sip of tea. He grimaced and said, "Ahh, for the love of… Let's go," he said, and they hurried out the door.

Grafton Street is a three-block-long pedestrian street populated by trendy shops. The top of the street is just two blocks from the Shelbourne. Dillon retraced his route along the Liffey and across the O'Connell Street bridge. Up past the entrance to Trinity College, where instead of following the street around the corner, he slowed and continued straight ahead, carefully rising over the curb and onto the pedestrian street. Fortunately, the McDonald's was just five doors up on the left-hand side.

Dillon came to a stop just before the McDonald's, pulled his phone out, and called Emily. She answered on the first ring.

"Dillon?"

"Yeah, are they still there?"

"I'm looking at the screen now, they should be right in front of the building. Two or three feet in front of the building."

Dillon double-checked, the only people standing in front of the McDonald's were a young mother and a little boy wearing a cowboy hat. He appeared to be five or six years old.

"Are you sure? I don't see anyone matching the Linnehan's description and—"

"Dillon, I never said it was the Linnehans. I just said the phone with that number is somewhere out in front of the McDonald's."

"Could they be inside?"

"Inside? Dillon, remember it's one hundred centimeters. Just thirty-nine inches. So theoretically, the phone should be thirty-nine inches from the front of McDonald's."

As she said that, the woman and little boy moved up the street, revealing a metal trash bin.

"I umm think I may have just found where it's located. I'll call you back," Dillon said and disconnected.

"Why do I think that didn't sound too positive?" Suel asked.

"Come on. I think they may have tossed the phone in the trash bin."

"What?"

Dillon climbed out of the car and reached into the back seat. He pulled two latex gloves from a box and tossed them over Suel's shoulder and onto his lap. He slipped his hands into a pair of latex gloves, grabbed an evidence bag, and said, "What are you waiting for?"

"Oh, for feck's sake," Suel groaned as he climbed out of the car.

They walked over to the metal bin. It was round and painted black with gold trim. Two rectangular holes were near the top where a person could drop trash. Beneath the holes was the word 'LITTER' in raised gold letters. Below that and in raised gold was the Dublin City coat of arms, three burning castles. Along the base at the bottom, again in raised gold capital letters, was the word, 'BUSCAR,' Irish for Litter.

The bin was solid steel, about a quarter of an inch thick, with a door. Suel pulled the door open. He let off a colorful bit of swearing and pulled out a gray plastic bin containing a blue plastic bag filled with trash.

"Start looking," Suel said, setting the plastic bin in front of Dillon.

Dillon glanced in the bin and moved a couple of McDonald's bags, a beer can, an empty half-pint bottle, a number of paper napkins, and then there it was, a black phone. Similar to the burner they'd found in McBaine's suit coat earlier, only this burner had Burgundy trim. Suel placed the phone in the evidence bag and slid the plastic bin back inside the metal bin.

"Happy?" Suel asked.

"We'll see what we get off this."

They headed back to the car. Suel nodded at two young boys who'd been watching them the entire time. "Good afternoon, lads. Trash patrol."

They were driving back to the office when Dillon's phone rang. He pulled it out and clicked on the speaker button.

"Yeah, Emily."

"Dillon, that phone is on the move."

"Yeah, I know, we got it."

"Mmm-mmm, sorry to bother you."

Once back at the headquarters building, Dillon brought the phone to Emily and asked her to examine it for any numbers, then he headed up to Special Branch. Suel had just hung up the phone and Dillon was settling in behind his desk when DCI McCabe stepped to his door and said, "Dillon and Suel, a moment of your time, please."

Dillon swore silently, and Suel rolled his eyes. Once he was in front of Dillon's desk, they headed into McCabe's office together.

"Have a seat, gentlemen," McCabe said as they stepped into the office. "Bring me up to date," he said once they were seated.

"Kevin McBaine, the American, was murdered at the Shelbourne Hotel last night between 10:15 and 10:45," Dillon said. "His body was discovered this morning when cleaning staff entered the room. Forensics and a medical team have been on-site. The body is currently at the morgue waiting for the autopsy. Cause of death is currently listed as asphyxiation. A sock had been shoved into McBaine's mouth, and he apparently choked on that while being tortured."

"Tortured?" McCabe asked.

"He was tied to a four-poster bed. He'd been severely beaten, and all of his fingers had been cut off," Suel said.

"Cut off?"

"Yes, some sort of garden shears are suspected," Dillon said.

"We've security tape of him in the Shelbourne, having dinner with Cillian and Padraig Linnehan last night. He paid for the meal, six hundred euros?" Suel asked Dillon.

"Six hundred and forty," Dillon said.

"We've just recovered a burner phone believed to belong to the Linnehans. The phone is down in the Tech Lab now."

"I want you to check on the address the Linnehan's gave when they entered the country. Let's make sure they aren't staying there. Now, to add to this ongoing saga, I received a phone call this morning from the head of security at Mountjoy Prison. Apparently, Cormac Doyle, the individual accused of strangling Tully Moran, was found dead in the shower room this morning. So far, no one has been arrested."

"Cormac Doyle was murdered? How? He wasn't someone you'd want to mess with."

"Beaten over the head with a floor tile in the shower room, and then his throat was slit. It would appear the Linnehans have at least the same amount of influence in The Joy as the Doyle family. I can't stress enough the need to locate Cillian and Padraig Linnehan. Airport and ferry security have been alerted should they try to leave the country. Now I'm depending on the two of you to find them."

FORTY

uel and Dillon were headed to Dalkey, an area on the south side of Dublin. Suel was driving and had his cellphone programmed to give directions to the address on Torca Road for Gemma Linnehan.

"You think we'll find these two idiots there?" Dillon asked.

"Would you be there if you were them? I'd think, if they had any brains at all, they'd have been on an early morning flight out of the country."

"What in the hell do you think McBaine did to warrant being cut up like that?"

"Maybe they didn't like the dinner," Suel said. "I don't know. Yet again, something isn't adding up."

"Something? How about nothing? None of it makes any sense starting with the murder of Liam McCabe and Jimmy Murphy. What purpose did that serve other than getting the Gardai all riled up and on a mission to deal with whoever was responsible?"

"Like I said before, you start looking at all of this, and none of it makes any sense," Suel said.

"In two hundred meters, turn right onto Torca Road," the GPS said.

All the homes on Torca Road appeared to be unattached and behind walls with gated entrances. Three or four of Dillon's home would have easily fit into any house they were passing.

"Looks like a pretty pricey area," Dillon said.

"If it's not the wealthiest area in town, it's in the top three," Suel said.

They drove along Torca Road for another couple of minutes as it gently curved, and then the GPS said, "Your destination is on the left in twenty meters." A moment later, the GPS said, "You have reached your destination."

Suel slowed and pulled over in front of the double wrought iron gates, effectively blocking the driveway. "Time to see how the other half lives," he said and climbed out of the car.

The home was a large two-story stucco structure that looked at least a hundred years old. The stucco was an off-white color. The windows, there were six, four on the second floor and two larger ones on the first floor, were surrounded with elegantly carved red stone. The front door was centered on the main floor. The door was painted a deep blue with stained glass panels above and on either side of the door. A brass door knocker hung on the door, and below that, toward the bottom of the door, was a brass mail slot.

There was a wrought iron gate in the brick wall and a sidewalk that led up to the front door. Suel lifted the latch on the gate, and they stepped into the front garden. He closed the gate behind him and followed Dillon up toward the front door. The winding sidewalk was lined on both sides by a neatly trimmed boxwood hedge. Every ten or twelve feet, there was a rose tree on either side of the sidewalk.

"Nice digs," Dillon said as he stepped up onto the granite stoop in front of the door. Two potted evergreens rested on either corner of the stoop. Dillon pushed the doorbell, and they heard chimes from inside.

A moment later, the door opened, and a woman, blonde and late thirties or possibly forty, opened the door. Her eyes were puffy, and her cheeks appeared flushed, suggesting she may have been crying. She gave a two-second study of Dillon and Suel and said, "I'm sorry, but we're not interested today."

Dillon detected an accent, European but not French and certainly not German. "Good afternoon. Sorry to disturb you. We're with An Garda Síochána," Dillon said and held out his ID. "We would like to speak with Gemma Linnehan."

"Who?" the woman asked with a questioning look on her face.

"Gemma Linnehan. I believe she owns this home."

"No," she shook her head. "We purchased this home two years ago from an estate. My husband and I have lived here ever since."

"So Gemma Linnehan doesn't live here?"

"No, we never met her. She died. Cancer, I think, but I'm not sure. As I said, the house was purchased from an estate. You could check with AIB. They handled the transaction." She began to close the door, and Dillon quickly said, "Thank you, may I have your name, please."

"My name?" She asked, suddenly sounding nervous.

"Yes, please, just to ensure AIB shows us the proper record."

"Oh, yes, of course. My name is Andris, Janina Andris. Would you like me to spell it for you?" she said meaning anything but.

"As a matter of fact, yes. That would help," Dillon said and pulled out a pen and a small notebook.

She bit her lower lip for a moment then slowly spelled out her name and said, "Is there anything else?"

"Lovely name, is that German?" Dillon asked as he took a business card from the back of his notebook and handed it to her.

"No, it's not German. I'm Lithuanian. Is that all? If you'll excuse me, I umm, I have something going in the oven," she said, raising her voice slightly as her cheeks took on a bit more color.

"Nothing else at the moment. Please feel free to call if you have any questions. Thank you, sorry to bother you."

She closed the door, and they heard the lock click.

"Amazing, you always seem to have that effect on women," Suel said as they headed for the front gate.

"Something isn't adding up. Why would the Linnehans give this address if it had been sold two years ago."

"Gee, let me think. Maybe so they could enter the country, and we would be unable to trace them," Suel said.

"Yeah, maybe. I want to check with Eric Bergman. He mentioned something about McBaine employing Eastern Europeans. They were doing tech work for him, and suddenly, they all disappeared."

"You mean they were killed."

"No, more like Martians took them from the planet. They left their cars, apartments, everything and just disappeared. He was wondering if maybe they had all come here and were going to set things up for McBaine to take over once he eliminated the Linnehans and the Doyles."

"And you think she's part of that group?"

"I'm thinking, at this point, anything is possible. I'll make a call as soon as we're back in the car," Dillon said.

FORTY-ONE

illon gave a quick glance toward the house as they headed out of the front gate. He caught a half-second movement at a curtained window. Someone had been watching them leave. He pulled the gate closed and waited until they were in the car. Once Suel started the car and headed down the street, Dillon said, "Someone was watching us leave. You think there was something wrong with that woman?"

"Yeah, she was bitchy," Suel said.

"Did she look like she may have been crying?" Dillon asked. "The puffy eyes. The red cheeks. Did you notice how she reacted when I asked if her name was German?"

"Yeah, but coming from one of those Eastern Bloc countries, she could have taken your question as pretty offensive."

"So, she's been home all day, we knock on the door, and she's offended?"

"No, I just meant your dumb German comment. Anyone from that area had family killed in the second war.

Obviously, she wasn't alive then, but you know, family history."

Dillon placed a phone call to Eric Bergman. He answered just before Dillon thought he'd be dumped into voicemail.

"Yeah, Dillon. What's up?"

"Hi, Eric. Hey, I've got a question for you. You mentioned a while back that Kevin McBaine had a half-dozen Eastern European employees working for him, and suddenly they all disappeared."

"Yeah, left everything. Cars, apartments, and vanished."

"You have any names on those people?"

"Not off the top of my head. I think I could find out if you really want them. Might take a bit of time. I'll have to contact a guy over in the States."

"Yeah, if you wouldn't mind. I'm looking for a woman named Janina Andris," Dillon said and spelled the last name for Bergman.

"Let me check into it. Hopefully, I'll be back to you by tomorrow morning."

"Thanks, Eric, much appreciated," he said and hung up. He scanned his contact list, came up with Kate's number, and called her.

"Dillon? Don't tell me you want to borrow that wig again."

"Surprisingly, no. Hey, I'm hoping you might be able to help me."

"Maybe. What's the problem?"

"Suel and I are coming back from Dalkey and—"

"Wow, you two have certainly come up in the world."

"Not to worry, they basically told us to leave."

"No surprise. So, what do you need?"

"Could you look up a name for me, Janina Andris? She lives at…" Dillon gave her the address. "Something just didn't seem right. Maybe she was having a bad day, or maybe something else was going on. Anyway, if you could check her out. Supposedly, she and her husband purchased that home two years ago from an estate. Could you check out that transaction as well?"

"And that address is in Dalkey?"

"It is."

"You heading back to the office now?"

"Yeah, but Suel's driving, so who knows when we'll get there."

Suel glanced at Dillon as Kate laughed over the phone. "I should have something for you by the time you get back."

"Thanks, Kate. Much appreciated," Dillon said and disconnected.

"What are you thinking?" Suel asked.

"I think I'm grasping at straws, but I can't come up with anything else. Did you put a BOLO out on Cillian and Padraig Linnehan?"

"I did, not that we've had any sighting, unfortunately. But it's out there."

"They gotta be lying low somewhere," Dillon said.

"Well, the logical place would have been with McBaine, but you know how well that worked out."

"You think the Doyles know those two are back in Dublin?"

"I would think so. Tully Moran, Shauna McNeese, Kevin McBaine, and now Cormac Doyle, they have to be involved in at least some of this."

"Yeah, you're probably right."

Ten minutes later, Suel parked behind the headquarters building, and they entered through the rear door. "I'll see you upstairs," Dillon said. "I want to check with Emily and see if she got anything off that burner we pulled from the trash."

"You'll probably find out they phoned in an order to McDonald's," Suel said and laughed at his joke.

FORTY-TWO

Dillon headed down the hallway to the Tech Lab and pressed the buzzer. A familiar-sounding voice answered, not Emily.

"Tech Lab," the voice growled. Dillon guessed it was Quinn O'Neal.

"Yeah, Jack Dillon to see Emily. If you could let her know I'm here."

No response, not so much as an 'okay.' Just a click as the intercom went off, ending the brief conversation. A couple of minutes later, the door to the lab opened, and Emily was there. She stared at Dillon, "Have you been waiting out here long?"

"Not really, just a couple of minutes. Was that your pal Quinn O'Neal who answered?"

"Yeah. I knew someone had called. He wanders over to the kettle, boils some water, makes a tea, complains there aren't any tea cakes, and then casually mentions that, oh by the way, you're out here waiting. I tell you, I want to kill that knacker."

"Save it for later," Dillon said.

"God, I'll put it on my list. Come on in. I've got some information for you," Emily said, and he followed her into the lab. The burner phone he'd pulled out of the McDonald's trash bin was hooked up to a computer. The computer screen was mounted on a stand set at eye level. Emily took up a position in front of the keyboard.

"Okay, so interestingly, there were a number of calls" she said, clicking on the keys. "There were two calls to this number." A number suddenly appeared on the screen. "Both calls were placed two days ago. The first one was made at 11:00 in the morning. The second one at 2:10 in the afternoon."

Dillon looked at the screen. The number looked familiar, but he couldn't place it. "I should know that number, but I'm drawing a blank," he said.

"Shauna McNeese," Emily said, and the image of little Rowen crying and raising his arms to be picked up suddenly appeared in Dillon's mind.

"2:10, you said?"

"Yeah, both calls lasted about ninety seconds," Emily said.

She ran her fingers over the keyboard again and said, "Then, we have four calls to this number, which is the burner phone that was recovered from the scene at the Shelbourne Hotel."

"Kevin McBaine's burner phone. They called him four times?"

"Yes. A call at 10:00, 11:15, 1:59, and the last call at 4:03 yesterday afternoon, no call longer than a minute." She ran her fingers over the keyboard again. "Now, we also have three calls to this number. It's located down in Dalkey. It's a landline. The number is registered to a—"

"Registered to Janina Andris," Dillon said.

"Half-right," Emily replied. "Actually, it's registered to a gentleman by the name of Rytas Andris. I looked up the name, and it's—"

"Lithuanian," Dillon said. "How long were the calls, and when were they made?"

"The first call was made yesterday just after the noon hour. It lasted almost two minutes. The next call was made just before 4:00 yesterday afternoon. That was a minute and a half." Dillon had his notebook out and was writing down the times. "The third call was made just before 11:00 last night. That lasted a total of four minutes and eight seconds."

Almost immediately after McBaine was murdered, Dillon thought and made a mental note to get CCTV footage on Grafton street from last night.

"One more interesting item. After the third call, this landline phoned Kevin McBaine's burner phone last night at 11:06. It was dumped into voicemail, and the caller didn't leave a message."

"The Andris landline called McBaine's burner?"

"Yes."

"I'll bet they were calling to see if McBaine was really dead."

"Oh, that's pretty creepy," Emily said.

"Anything else?" Dillon asked.

"No, sorry it's not better news. Whoever was making those calls to Shauna McNeese, Kevin McBaine, and the Andris house does not sound like a very nice person."

"Anything on fingerprints?"

Emily flashed an evil smile and said, "Now it's my turn to tell you that your close personal friend, Quinn O'Neal, has the fingerprints, and he's running them through the system as we speak. His area is just around the corner if you would care to check with him," Emily said.

"Thank you, Emily. I'll do that now," Dillon said and walked down to the end of another counter and took a left. He could see Quinn O'Neal standing in front of a computer screen. "Quinn," he called as he approached.

O'Neal didn't bother to look. He remained focused on the screen and said, "Running fingerprints from that burner phone from McDonald's. Was it left on a table?"

"No, it was tossed in a trash container just outside."

"That explains it, traces of catsup and residue from cooking oil, either french fries or onion rings. I got three matches, with three more to go on some pretty good partials."

"You have a name?"

"The three matches are all from an individual named Cillian Linnehan. Bit of an extensive record up until maybe two years ago and then, surprisingly, nothing."

"Yeah, that's because he fled down to Costa del Sol with other members of his family and, as far as we know, hasn't been back since."

"More's the pity he decided to return," O'Neal said.

"How long do you think before you have those other three fingerprints?"

O'Neal looked over at Dillon, "I'm running one now. With any luck, I should have them all identified in maybe ninety minutes."

Dillon tossed a business card on the counter and said, "Please call me when you're finished. Thanks in advance for all your work."

"Glad to be of service. We aim to please," he said.

"Much appreciated," Dillon said and hurried out of the lab and up to Special Branch. Suel and Kate were both on the phone when Dillon entered. Apparently, things were getting back to normal because there were two candy bar wrappers, a dirty bowl, and a half-empty tea mug left on his desk. He gathered them up without stopping and dumped them in the sink in the break room.

Just as he sat down at his desk, the phone rang. "Marshal Dillon," was how he answered.

"Hi, Jack. Eric Bergman. Hey, I had a little luck and was able to talk to someone on those folks disappearing. I'm just sending a file your way. You can read up on it."

"Did you look at the file?"

"I skimmed it, but I wanted to get it over to you as soon as possible because, well, I'm a real professional, and it looks like you can use any help you can get right now." He laughed at his joke.

Dillon's computer dinged, alerting him to an incoming email.

"I think it just came through. Do you recall the surname Andris in the file?"

"Yeah, that seems to ring a bell. As a matter of fact, there were two individuals by that name. Are they married, siblings, or—"

"I believe they're married, but I don't know that for sure. Let me open the file, and I'll get back to you if I have any questions."

"Okay, you'll have to wait until tomorrow. We've got a half-dozen members of the House of Representatives here tonight, and I'll be dealing with them in about thirty minutes."

"Enjoy yourself," Dillon said.

"Yeah, just what I wanted to do tonight, not. Chat tomorrow," Bergman said and hung up.

FORTY-THREE

Dillon started in on the file Eric Bergman had sent him. Janina and Rytas Andris were mentioned, along with three other people. Janina's name had an '(F)' following her name, and the other four individuals' names were followed by an '(M),' eliminating any question regarding sex. The Andrises were listed as a married couple. The other three individuals were apparently single males.

The Andris home had been in Newark, New Jersey. They had resided for five years in apartment 203 in the Colonnade, an apartment building at 25 Clifton Avenue in Newark. They, along with the other three males, had disappeared in early 2018. Pictures followed of a decent-looking two-bedroom apartment. Dillon found it interesting that the photos of the apartment showed beds with linens and bedspreads. A bathroom with toothbrushes and a hairdryer. A kitchen with frying pans stacked next to the stove and cabinets filled with glasses and china. The dining area had a table with six chairs and what appeared to be two silver candlesticks on the dining table. A flatscreen TV rested on a stand opposite a couch and two matching chairs. A handwritten notation mentioned that the apartment and furnishings, along with a 2014 Toyota, had apparently all been abandoned.

Did they just show up in Ireland and purchase a home in the wealthiest part of Dublin? Housing costs for an unattached home in Dalkey would have easily been upwards of a million euros. Dillon moved back a page and viewed images of the dining area and the living room. Framed photographs that appeared to be parents and family were apparently left behind. There almost had to have been family heirlooms there, china, possibly silver, maybe photos. They literally disappeared off the face of the earth and then show up in Dublin and purchase a home for over a million euros? It didn't make any sense. He saw Kate hang up the phone, and he hurried over to her desk.

"Just a moment, Dillon, let me make a note here, so I don't forget the number I just got," she said, writing down a number on a yellow tablet. The page was half-filled with notes.

"All right, here's what I know, and I'll email you passport photos of Janina and Rytas Andris. They purchased their home in Dalkey on Torca Road in March of 2018. Purchase price was a million five. That's roughly a million eight in US dollars at today's rate. No contingency, and the home was purchased for cash."

"Any idea how they had that amount of cash?"

Kate shook her head. "Rytas Andris, age forty-one, was born in the city of Kretinga, the third-largest city in

Lithuania. Janina Andris, age thirty-seven, maiden name Matas, was born in the resort town of Palanga on the Baltic coast. Both attended Oxford University, where they apparently met. They arrived in the US on student visas to attend Harvard University, where they both obtained advanced degrees in computer science. They worked five years for the US government, no information available." She glanced up at Dillon. "Which suggests some top-secret nonsense, your CIA, FBI, or ABC."

"ABC?" Dillon asked.

"That was a joke, Dillon. Following their stint working for the US Government, they were employed by an organization named Digital Necessity, located in Queens, New York. You want to guess who was the CEO of Digital Necessity?"

"Kevin McBaine?" Dillon asked.

"You are so smart. You know, I want to take back some of the things people have been saying about you."

Dillon smiled.

"That pretty much does it. They're listed as self-employed here in Dublin. The only other thing is that Janina Andris delivered a stillborn child, a boy, in 2019, about a year after their arrival here. That delivery was at the National Maternity Hospital. I know you and Suel are working a drug angle on this, but nothing came up in that regard either here or in the information I was able to obtain in the US. Sort of a big fat nothing, I'm afraid."

"Anything on travel outside Ireland, maybe back to Lithuania?"

"I checked and came up empty-handed. Either they are really good at keeping a low profile, or they're not involved."

"And yet they were able to pay cash for the home in Dalkey," Dillon said and shook his head.

"I'll keep looking, but I may turn up more of the same. A combination of US government contacts and the tech from McBaine's Digital Necessity, it could be possible. Wish I had more for you, Dillon, but they appear to be two upstanding individuals."

Dillon seemed to think for a moment and said, "I have the names of three other people who left the Digital Necessity organization at the same time and under the same circumstances. Would you mind if I sent you their names, and you could check them out?"

"Three more?" she asked.

"Yeah, disappeared at the same time back in 2018. They all worked for McBaine at Digital Necessity."

"Okay, send me the names, and I'll check them out. But then I have to get back to my own headaches. Oh, and by the way, you're going to owe me dinner at a very nice restaurant."

"That would be my pleasure, Kate."

"Send me the names, and I'll get on it."

Dillon hurried back to his desk and emailed the three other names to Kate. Suel was just hanging up his phone, and Dillon phoned him.

"What?"

"You want to meet me in the break room, and we can compare notes on what little we know?"

"Give me a minute, and I'll join you," Suel said. Dillon headed into the break room. The coffee pot was still on the burner containing less than a cup of coffee, just enough to cover the bottom of the pot. Dillon dumped the contents in the sink, rinsed the pot, and made a fresh six-cup pot. He was in the process of filling his mug when Suel walked in.

"Please tell me you've got something we can act on," Dillon said and took a sip from his mug. He grimaced at the bitter taste.

"I've come up empty-handed. You learn anything?"

"Yes and no. That burner phone we recovered made four calls to McBaine yesterday. The last one was around 4:00, maybe lining up their dinner. There were two calls to Shauna McNeese, one around 11:00 and another one just after 2:00. And calls to the Andris house out in Dalkey, three calls to be exact. The first two were just a minute or so. The third call lasted four minutes, and it was made just before 11:00 last night. Hugh Healy estimated the time of McBaine's death between 10:15 and 10:45 last night."

"So, the Linnehans are calling these folks out in Dalkey and telling them what? Mission accomplished?"

"Maybe, except there is absolutely nothing that suggests the two of them, husband and wife, are involved in any way, shape, or form in the drug trade or with the Linnehans for that matter. That said, after the 11:00 call from the burner to the Andris residence, the Andris land-line phoned McBaine's burner phone and got dumped into voicemail. They didn't bother to leave a message."

Suel shook his head. "So, you're telling me the Dalkey folks are clean? Well, except for the fact that they worked for McBaine, who was great pals with the Linnehans. His fingerprints are on the weapon and one of the shells used to murder Liam McCabe and Jimmy Murphy. Oh, and let's not forget, they bought that Linnehan house from an estate."

"Yeah, there is that. Paid cash, as a matter of fact, a million five euros."

"Cash? And you're telling me they're not involved in the drug trade?"

"I'm saying I don't know. Kate's doing a search on the other three guys who disappeared at the same time as the Andris couple. Maybe she'll be able to shed some light on it. Right now, I can't figure out a damn thing."

"So, what are you thinking?" Suel asked.

"I'm going to request CCTV footage on Grafton Street, see if we can't get an image of the Linnehans tossing the burner in the trash. Quinn O'Neal is checking the last three fingerprints on that burner. I'm thinking there's a pretty good chance they'll come up as belonging to Cil lian Linnehan. Kate is running a check on the three other Eastern Europeans who were working for McBaine. They all seem to have disappeared at the same time. We'll maybe see where that leads. I'm going to go home, take a deep breath, and be back here early tomorrow morning."

Suel nodded and said, "That doesn't sound like such a bad idea. It's been a long day. Get out of here while you can."

Dillon tidied up his desk, checked a couple things online, and headed out the door. It was just a little after 6:00 when he climbed behind the wheel. He started the car and then decided on a quick stop on his way home.

FORTY-FOUR

S aint Joseph's Home was located in the Clontarf area of Dublin. It was where social services placed children when a family member couldn't be located to care for a child. Rowen McNeese had been removed from his mother's home and placed there until such time as a family member could be found. It was half-past-six when Dillon entered the grounds and pulled into the parking area. The building was built of granite with four pillars at the top of the five steps leading to the front door.

Dillon climbed out of his car, the only car in the dozen parking spaces opposite the building. He draped his An Garda Síochána ID around his neck and climbed the five steps to the front door. A cornerstone with the date 1854 was next to the pillars on the right-hand side.

He opened the door and stepped inside. A receptionist counter was just ahead. A gray-haired woman dressed in a light blue nun's habit stood behind the counter. She flashed a half-second smile and said, "We're closed for the day. Our hours are from ten until four, with an appointment."

Dillon held up his ID and said, "I'm here to check on a small boy who arrived just yesterday, Rowen McNeese, age two years."

"Is it really necessary at this hour?"

"I'm afraid so, court order," Dillon lied.

She gave a loud exhale, studied Dillon's ID, wrote his name on a notepad, and said, "You'll have to take a seat, please, while I make a call and try to find someone." She pointed to an area behind Dillon.

"Thank you," Dillon said and headed toward a wooden bench, one of three, positioned against the wall.

The nun picked up the phone and spoke for a minute or two. Dillon was unable to make out what was being said. When she hung up, she said, "Someone will be down in just a moment."

It was more like fifteen minutes, but eventually, a woman in a similar habit and at least twenty-five years younger stepped into the hallway and walked toward Dillon. "Hello." She smiled as she drew closer and said, "You're here to check on the McNeese child?"

"Yes, Rowen McNeese."

"Is there a problem?"

"I hope not. I'm working under a court order. He was present, in the same room actually, when his mother was murdered and then remained alone in the room for two or three hours. I just need to check on him."

She seemed to think about that for a moment and eventually nodded. "All right, if you would follow me.

I'm Sister Jovanna," she said and held out her hand as they headed down the hall.

"Jack Dillon," he replied and shook her hand.

"The boy seems to be doing well. All things considered. He slept last night. Soundly, I might add."

"Bit of a tragic day for him," Dillon said.

"You were there, on the scene?"

"As a matter of fact, I was the first one. His mother had been murdered. As I mentioned, dead for at least two hours, probably more. I could hear him crying, screaming, actually, while I was outside knocking on the door. When I stepped into the kitchen, he focused on me and raised his arms to get him out of the highchair he'd been stuck in. I just got him out of the room and tried to calm him down."

"That was the right thing to do," she said and opened the door to a stairway. They began to climb a set of granite stairs. "At his age, it's quite possible he'll have no memory of the incident. Do you know anything of the circumstances?"

"Well, she was murdered. Shot between the eyes. I would say that, from the little I know, the home life was not the best. I believe there were financial problems. She had expressed a fear of eviction to me on an earlier visit. That said, she appeared to be a loving mother. The first time I saw him, his face and hands were covered in chocolate."

She chuckled at that and then opened a door on the second floor. As they stepped into the hallway, she asked, "You're American?"

"Yes, although I've been here in Dublin assigned to An Garda Síochána for the past few years."

"Oh really, interesting," she said, sounding sincere as they walked down a hallway. "Well, Rowen's time here will be limited, like all children. We're basically the first place they land, then one of three options occurs. They're returned to the family, they're placed in foster care, or if they're lucky, they're adopted."

She stopped at a door and said, "He's just in here with some others approximately the same age." She opened the door to a large room, maybe the size of a grammar school classroom. One wall was covered with a chalkboard that looked like it had been there for a hundred years. Built-in shelves ran along a wall. For a brief moment, Dillon recalled the conference room at Mountjoy Prison. The shelves were mostly empty, and the floor was covered with toys, books, and wooden puzzle pieces. Dillon counted seven kids, ranging in age from two to three years old, four boys and three girls.

Another nun was seated in the corner, reading. She looked up as they entered. "It's all right, just checking on the McNeese child," Jovanna said.

Rowen was by himself in the far corner pushing a red plastic dump truck. He looked up and focused on Dillon. He suddenly leaped to his feet and ran toward Dillon, yelling something no one could understand. Dillon stepped toward him, picked him up in mid-stride, and hugged him.

Rowen gave him a big kiss and wrapped his arms around Dillon's neck.

"Oh my," Jovanna said, "he really remembers you. It's obvious he feels safe with you."

"We're best friends," Dillon said and patted Rowen on the back as he held him.

"They'll be getting ready for bed in the next fifteen or twenty minutes. How would it be if I gave you some private time? You could read him a book or play with a truck. Right now, just the gentle interaction is what is most important for him."

"Yeah, I'd like that," Dillon said.

"I'll leave you boys to it. I'll be back when it's time for bed," she said and left the room.

Dillon looked around the room. There was a rocking chair in the far corner and a couple of books on the shelf next to it. He settled into the rocking chair with Rowen on his lap and reached for a book, <u>I Love You to the Moon and Back</u>. The book cover featured a polar bear and a cub staring up at a large full moon. Dillon turned to the first page and began reading the rhyming words.

Rowen pointed at each picture when Dillon turned the page.

He could detect the child beginning to nod off, all the while attempting to fight off sleep. When he finished the last page, he turned back to the first page and began again. Halfway through the second reading, Rowen was sound asleep, breathing deeply. Dillon continued reading. He'd lost track of how many times he'd read the book by the time Jovanna returned with two other women. They herded the children out of the room and down the hall. Dillon handed Rowen to Jovanna and said, "I can see myself out if you want to put him to bed."

"Thank you, that will help. You seem to have a touch with this one."

"Hardly. He's probably just exhausted with all the changes."

"Well, he certainly felt safe with you. If you would touch base with Sister Francis at the front desk on your way out, please. You're welcome to visit Rowen at any time," Jovanna said and indicated the door.

Dillon followed her to the door, opened it, and they stepped into the hallway. The other children were at the far end of the hall, and Dillon was reminded of the phrase 'Herding cats.' He said his good-bye and took the stairs down to the main floor. He checked in with Sister Francis, the older nun at the front desk. He gave her a hearty, "Thank you," and headed out the door to his car. Once in the car, he wrote down the names of Sisters Jovanna and Francis. He was home fifteen minutes later.

FORTY-FIVE

Dillon was up before his alarm went off. He turned on the coffee, shaved, and grabbed a quick shower. He checked his computer, hoping to find an email from Kate with information regarding the three individuals who disappeared from McBaine's organization, Digital Necessity. Unfortunately, there was nothing.

He went upstairs, gently woke Lucifer, and enticed him downstairs with the promise of a biscuit. He tossed the biscuit out the door, and Lucifer followed, although nowhere nearly as quick as usual. Dillon ate a quick breakfast of three pieces of toast slathered with blackberry jam. He lured Lucifer back in the house with another biscuit, filled the food and water dishes, and was on his way.

Tara's home, along with all the others on the lane, was still dark at this early hour. Dillon headed to the office, possibly making the quickest trip he could remember. When he stepped into Special Branch, he appeared to be the only person in the office. He went into the break room and turned on the burner to reheat the pot of coffee he'd made the night before.

He fired up his computer and poured himself a mug of coffee. The coffee turned out to be just as bad as he remembered, and he carried his mug out to his desk. He brought up the file Eric Bergman had sent him regarding Janina and Rytas Andris. Once again, other than having been employed at one time by Kevin McBaine, nothing raised a flag.

It was just before 7:00 when two members of Special Branch wandered into the office. One of them gave a friendly wave to Dillon, but neither one said anything.

It was almost 7:30 when Kate stepped into the office. Dillon waited for her to get settled in at her desk. Just as he was about to approach, she picked up her mug and headed for the break room. "I've got a couple of emails to go over. It'll go a lot better after a tea. I'll let you know when I have something. No need to bother me," she said and headed into the break room. It was a good five minutes later before she wandered back to her desk.

Dillon left messages for Hugh Healy, Eric Bergman, and Suel.

Suel replied about sixty seconds later. "For lord's sake, it's not even 8:00, and you're leaving me a message wondering where I am. I'm on my way into the office. I'll be there in seven minutes if I don't have to wait for the stoplight on North Circular Road. Do you think you'll be able to stay on the line for that long?"

"I'm just checking in. Stop at my desk once you're here. I have an idea."

"God deliver me. I can hardly wait," Suel said, meaning anything but. "Damn it. The light just turned red. Add two minutes to my arrival time." Suel disconnected, and Dillon tossed his phone on the desk.

True to his word, Suel entered the office ten minutes later. He grabbed his mug, headed for the break room, and placed an index finger to his lips, signaling 'quiet' as he passed Dillon's desk. He returned with a steaming mug a few minutes later.

"You mentioned you had an idea. I can hardly wait. What is it?"

"The couple down in Dalkey. They—"

"The Andris couple, Janina, and what's his name, Rytas?"

"Yes, what if they—" Dillon's phone rang. "Hang on," he said to Suel. "Marshal Dillon," he answered.

"Dillon, it's me, Kate." Dillon glanced over at her desk. She smiled and gave him the finger. "I'm sending two files your way. Information on two of the three gentlemen who were employed in McBaine's firm."

"What did you find out?"

"One is employed by the US government. At no surprise, there is very limited information on him. The other has taken up residence in the US Witness Protection program, and there is even less information on him."

"Witness Protection, what did he do?"

"From what I was able to determine, he testified."

"Testified?"

"Yes, against this McBaine individual. Whatever he said, apparently, it was enough to grant him protection. Doesn't the protection program mean he has an assumed identity, and basically no one knows where he is?"

"Yeah, pretty much. More reasons to wonder about McBaine and no way to get an answer. What about the third individual? Is he even alive? Could you find him?"

"Yes and no."

"Meaning?" Dillon asked.

"Meaning, yes, he's alive. No, I couldn't reach him. I gave your contact information to someone I know in the US Justice Department. They promised to pass the information on to him. Unfortunately, it's up to him to contact you. Hopefully, you'll hear something sooner rather than later."

"Sounds like another dead end," Dillon said.

"Possibly," Kate said. "It took a good deal of groveling on my part just to get this information. There seems to be a number of closed doors around this McBaine person."

"Shit," Dillon said just under his breath. He finished up with, "Well, thanks for your effort, much appreciated, Kate. If you pick up on anything else, please let me know."

"I'll be sending you a list of the evenings I have available for that special dinner you promised."

"I'll be looking forward to that," Dillon lied.

"That didn't sound too positive," Suel said as Dillon hung up his phone.

Dillon seemed to think for a moment. "Actually, it fits into what I've been thinking. This Andris couple. What if they, and the other three individuals who all disappeared, what if they disappeared because they didn't like what McBaine was doing? What if they didn't want to be involved with him, and they simply took off?"

"So, they quit, or resign, or whatever. They disappear off the face of the earth, and the Andris couple lands here in Ireland, and they buy a house for a million five?"

Dillon shrugged. "Maybe they disappear because they don't like whatever it is McBaine is getting involved with. One guy is in witness protection after apparently testifying against McBaine. Another is with the government and can't be contacted. The third guy we don't know about, but he can be contacted by someone in the Justice Department. It's all very strange and, at least to me, suggests they may have turned government witnesses or something."

"I agree with the 'very strange' part. Just like everything else in this fiasco, starting with the murder of two Gardai officers," Suel said.

FORTY-SIX

Dillon went through the files Kate sent him twice more and never came up with anything new. It was close to 11:00 when Niall Reid phoned him. "Yeah, Marshal, just checking in. We're in the process of going through McBaine's items, such as they are."

"The way you're describing that makes me think you haven't found anything of interest."

"You mean besides his body strapped to the bed?"

"What do you know so far?" Dillon asked.

"Much of what we know, or think we know, is a presumption. The man was clearly tortured, brutally tortured. It's our suspicion whoever was responsible was looking for answers of some sort. At this stage, and there's no way to confirm, but it would appear whatever information they wanted, they never received. Experience suggests that, after the removal of a finger or two, the victim would be more than willing to offer up any information they wanted. The fact that they removed every finger suggests they never received answers and, at some point, switched to more of a torture."

"What if it was just some whacko psychopath who enjoyed what he was doing?"

"That's the part we don't know. What we do know is that McBaine ended up dead. That suggests he did not provide whatever information they were attempting to obtain."

"But he choked to death on a sock. How does he give them information with a sock stuffed in his mouth? Doesn't that suggest they were just enjoying themselves and kept at it?"

"Possibly. We don't know when the sock was used. Was it at the start? Halfway through? The use of the sock may mean they didn't realize he was choking, and his death cut the operation short."

"I don't know. He lost all his fingers. He had the hell beat out of him. I'm thinking the Linnehan brothers are a pair of real bastards, and that was simply their idea of a fun time."

"You'll get no argument from me. Oh, there is one thing we recovered. A briefcase was under the passenger seat of the rental car. Not sure if it just slid there or if McBaine attempted to hide it there. The briefcase had combination locks and contained financial information on a series of accounts in Romania, Bulgaria, and the Republic of Moldova. All key places in Eastern Europe for money laundering."

"Was there a lot of money in the accounts?"

"Depends on your definition of a lot. A few hundred thousand euros in the accounts in Romania and Bulgaria, maybe fifty thousand in the Moldavian account. From there, the trail becomes pretty blurry. Suffice it to say, millions of euros had gone through, and it's going to take a lot of work to find out where they ended up. If we can even find that information. Accounting is working on all that now, but it's going to take some time."

Dillon thought back to the Andris couple and the three Eastern Europeans. Had they set this up? Was this where the Andris couple got the money to purchase their home in Dalkey? "Okay, Niall, thanks for the update. Keep me posted should you learn anything on the Eastern European accounts."

"I will, Marshal, but don't hold your breath. We're looking at years, not months, to get any information at all."

FORTY-SEVEN

Dillon was eating lunch at his desk, a Yorkie candy bar, while reviewing the autopsy results Hugh Healy had sent over fifteen minutes earlier. Asphyxiation had been ruled as the official cause of Kevin McBaine's death, but there was a laundry list of additional injuries that occurred just prior to his death.

McBaine's nose had been broken. His skull was fractured due to a serious blow to the back of his head that had caused bleeding on the brain. His jaw was fractured, and two of his ribs were broken. All this, plus the removal of his fingers, in short, he'd had the hell beaten out of him. McBaine had been tortured and beaten. Dillon was pretty sure this hadn't been an effort to obtain answers but rather a punishment. Did that suggest that the Linnehans had determined McBaine was playing both sides of the street? Reigniting the war between the Linnehans and the Doyles so he could pick up the pieces and be in charge?

Dillon clicked on the link he'd received for the CCTV footage of the Linnehans strolling down Grafton street at 11:15 in the evening. They'd murdered Kevin McBaine thirty minutes earlier, and there they were, laughing and joking as they wandered down the street, ogling various women along the way.

They'd stopped in front of the McDonald's and tossed the burner phone into the black and gold litter bin. Quinn O'Neal had left an email for Dillon confirming that all six partial fingerprints on the burner phone did indeed belong to Cillian Linnehan.

Dillon paused the CCTV footage of Cillian Linnehan tossing the burner phone into the trash bin. He was a muscular blonde-haired man with a short ponytail at the back of his head. He had a large tattoo of some sort on the back of his right hand, but when Dillon enlarged the image, it became too blurry to identify the design.

He kept thinking about the Andris couple, wondering how they fit into this entire mixed-up affair. Dillon's phone rang. "Marshal Dillon," he answered.

There were a number of clicks, and then an accented voice said, "My name is Vitas Matas. I have received information that you have some questions regarding a man by the name of Kevin McBaine and his company, Digital Necessity."

"I'm sorry, could you repeat your name for me?" Dillon said.

"I'm taping this conversation," the man said. "Do you agree to me taping?"

"Yeah. Yes, I agree. Tell me your name again, please."

"Vitas Matas."

The name rang a bell with Dillon, but he couldn't place it at the moment. "You worked at Digital Necessity? For Kevin McBaine?"

"Yes, I was there for approximately five years. You are in Ireland, Mr. Dillon?"

"Yes. I'm a US Marshal assigned to An Garda Síochána, the Irish police force."

"Do you have knowledge of my sister, Janina Andris?" There it was. Her maiden name was Matas. That's why the guy's name rang a bell.

"A little knowledge. I saw her yesterday, at her home, for all of a minute or two."

"How was she?"

"Not very talkative. She and her husband worked with you at Digital Necessity, correct?"

"Yes, along with two other gentlemen from Lithuania, we all… left at the same time."

"You literally disappeared. Left your apartments, possessions, everything."

"We were involved in a project that suddenly became very dangerous, and we didn't want to be involved in any way. We had the funds that allowed us to flee and not be traced, and that was what we did."

"But your sister and her husband came to Ireland, correct?"

"That's correct."

"Why over here? You and the other two gentlemen are still in the States."

"We, the two men and I, were involved with a, umm, governmental contract. It only made sense to continue in that vein. Janina and Rytas had been working on a European project, and Ireland seemed to be the logical location. Unfortunately, our former employer, Kevin McBaine, discovered that was where they had settled."

"They purchased a home for a large amount of money," Dillon said.

Matas chuckled at that. "Are you familiar with Bitcoin?"

"Only by name."

"Back in, I think 2012, Rytas spent a thousand dollars on Bitcoins. The going rate at that time was maybe seven and a half dollars. Move to the year 2018, just six years later when they purchased that home. The value of Bitcoin had risen to more than fifteen thousand dollars. He sold his shares to an investor he knew in Kretinga, his hometown, and they paid cash for the house. A wonderful deal, however, if he'd held on and sold in early 2021, well, he could have retired in his early forties and never have had to work again."

"Tell me about Kevin McBaine."

"I don't wish to discuss him except to say that he is a very bright individual who decided to head in a direction none of us were interested in following."

"Have you had any dealings with him since you left?"

"It has been everyone's intention to have no contact whatsoever."

"Does the name Linnehan mean anything to you?"

"I don't wish to answer that."

"Are you aware Kevin McBaine was murdered here in Ireland in the last day or two?"

Click

"Hello? Hello?" Dillon said but didn't get an answer. He pushed three keys on his phone to return the call but got a recording instead. "We're sorry, but the number you wish to reach is not available."

FORTY-EIGHT

Dillon looked around for Suel. He wasn't at his desk or in the break room. Dillon thought for a long moment then grabbed his jacket and headed out of the office. He got into his car and wondered for a brief moment if this was a good idea. He decided it was, programmed the GPS on his phone, turned on his car, and drove out of the parking lot. He took the bridge across the Liffey and headed south to Dalkey. Twenty minutes later, the GPS said, "In two hundred meters, turn right onto Torca Road." He followed the road along the gentle curve until the GPS said, "Your destination is on the left in twenty meters." A moment later, the GPS said, "You have reached your destination."

Dillon pulled up onto the sidewalk where Suel had parked the other day, blocking the double wrought iron gates to the driveway. He climbed out of the car, locked the door, and headed for the gate leading up to the front door.

As he walked up the winding footpath, he watched the stained glass panels on either side of the front door, looking for anything that suggested movement. He didn't see any sign of someone watching his approach. He rang the doorbell, heard the chimes from inside, and waited. He was about to ring the doorbell again when he heard the lock turn, and the door opened slightly. Janina Andris peeked out with a surprised look on her face and then opened the door a bit more.

"Hi, Mrs. Andris, Jack Dillon. I wonder if we might chat. I just have a couple of questions, and I—"

She shook her head and said, "I'm sorry, but now is not a good time to chat. Perhaps some other time would work. Thank you for stopping. Sorry I couldn't be of more help." As she spoke, her eyes blinked nonstop.

Dillon was about to ask if there was something in her eye when it suddenly dawned on him. "I see, well, sorry to bother you. I was just in the neighborhood and thought I'd stop and see if you had a moment. You take care. Everything is fine on our end. Just wanted to tell you all our questions have been answered. You enjoy your day," he said as he stepped off the stoop and headed back to the front gate. His ears were perked for the slightest hint of a sound suggesting trouble, but fortunately, he didn't hear anything.

He closed the gate behind him, glanced at the stained glass panels on either side of the front door, and thought he may have detected movement but couldn't be sure. He climbed back into his car and drove away. He checked the rearview mirror for the sign of a vehicle following, but thankfully he didn't see anything.

He turned onto the first side street he came to and drove around the bend until his car was hidden from anyone driving on Torca Road. He pulled out his phone and pressed speed dial.

Suel answered on the second ring. "Yeah, Dillon, where in the hell are you?"

"I'm down in Dalkey at the moment. I think I found them."

"Found who?"

"The Linnehan brothers."

"Where? What are they up to? Did they see you?"

"I think they're at the Andris house on Torca Road. I was—"

"What in God's name are they doing there?"

"I didn't have time to ask any questions, Paddy. Stop interrupting and let me tell you what happened." Dillon went on to explain his phone call with Vitas Matas. How he hung up after Dillon asked if he knew McBaine was dead. "So, I drove out here to Torca Road. Same as before, Janina Andris seemed less than happy to see me, only this time she kept blinking her eyes."

"What? She have something in them? Was she crying because she had to see you again?"

"No, Paddy, she was blinking SOS."

"What the hell?"

"Three short, three long, three short. I'm telling you she was blinking SOS. They're in there, the Linnehans. They've got her and probably her husband held prisoner. That's why we haven't been able to find those two

Linnehan bastards. They're holing up down here in Dalkey."

"Are you sure? I mean, did you see them? Did—"

"Paddy, we need people down here now. Before these guys do any more damage. Before they kill someone else."

"Dillon, I don't know if we should—"

"Paddy, there's about a hundred percent chance whenever these guys are finished with this couple, they'll kill them. That may be tonight, might be next week, but they'll kill them, they have to. We need a team down here, now."

"Dillon, we're going to require a little more proof than some poor woman blinking her eyes before we send—"

"All right, forget it. But I'm going back. I'm telling you, they're in there, the Linnehans. You saw what they did to McBaine. You want to be responsible for a husband and wife getting murdered?"

"I just think—"

"Paddy, we're running out of time to think. These guys mutilated McBaine. God only knows what they'll do to this couple. I'm heading back there now. I'll—"

"All right, Dillon. Okay, okay, I'm coming down there. Jesus H. Christ. Let me see if I can get anyone else to join me. After all, misery loves company."

"Thanks, I'll be parked on Torca, a couple of lots past the Andris house."

FORTY-NINE

D illon was parked four lots down on Torca Road, in front of a two-story stone house. Fortunately, there was a seven-foot wall across the front of the lot, so if the owners were home, they most likely hadn't seen him parked outside their house for the past hour and a half.

He finally saw Suel's car coming down the road. He stepped out of his car and gave a slight wave. Suel drove past the Andris house without slowing and pulled in front of Dillon's car. Kate and another Special Branch officer named Connor Reilly were in the car with Suel.

Suel lowered the driver's window, and Dillon walked over.

"Anything happening?" Suel asked.

"Nothing," Dillon said.

"And you're still sure about this?"

"Yeah, Paddy, I am. Something's not right. She was doing this the entire time I was talking with her," Dillon said and proceeded to blink three short, three long, and three short, over and over again.

"Okay, okay, I get it. Oh, for Christ's sake. I don't suppose you phoned their house?"

Dillon shook his head. "No, I did get a call from her brother. One of three folks who disappeared from McBaine's business along with Janina and Rytas Andris."

"So, you talked to this guy?" Suel asked.

"Yeah, for a minute or two. Kate passed our information on to someone in the States, and the guy called. That's what led me to come out here."

Suel looked in the rearview mirror at Kate. "I didn't know he called," she said. "Everything was top secret over there in the States. I couldn't get a straight answer from my contact except he said he'd try. Apparently, it worked."

Dillon nodded. "The guy's name is Vitas Matas. His sister is Janina Matas Andris. He told me they all fled the scene and disappeared because whatever McBaine was doing was not going to end well. That was back in 2018. They had connections with the government, and the three guys ended up doing some black ops shit or something. Janina and Rytas Andris came over here. He sold a bunch of Bitcoins to someone in Lithuania and used that money to pay cash for the house they're in now."

"When did you learn all this?" Suel asked.

"A couple of hours ago. You were hiding in the break room or somewhere."

"You said you've got her phone number?" Suel said to Kate.

"Yes."

"Make a call. Ask her, umm, some computer question. See if she'll respond."

"I know just the thing to ask. You want me to call now?"

"Yeah, just remember, if the Linnehans really are in there, they're probably going to be listening. Put the call on speaker," Suel said as Kate pulled out her phone. She leaned forward and placed the phone on Suel's center console and brought up the Andris phone number.

"That'll go through as unknown?" Dillon asked.

"Yeah, so just relax. Okay, quiet on the set," she said then tapped the screen calling the number and put the phone on speaker. They could hear it ringing.

After the fourth ring, Janina answered, "Hello."

"Yes, Janina Andris, just calling to check security on your phone system. We have three dots, three dashes, and three dots, is that correct?"

There was a pause, and then Janina Andris said, "Yes, that's correct."

"Okay, everything is fine on your system. Sorry to bother you," Kate said and disconnected. She turned her phone off and said, "Well, there's your answer, Paddy. Sounds like it's for real."

Suel nodded and said, "Connor, bring up that address on Google maps. See if we can get an aerial view of the property. You remember what the house number is, Dillon?"

"Relax, I've got it," Connor said and started tapping keys. A moment later, he turned his computer screen toward Suel. Dillon leaned in the driver's window to get a closer look. The aerial view showed the structure was 'L' shaped and on a triangular lot. Hedges and trees lined both sides of the lot. There was a small grassy area along the right side of the house, far enough back so it couldn't be seen from the street, and Dillon thought the area looked large enough to park a car.

"What are you thinking?" Dillon asked.

"I'm thinking we need more people, but if we do that, there's a good chance whoever is in there will be alerted.

"If we went in on our own, maybe along either side of the house, we might be able to catch them unaware," Dillon said.

Suel nodded and said, "Kate, I want you to stay here with Dillon. Connor and I are going to park on the other side of the house. That way, if they leave, no matter the direction, one of us can immediately follow. If they remain in there, we'll advance through the neighboring gardens at dusk. Everyone turn your phones to silent. Protective vests from here on in. At dusk, we inform the neighbors on either side, not before. Clear?"

Everyone nodded. Kate opened the rear door of Suel's car and climbed out. Suel backed up a few feet then drove around the bend until he was out of sight. He made a U-turn and parked three lots on the far side of the Andris house but still in sight of Dillon's car.

They sat in the cars for the next five hours. At 9:15, Suel sent a text:

Approach through neighbor lot.

Dillon and Kate already had their weapons lying in the back seat. Dillon turned on the car and moved forward to the house next to the Andris residence. He reached into the back seat and handed Kate's pistol to her. He grabbed his personal defense weapon, a Heckler & Koch MP7. It featured a twenty-round magazine and a reflex red sight.

They stepped out of the car and hurried up the front sidewalk of the three-story brick house next to the Andris residence and rang the doorbell. A moment later, a man opened the door. He was wearing navy blue trousers, a starched white shirt with an unbuttoned collar, and a loosened red striped tie. He held a crystal glass in his hand with what looked like whiskey. "How may I help—" He stopped and stared when he saw the protective vests and the weapons.

"An Garda Síochána. We'd like you to remain in the house. We'll be walking along the side hedge," Dillon said, indicating the left side of the house.

The man nodded and drained his whiskey glass as Dillon pulled the door closed.

The half moon was just beginning to rise as they hurried to the side of the house and walked along a privet hedge with green and yellow leaves. From what they could see, the Andris house appeared dark inside. They passed the green lawn patch Dillon had noticed on Connor's computer screen. A gray SUV had been backed onto the lawn.

"Hold up here, Kate," Dillon said. "Let's see if we can find a way through, and we can hide alongside that SUV."

"Over there, Dillon," she half-whispered and pointed to an opening at the bottom of the hedge, maybe large enough to crawl through.

Dillon nodded and headed toward the opening. Kate pulled him back and said, "Let me go first. You'll make too much noise. Meet me at the SUV."

Dillon watched as she climbed through the opening. She made it, but with little room to spare, which meant he was bound to have a tougher time. He laid down on his back and slowly began to work his way through the opening. He was nearly halfway through when he heard a branch crack and felt something sharp scraping along his left side. He had to wiggle back and forth and just when he thought he was really stuck, he suddenly broke free and was able to quickly roll to the side. He was up with Kate and next to the SUV a few seconds later.

"You okay?" she asked.

"I'll live. Hang on a minute. Let me check something." He crawled alongside the SUV to the front of the vehicle. He lifted his head and checked the windshield. Over on the driver's side in the corner of the windshield was a sticker for a car rental agency. He pulled his phone out and sent Suel a text message:

Rental Car SUV flatten tire?

Suel sent a one-word reply:

Yes

Dillon began unscrewing the cap on the tire valve.

"What are you doing?" Kate whispered.

"I'm going to flatten the tire in case they try to drive away."

She shook her head and said, "Move away. Honest to God." She reached into a pocket in her protective vest and pulled out what looked like a long metal nail file. It had a pink plastic handle and a point at the end. She held it against the tire and then shoved it into the side, about an inch from the chrome rim. When she pulled it out, there was a slight hissing sound, but nowhere near as loud as letting air out of the tire valve.

"Smart move," he said and then glanced over the hood of the SUV.

The house was dark. Most of the drapes appeared to be drawn. Dillon was looking at the windows when he saw what looked like a flashlight beam in a window half-way up the side of the house, most likely a staircase, maybe a landing. He ducked down, whispered "Flash-light," to Kate and then texted the same word to Suel.

Suel sent a text a couple of minutes later:

Light on at rear of house.

Dillon signaled Kate to follow him, and they crawled up next to the house then moved toward the rear, squatting below the windows. They could see a blueish light flickering from what appeared to be a back porch. A brick patio surrounded the rear of the house.

Dillon crept on the patio toward the porch. The walls were all glass, from the floor to the ceiling. The roof was glass as well. He cautiously peeked in and saw two men. One was sitting in a cushioned wicker chair. The other was stretched out on a wicker couch. A glass-topped coffee table rested between them with an empty pizza box, a half-dozen empty beer bottles, and an automatic pistol. A glass door leading outside to the patio was at the corner of the back wall closest to Suel.

"Now what?" Kate asked.

FIFTY

They remained in the same position for the next forty-five minutes, kneeling at the corner of the stucco house, staring into the glass room. They watched as the two Linnehans went through four more beers. Finally, the one sitting in the cushioned wicker chair drained his current beer and stood. Dillon recognized him from the CCTV footage. He was the muscular blonde brother with the ponytail. He glanced at his brother, who appeared to be asleep on the couch, then headed for the rear door. He left the door open when he stepped outside onto the patio.

Dillon and Kate pressed themselves firmly against the stucco. Dillon positioned the Heckler & Koch MP7 against his shoulder and waited as Ponytail headed across the patio toward a flower bed. He unzipped his jeans and proceeded to urinate.

"Go," Dillon whispered as he rose to his feet and rushed toward Ponytail. Suel was up and running along the other glass wall. He pointed toward the door and stepped inside the glass porch with Connor behind him.

Ponytail gave a casual look over his shoulder. His eyes grew wide for a half-second as Suel and Connor hurried into the porch. That was all the time Dillon needed to raise his weapon and bring the butt crashing down on the back of Ponytail's head, knocking him headfirst into the recently sprinkled flower bed.

Kate was right behind Dillon. She planted a boot into the middle of Ponytail's back and growled, "Don't even think of moving."

Dillon grabbed his handcuffs and slapped them on Ponytail's right wrist, then twisted and pulled the left arm behind Ponytail's back.

"Ahh, God. You're breaking my damn arm. Would you ever calm down?" he said as Dillon clamped the handcuff onto his left wrist.

"Let him stay there and enjoy the flowers. He so much as moves, blow his brains out," Dillon said and hurried into the glass porch.

Suel was just getting up after rolling the other brother off the couch and onto the floor. Connor had the barrel of his pistol pressed against the left side of the man's head.

"Anyone else with you?" Suel said.

"No, no, will you get that damn gun off me head? I'm not about to go anywhere, you bleedin' eejit."

"You got that right," Suel said.

"Where's the couple that lives here?" Dillon asked.

"I don't know who you's are talking about. We were just visiting and—"

Dillon kicked his shoe between the man's legs and began to add pressure.

"Ahh, God, upstairs. They're upstairs," he shouted.

"Call Special Branch, Connor, and watch him. He moves, shoot him," Suel said as he and Dillon hurried up two steps and into the house.

Suel hit the light switch as they entered, illuminating a hallway leading all the way to the front of the house. They took their time, clearing each room along the way until they were at the front entry and a stairway leading up to the second floor. Suel headed up the stairs with Dillon behind him. Dillon kept his weapon focused on the upstairs hallway.

Suel turned on the light, and they repeated the process, clearing the first two rooms as they went. When they opened the door to the third room, Suel turned on the light, and Dillon quickly aimed his weapon around the room.

Two individuals were lying on the floor, wrapped in silver duct tape. Their eyes grew wide as they focused on Dillon and Suel and made incomprehensible sounds from behind the duct tape wrapped around their heads and over their mouths.

Suel slowly removed the tape from Rytas Andris's head. He gasped as the tape was removed from his mouth.

"Oh, thank God. Thank God," he said. "Please undo Janina. Take care of her."

Dillon set his weapon off to the side and carefully removed the tape from around her head. It pulled out some hair as he eased it from her head and then off her face. The duct tape left a red mark on her cheeks and over her mouth. Tears were running down her face, and she was sobbing. Her arms were pulled behind her back and taped along the wrists.

As soon as Dillon unwrapped the tape from her wrists, she began to crawl toward her husband, wrapping her arms around him and sobbing louder.

Suel undid the tape around his arms, and the moment they were free, he wrapped his arms around Janina and began repeating something that must have been in Lithuanian because neither Dillon nor Suel could understand it.

They undid the tape around the couple's legs, but they remained on the floor, hugging one another tightly and crying.

In the distance, Dillon could hear the first of a number of sirens.

FIFTY-ONE

Dillon slept until almost 8:00 the following morning. He shaved, showered, dressed, and found Lucifer waiting for him at the front door. He let him out and filled his food and water dishes. He made a quick breakfast of frozen waffles in the microwave, let Lucifer back in the house, and drove to Headquarters.

As he pulled into the parking lot, the guard at the gate gave him a thumbs-up. He let himself in the back door to the building and got a "Well done" from three different people on the way to the elevator.

Connor Reilly was the only one of the four of them at his desk. A cupcake with white frosting and little colored stars was sitting on the corner of his desk. "Were you able to get any sleep last night?" Dillon asked him.

"Like a baby, once the wife was finished with me," Connor said and flashed a smile.

"What's with the cupcake?"

"We all got one, compliments of a secret admirer, I guess."

Dillon glanced around, and sure enough, there was a cupcake on Suel's and Kate's desks along with Dillon's as well. Amazingly, there weren't any dirty dishes or mugs on Dillon's desk. Just the cupcake on a plate in the middle of his desk. He headed into the break room, filled his coffee mug, and then settled in his chair. The light was flashing on his phone, and he checked his messages. He had three. Congratulations from Eric Bergman, Hugh Healy, and Emily. Suel and Kate arrived over the course of the next thirty minutes. The morning and early afternoon were filled with interviews and statements regarding the arrest of the Linnehan brothers and the release of the Andris couple. All four individuals were placed on administrative leave for seventy-two hours, which was standard policy. At the end of the day, Dillon took a slight detour and headed for Saint Joseph's Home in Clontarf. This time when he parked, there were two other cars in the parking area.

He checked his notebook for names, draped his ID around his neck, and headed up the front steps and into the building. The same elderly nun from his previous visit was at the front desk. "Good afternoon, Sister Francis. I'm Marshal Dillon with An Garda Síochána."

"How could I forget," she said and didn't smile.

"I'm here to see Rowen McNeese. I believe Sister Jovanna had escorted me at my last visit."

"Mmm, let me see if she is available. Take a seat," she said, instructing rather than suggesting. As he headed for the bench against the far wall, Dillon immediately flashed back to one of the many times he'd been sent to the principal's office as a child.

Sister Jovanna appeared five minutes later.

"Marshal, what a pleasant surprise. Is this business or pleasure?"

"Pleasure, I hope. I was wondering if I could read Rowen a story."

She smiled and said, "I think that would be wonderful."

As they headed up the staircase to the room with the books and toys, Dillon asked, "Any word on an adoption?"

"For Rowen?"

"Yes."

"Oh, I'm afraid that's not going to be an easy task. Due to the circumstances of his arrival, namely the murder of his mother, it makes it rather difficult to find a couple who would be interested."

"But he's barely two. He obviously didn't have anything to do with that situation."

"Oh, believe me, we know that. But the law requires us to provide as complete a history as possible. Unfortunately, Rowen's history, at least at the moment, will be very brief and defined by that awful incident. There's nothing we can do about that, I'm afraid. Well, here we are. I'll be back, oh, in twenty minutes or so. It's bath night," she said as she opened the door.

This evening, there were three other children in the room, two girls and a little boy. The same woman was reading from a different book. All three looked to be at least a year older than Rowen. He was seated on the floor in a far corner with his back to the door.

"Oh, Rowen," Jovanna called. He half-turned to look over his shoulder, and then his eyes grew wide as he focused on Dillon. He jumped to his feet and hurried toward him, yelling something unintelligible.

"Oh, you are so lucky," Jovanna said as Dillon stepped forward and scooped Rowen up in his arms. He got a kiss for his effort and gave Rowen a kiss and a big hug in return.

"We'll be in the rocking chair," Dillon said and headed for the corner of the room. There were three books on the floor next to the rocking chair. Dillon sat down with Rowen on his lap and reached for the books. One of the books was the one Dillon had read the last time, with the polar bear and a cub staring up at the large full moon on the cover. Rowen grabbed that book from the three and opened it up.

Dillon proceeded to read the book. He was on his fifth time through when the door opened, and Jovanna entered with another woman. Rowen immediately snuggled up against Dillon.

"Would it be all right if I carried him down the hall for you?" Dillon asked.

"That's a great idea," Jovanna said.

As they walked down the hall, Dillon asked again about the adoption possibilities for Rowen.

"Oh, I'm afraid it could well be the perfect storm. Because of the particular circumstances, there won't be much interest, and then as time goes on, people will look, and whether they admit it or not, they'll feel that something with the child just isn't quite right and assume that's why no one has expressed an interest. Suddenly, he's eight, then ten or twelve. As the child grows older, the option for adoption decreases. At age eighteen, they leave whatever facility they're in, and they're on their own. It's not right. It's not fair. But that's our current system."

"If someone expressed an interest, could I suggest they talk with you?"

"You know someone who might be interested?"

"I don't know, but I intend to find out."

"By all means, have them contact me. If they want to call here, have them ask for me. I would love to talk with them."

"Thanks, I'll see what they say," he said and handed Rowen to Jovanna. The child started to put up a fuss but then seemed to relax as she wrapped her arms around him and patted him on the back.

"Enjoy bath time," Dillon said and gave Rowen a kiss and a wave goodbye.

Dillon drove home, changed clothes, and took Lucifer for a walk. They did three laps of Albert Park, roughly three and a half miles, and headed home. Dillon pulled leftover chicken from the refrigerator, fried up a red pepper, and sat down in front of the TV. He woke a little after eleven. Lucifer was already upstairs, asleep in bed. Dillon climbed into bed and slept soundly.

FIFTY-TWO

It was the final day of their administrative leave. The Linnehan brothers were being held in Mountjoy Prison and were being interviewed beginning at 9:00. Dillon and Suel, twiddling their fingers on administrative leave, planned to watch at least the morning interviews.

Suel drove them to Mountjoy parking on the same side street they'd parked during the brief Tully Moran interviews. Dillon decided to watch Cillian Linnehan's interview while Suel watched the interview of Padraig Linnehan.

Cillian attempted to place all responsibility for the murder of Officers Liam McCabe and Jimmy Murphy on McBaine. He insisted he had nothing to do with the murders of Tully Moran, Kevin McBaine, or Shauna McNeese.

Dillon had seen and heard countless versions of the same sort of denials over the years. It always amazed him that the guilty parties never seemed to grasp the fact that they'd left fingerprints and DNA behind, made payments that could be tracked, and almost always appeared on CCTV footage placing them at or near the scene of the crime.

When they finally broke for lunch, Suel and Dillon headed over to Two Boys Brew and ordered Reuben Toasties. Halfway through the sandwich, Suel asked, "You interested in going back to The Joy this after-noon?"

"To tell you the truth, no, I'm not. I don't need to sit and listen to either one of those idiots tell lies and pre-tend they had no involvement."

"Between the murders and the kidnapping, I doubt they'll ever get out," Suel said.

"Which is just fine with me," Dillon added. "The pistol we recovered the other night has been linked to the murder of Shauna McNeese."

"And don't forget the Shelbourne dinner tapes with McBaine. With any luck, they'll never see the light of day," Suel said.

"What do you say we head back to the office? I've got a couple of files I need to update, and after the last two weeks, it might be nice to leave just a little early and, God forbid, enjoy a pint."

"That sounds like a much better plan," Suel said.

They'd been back in the office for almost an hour when DCI McCabe stepped to his office door and said, "Officers Dillon and Suel, a moment of your time please."

As Suel headed for Dillon's desk he shrugged and held his hands out suggesting he didn't know what McCabe wanted. "Now what did you do, Dillon?"

"Probably didn't keep a close enough eye on you," Dillon said.

"Take a seat gentleman," McCabe said as they entered. He cleared his throat a couple of times as he settled into his chair.

All was quiet for a moment. McCabe cleared his throat again and then said, "I would just like to— I would like—" He cleared his throat again, took a deep breath and said, "On behalf of my family I want to thank you both for all you've done. You're pursuit and the arrests you made the other evening brings this—" A tear suddenly ran down his cheek. He stared at the open file on his desk. A black and white photo of Liam McCabe and Jimmy Murphy lying in Mountjoy Square was paper clipped on the file. McCabe's bottom lip suddenly began to tremble.

"God bless, Liam and Jimmy," Suel said.

"It was an honor, sir. Thank you for giving us the cover to pursue this," Dillon said.

McCabe nodded and continued to stare.

After a bit Suel signaled with a wave of his head that they should leave. As they stepped out of the office Dillon heard McCabe begin to sob.

FIFTY-THREE

A half-hour later Dillon walked over to Suel's desk and said, "I'm going to meet up with someone. You want to grab a pint at the end of the day?"

"That sounds like the perfect idea. We're back on the front-line tomorrow. Be nice to have a pint or two, just from the good health aspect," Suel said.

"I'll meet you at The Palace around five. If the weather stays as nice as it is now, we can drink them outside."

"Sounds good. Thanks in advance for buying the first round," Suel said.

"Be happy to," Dillon replied and headed out of the office.

Dillon didn't need to put the address into his GPS system. He drove across the Liffey and headed south down to Dalkey. He turned onto Torca Road and followed the curve of the road until he pulled in front of the Andris house. This time when he parked, he didn't feel the need to block the entrance gates. He walked up the winding path with the trimmed boxwood hedge and the rose trees and rang the doorbell. Janina Andris answered the door a minute later. Her face broke into a large smile, and she yelled, "Rytas, come see." She wrapped her arms around Dillon and said, "Oh God, but we can't thank you enough."

Rytas stepped into the entryway and said, "To what do we owe this pleasure? Come in, come in, Marshal. So wonderful to see you."

Dillon shook hands, and then Janina linked arms with him and led him into the kitchen. "Your timing is perfect. I just put a kettle on, and we're about to have tea and cakes. Please say you'll join us."

"I would love to," Dillon said.

They sat in a den off the kitchen, sipping tea, chatting, both Rytas and Janina giving their versions of events. All and all, given the ordeal they'd been through, they seemed to be doing quite well.

Dillon finally mentioned that he had received a phone call from Janina's brother, Vitas. "Yes, yes, we know. We spoke with him last night, and he told us all about it."

"He told me you purchased this home using Bitcoins?" Dillon said.

"Partially correct," Rytas said. "I sold our Bitcoins to a gentleman in Kretinga, the city I grew up in. He was actually a teacher of mine, owns a bank now. Anyway, he purchased the Bitcoins, and with those funds, we were able to purchase this house."

"It's a lovely home. Be a great place for kids," Dillon said and held his breath.

"Oh, I wish," said Janina. "But that's not an option. I lost our first child, stillborn, actually. I'm unable to get pregnant now. It's something we've had to deal with, unfortunately."

"That's a shame. When was that? A couple years ago?"

"Yes, two, to be exact. A very dark time, I'm afraid. I have the sense you're thinking of something here. What is it?"

Dillon took a deep breath and said, "I know of a child. A little boy who recently lost his mother. As a matter of fact, his mother was most likely murdered by the Linnehan brothers. He's just two years old. He's in Saint Joseph's Home at the moment, and I occasionally go there and read him stories."

"Saint Joseph's Home? We don't know of this place," Rytas said.

"It a place where children are sent when the parents have been lost or the home life is such that they shouldn't remain. I don't believe they've had much luck in finding a relative of the child."

"The Linnehans killed the mother?"

"We're pretty sure of that. They had a burner phone and called her twice a couple of days ago. The second call was a short time before she was murdered. The pistol we took from them has been linked to the mother's murder. I was first on the scene and found the child crying in a highchair. His mother was dead on the floor."

"Oh, the poor little darling," Janina said and bit the knuckle on her index finger.

"Yeah, he's really a sweet little guy."

"Rytas?" Janina said as her eyes began to water.

"We'll talk of this later, darling."

Dillon pulled out a business card and wrote *Saint Joseph's Home* on the back, followed by *Sister Jovanna.* "If you're interested, give them a call, ask for Sister Jovanna, and please mention my name. She's very familiar with the little boy."

They chatted for another ten minutes, and then Dillon left, not sure if he'd done the right thing by mentioning Rowen's situation. He drove home and let Lucifer out into the front garden and encouraged him back inside with a biscuit ten minutes later. He sent Suel a text message saying he'd be down at The Palace in fifteen minutes.

FIFTY-FOUR

Dillon had to park a block away. As he walked around the corner and onto Fleet Street, The Palace Bar was right there. Four large fifty-gallon whiskey barrels stood out in front of the pub. Suel was just stepping out the door, carrying a pint of Guinness in each hand. He caught sight of Dillon and set the pints on top of one of the whiskey barrels.

"Well, what do you know?" Dillon said. "Perfect timing on my part. You bought the first round."

"Not to worry," Suel said. "Luckily, the barman read about the Linnehan brothers ending up in The Joy and poured the pints for free. So, you can still get the first round that has to be paid for."

"It never ends," Dillon said and raised a glass toward Suel.

"I told Kate and Connor we were meeting here. Connor can't make it, but Kate said she'd show."

They sipped Guinness and talked about everything except the activities of the past two weeks. Kate joined them a little later with apologies for being late. She purchased a fresh round of Guinness.

They'd been there for the better part of two hours relaxing when Hugh Healy and Niall Reid showed up. "Here, join us, Lads. We'll make room," Suel said. "What is it you're drinking? I'll get the first round for ya's."

"No need, Suel," Reid said.

"No, I owe it to the both of ya's. The work you did and the speed you did it in. Now, I'm buying. What'll it be?"

"Pint of Guinness," Reid said.

"I think I'll have a Pina Colada with a little umbrella," Hugh said and gave a quick wink to Dillon.

"The feck you will," Suel said.

"Oh, okay, then a pint of Guinness will do me just fine."

"Ahh, you're a right plonker," Suel said, and everyone laughed. He was back a few minutes later with the two Guinness. One of them had a small blue paper umbrella in it, and he gave that to Healy. "It took some doing, but I got it just the way you like it," Suel said.

"Serves me right," Healy laughed and pulled the umbrella from his pint.

They were there for the better part of the evening, and then it was time to head home. Gradually, everyone began to say goodnight.

"Hugh, thanks for the work you did on Mountjoy Square. You finding those two shell casings made a real difference. Glad you're on our side. Anyone gives you a hard time, you send them to me, and we'll have a little

'Come to Jesus chat,'" Suel said and extended his hand to Healy.

"Thank you, D.I.—"

"No, you're a mate, Hugh. You can call me Paddy. Besides, we need everyone on board, keeping an eye on that knacker Dillon."

EPILOGUE

I t was two months later. With all the cars parked on the road, Dillon pulled onto the side street, parked, then walked back to the house with his gift in hand. The front door was partially open and had a flowered wreath hanging from it with a sign that read 'WEL-COME.'

He stepped inside and looked down the long hall-way. He could see people out on the patio, and he headed in that direction, past the room with children's toys and the kitchen with the highchair. He stepped down the two steps into the glass porch and then out the door and onto the patio.

A woman in a blue skirt and a white vest ap-proached. She held a silver tray with a half-dozen chilled champagne flutes.

Dillon smiled, shook his head, and asked, "Are the parents out here?"

"Just over by those flowers," she said then turned and presented the tray to a couple behind Dillon. Dillon placed his gift on the pile of gifts stacked on a card table and strolled over toward the flowers. There was a group of a half-dozen people sipping champagne and smiling next to the bed of flowers. Dillon recognized two of them as he approached.

"Oh, he's so good. You're lucky, a wonderful match, and already into books. Oh my," one of the women said, and everyone chuckled.

Dillon stepped up to the edge of the group. Two or three of the people had that look on their face that suggested, 'Who is this?'

But then Rowen glanced up and suddenly held out his arms. The book with the polar bears under the moon was in his right hand.

"Oh, people," Janina Andris said, "let me introduce a special friend, Marshal Dillon. He made all this happen. Marshal, you're just in time to read our son his favorite book," she said and handed Rowen to Dillon. Rowen wrapped his arms around Dillon then leaned back, grinned, and gave Dillon a kiss.

THE END

Thank you for taking the time to read <u>Dublin Moon</u>. If you enjoyed the read, please consider taking a moment to leave a review. Even if it's just a short line it really helps.

Don't miss the sample of the next book in the Jack Dillon Dublin Tale, <u>Mystery Woman</u>.

PROLOGUE

The two-story house was white and nestled on the side of a hill in West County Cork. Dennis Sheehan followed the winding road up through the open gate and parked next to the house. "We made it, Maureen," he said, glancing over at his wife in the passenger seat.

"Oh, thank God! Yesterday's flight from the US to Amsterdam, spend the night in the airport, fly to Ireland this morning, and a four-hour drive today from Dublin. I'm ready—"

"You're ready to take it easy and relax. We've got two weeks to do whatever we want. Let's check the place out," Dennis said, and they climbed out of their rented car.

A brick path led to the front door. He pulled the rental agreement from his coat pocket and focused on the security code. He input the code on the keypad. A half-second later, the front door unlocked, and they stepped into a paneled entry. Off to the right was a sitting room with two black leather couches arranged on either side of a fireplace. A coffee table rested between the couches. A bottle of white wine with a ribbon around it and two wineglasses were on the coffee table.

"Oh, isn't that nice," Maureen said, nodding at the wine bottle.

"Perfect, just what the doctor ordered. How about I pour us each a glass, we toast our tenth anniversary, and check this place out?"

"I thought you'd never ask," she said and kissed him on the cheek.

Thankfully it was a twist-off cap on the wine bottle. He opened the bottle, filled both glasses, and handed one to Maureen. "To another fifteen years," he said and raised his glass.

"Only fifteen?" she said and clinked glasses with him.

They wandered from room to room. Everything looked to be just as promised. A lovely bedroom, bathroom with a jacuzzi, steaks on a platter in the refrigerator, brie and crackers on the kitchen counter, and more wine in the wine rack.

Dennis carried their suitcases up to the bedroom while Maureen arranged the brie and crackers on a small cutting board. She opened the curtain on the back window in the sitting room and took in the view of a gorgeous hillside.

He cooked the steaks on the grill in the back garden. They kissed a number of times, began to relax, and started in on a second bottle of wine. The next two weeks promised to be everything they'd hoped for and more.

It was almost 10:00, and they were in the sitting room focused on the moon rising above the hillside. It wasn't quite full, but by the end of the week, it would be. Dennis was considering a third bottle of wine. Maureen was thinking wouldn't it be fun to make love on the leather couch with the Irish moon shining through the window.

The knock on the door snapped them back to reality.

"I'll get it. Probably the owners just checking to see if we need anything."

"Hurry back, darling," Maureen said as she pulled her top over her head and tossed it on the coffee table.

"A half-minute, don't start without me," Dennis replied and hurried to the door. He pulled the door open and looked at the couple standing on the front stoop. He'd only seen a photo of the owners. Neither one of these people seemed to resemble what he recalled.

The young man smiled and said, "Well, Punchy, welcome to Ireland."

"Excuse me?" Dennis said.

"You're Dennis Sheehan?" the woman asked in an Irish accent.

"Yes, and you are?"

"Judge and jury," the young man said, pointing a pistol at Dennis's head and firing. With the silencer, the shot almost sounded like someone spitting.

Maureen heard it, thought about pulling her slacks back on, and called, "Dennis?" After a few seconds, she sat up and stared over the back of the leather couch just as the couple stepped into the sitting room. "Where's Dennis?" she asked and then focused on the pistol the man pointed in her direction. "No," was the only word she got off before he began to fire.

The young man strolled over to the couch, gazed down at Maureen, and shook his head. "Too bad, she could have been fun. I never thought of Sheehan and his wife being this young. What do you think, maybe forty, forty-five?"

"Well, they're Americans, so it's gotta be them. You heard her call his name. Well done. Accomplish the task and leave the scene, two basic rules. Oh, and don't touch anything." She glanced at the naked woman on the couch, shook her head, and thought, *'Sorry, dear, I know the feeling.'*

ONE

Not for the first time, Dillon gave Suel an elbow in an effort to stop his snoring. They were on the third night of a stakeout. Thus far, absolutely nothing had happened. They were parked on the street waiting for the suspected arrival of Boston gangster Dennis Punchy Sheehan. From where they were parked, they could see the entrance to the Westbury Hotel on Balfe Street. Sheehan was supposed to have arrived two nights earlier.

Dillon got on the radio and called McCarthy. He was positioned inside the hotel near the reception desk. Two clicks on the handheld radio and then one word, "Anything?"

"No. No one claimed the room. I'm thinking this reservation might have been a diversion."

Suel snorted a couple of times and readjusted his position in the passenger seat.

"What the hell was that?" McCarthy asked.

"Who do you think? Snoring his ass off."

"Serves you right," McCarthy said and disconnected.

Two hours later, 5:30 in the morning. The sun was rising as Dillon watched the car pull around the corner and park behind them. Two figures were seated in the front. He heard the clicks on the radio and then, "Good morning," a voice said.

"Glad to see you. Another night of absolutely nothing," Dillon said.

"We're thinking it's a bust."

"I wish I could disagree, but I'm thinking the same thing," Dillon said.

Suel groaned, then opened his eyes and stretched.

"Well, good morning, DI Suel. Care for a full Irish breakfast, or maybe a tea and some scones?"

Suel smacked his lips, glanced around, and said, "Another waste of a night. For feck's sake."

"Good luck," Dillon said into the handset. He turned on the car and pulled away from the curb. As he drove past the Westbury Hotel, Suel glanced out the window, shook his head, and said, "I'm thinking we should put this down as bad information and come up with something else."

"Three days late, if he's coming at all. I'm afraid we've wasted enough time, and we're back to square one."

"Ahh, the bastard," Suel focused for a moment on a blonde woman just getting off a bus. He shook his head and said, "I honestly don't know how someone can work that overnight shift, day in and day out. We've been at it for three days, and my sleep schedule is so screwed up it's going to take me a week to get back to whatever normal is or was."

"Preaching to the choir," Dillon said. "O'Brien's is the only place open at this hour. You up for it?"

Suel yawned and said, "Breakfast there three mornings in a row. You almost make it sound like a dare."

"Not far from the truth," Dillon said. He drove another block, turned at the light, and then took a left. They drove along the Liffey for a bit and took the Heuston bridge across the river. O'Brien's was on the corner, on the far side of the bridge. The building was a good hundred years old. The food would never be described as special, but there was plenty of it. At this hour, Dillon parked on the street almost in front of the diner, and they went inside.

They weren't the first ones in this early. Maybe a half-mile from the An Garda Síochána headquarters, they recognized two individuals as they entered. Dillon gave a nod and headed for a table on the opposite side of the room. The place smelled of strong coffee and fried bacon.

"Hi, ya's," the waitress said as they sat down. She held a couple of menus, but instead of placing them on the table, she asked, "The usual?"

"Yeah," Dillon said and followed up with a yawn.

"Same, and coffee, black, no tea," Suel said.

She left as Dillon gave another yawn and said, "I think we're past the point where we might be wasting time. We're definitely wasting time. I'm thinking we talk to McCabe and suggest we call it off and refocus. If Punchy Sheehan flew into Dublin three days ago, we've missed him."

"Be best to see McCabe on a full stomach. What do you say to a leisurely breakfast, and we catch him first thing? He's usually in by 7:30."

Dillon nodded and said, "Yeah, I don't see anything happening. You think Sheehan might have come in on a ferry from the UK or France? Maybe even a private jet?"

Suel shook his head. "Maybe a ferry, but that would be a surprise. We can check with the airlines again. A private jet? The guy is notoriously cheap. I can't see him spending that kind of money."

"He's gotta be somewhere. The one thing we know is that he isn't in the Westbury hotel."

"Ain't that the truth," Suel said just as the waitress arrived with two full Irish breakfast platters and two mugs of coffee.

She set the platters down in front of them and then the mugs. When the coffee spilled over the sides of the mugs, she didn't so much as blink. "Anything else?" she said as she set a handwritten bill on the table.

Both Dillon and Suel shook their heads and shoveled in forkfuls of fried egg.

She was back four more times over the next half-hour, topping up their coffee mugs. Each time she dribbled coffee onto the table.

"She's the reason they don't have tablecloths in this place. The laundry bill would put them out of business," Suel said.

Suel's platter was clean, and Dillon had eaten everything except the baked beans. "You going to finish those?" Suel asked.

"No, help yourself," Dillon said and handed his platter across the table.

Suel scraped the beans onto his platter and handed the empty one back to Dillon. Ten minutes later, they were in the car on their way to headquarters. They were early, and DCI McCabe had yet to arrive. Dillon grabbed a razor and shaving cream from his desk and headed for the restroom. Suel set about making a tea.

They spent the next half-hour discussing how Dennis Punchy Sheehan might arrive in Ireland and came up with the same answer they'd always come up with. He'd fly and make someone else pay for the flight.

DCI McCabe arrived just before 7:30. Dillon gave him a couple of minutes to get situated before he and Suel approached his office and knocked on the doorframe.

McCabe motioned them in and continued his phone conversation. "No, six officers a day, Brennan. They're out there waiting for something, anything to happen, and the only thing that's happening is they're exhausted. I'm going to pull it today, and we'll think of something else. Clearly, this isn't working. Yes. I will. Okay, thanks for listening. Yes. As soon as I know. Thank you," McCabe said and hung up.

"Good morning, sir," Dillon said.

McCabe shook his head. "Nothing good about it. I'm going to pull the Sheehan stakeout. It's been three days, and all we've got to show for it is a wasted budget, three wasted days, and six people who already have more than enough to deal with. I'll contact the team in a moment and call them in. In the meantime, put your heads together and come up with what we're going to do next. He has to show up here sooner or later or risk losing control of his entire operation."

"So you're saying we're not on tonight?" Suel asked.

"No, I'll pull the day team off now. You two head home, get some rest and be back here tomorrow morning. Any questions?"

Dillon shook his head. "No, sir. Sorry it didn't work out. We've discussed it, and we can't see Sheehan taking an alternative way into the country."

"He's such a cheap bast…err, individual," Suel said. "We can't see him arriving by ferry and certainly not by a private jet."

"Home to get some sleep, gentlemen. Anything changes, I'll be the first to call."

Dillon and Suel both rose and headed out the door. Suel gave Dillon the thumbs-up and hurried to his desk. They walked out together ten minutes later and drove home.

TWO

Dillon was met at the front door by his aptly named dog, Lucifer. As he opened the door, Lucifer jumped off the front stoop and assumed the position next to Dillon's car. I know the feeling, Dillon thought and stepped into the house. Amazingly, there didn't seem to be a mess anywhere. He thought about making some coffee and decided sleep was the better option.

He grabbed a biscuit from the cookie jar and used it to coax Lucifer back into the house. He filled the food and water dishes and made his way upstairs to the bedroom. He set his alarm for noon, thinking four hours of sleep would probably get him through the day. After the four hours, if he could stay awake until 10:00 tonight, he'd be back on schedule tomorrow morning.

Five minutes later, he was in bed and vaguely aware of Lucifer settling in next to him. His cellphone ringing interrupted his dream. At first, a distant ring, but then each time it rang, it seemed to be slightly louder until he opened his eyes and pulled the phone from the bedside table.

"Hell—" He cleared his throat twice and tried again, "Hello."

"Hope I woke you, you lousy knacker," Suel said. "Just off the phone with McCabe. Apparently, they've found Punchy Sheehan down in County Cork."

"County Cork? How in the hell did he get down there?"

"I presume he drove. They're in a little village called Desertserges."

"How many are with him?"

"Just one. A woman. Oh, and they're both dead."

"Dead?"

"Our man Punchy was apparently shot in the head. The woman was shot mutiple times. Desertserges is barely a village. It's outside of Enniskeane. We're to go down there and head up the investigation."

"What?"

"There's no local Garda. Enniskeane is the nearest, but they're stretched—"

"Oh, and we're not?" Dillon asked.

"I'm just repeating what I've been told. Besides, you as an American, it's only natural you'd be involved in the investigation of the death of a brother."

Dillon took a deep breath and exhaled. "Why do I get the feeling we're not to wait until tomorrow to head down there?"

"It's that marvelous intuition you have. Pick me up in an hour. It's going to take three hours to get to the place."

"Gee, I can hardly wait. Okay, see you in an hour."

"I could go for a coffee when you arrive," Suel said.

"Goodbye," Dillon said and disconnected. He remained in bed, staring at the ceiling. He thought maybe fifteen more minutes might help and closed his eyes. After five minutes, he climbed out of bed and headed toward the bathroom. He showered, dressed, and packed an overnight bag. He let Lucifer out into the front garden and tossed him a biscuit for added encouragement. He refilled the food and water dishes and then wrote a note to Tara, his neighbor across the street, asking her to check in on Lucifer.

He walked across the lane and rang Tara's doorbell. Her car was gone and, at no surprise, she didn't answer the door. He slipped the note through her mail slot and walked back to his house. Lucifer was investigating a corner of the front garden. Dillon went inside and then encouraged Lucifer back in with another biscuit. He grabbed two slices of cold pizza from the refrigerator, wolfed them down, then tossed his overnight bag in the car and headed to Suel's.

Suel answered the door with a cup of coffee from the shop up the street and handed it to Dillon. He grabbed his suitcase and another coffee, locked the door behind him, and headed for Dillon's car.

"Since when did you become so organized? Oh, thanks for the coffee, much appreciated."

"Yeah, well, thanks for driving. I figured, for the price of a coffee, I can be guaranteed a safe drive down to Cork."

"You find out anything else?"

Suel shook his head. "I put a call into my pal, Jamie McCormick down in Bandon but haven't heard back. Hopefully, he'll call when we're on the road. All I know is there are two bodies, and one of them is Dennis Punchy Sheehan. They've got the site locked down, and we'll be leading the investigation."

Dillon shook his head as he backed out of the driveway and headed for the M50.

"Take the M50 to the N7 and head south. I'll give you directions as we—"

"How about I just listen to the GPS on my cellphone," Dillon said.

As if in reply, the GPS voice suddenly said, "In five hundred meters, take a right turn."

"Perfect, you finally have a relationship with a woman. That means I can nap and—"

Dillon took a sip of his coffee and said, "I think the safer thing might be for you to make sure I don't fall asleep."

"Don't fall asleep? That's why I got you that coffee, for lord's sake."

"That will keep me going for at least a half-hour. Remember, Paddy, you were the one snoring in the car last night while I kept watch."

"Well, all right, if you insist. I think we could stop for a late lunch and—"

"Let's just get there. It's going to be close to 4:00 before we get to Enniskeane, and who knows how long it will take to find the place after that."

"I've got the address in Desertserges. We can reset your GPS once we get to Bandon. Enniskeane is on the far side of the murder scene, and we need to check in with Jamie McCormick and the Bandon Gardaí anyway. They're the local force."

Dillon reached for his coffee. It was warm, and he took a couple of large swallows. It was shaping up to be a long journey, and they were still on the Dublin city streets.

"Turn right at the next corner and remain in the righthand lane," the GPS instructed.

It was almost three hours before they pulled in front of the main Garda Station in Bandon. The building was a two-story white stucco structure with blue trim on the windows. Two lamp posts with the Garda logo stood on either side of the entrance. A ramp for handicapped individuals leading up to the front door was on the righthand side, and a flowerbed filled with white flowers was off to the left.

They pulled the lanyards with the IDs from their pockets, slipped them on, and walked up the four steps to the front entrance. The word 'GARDA' in large blue letters along with the Garda logo was centered on the front of the building. Dillon held the door open for Suel and followed him inside.

A reception counter with a uniformed officer seated behind it was fifteen feet in front of them. As they approached, Suel did the introduction. "DI Paddy Suel and US Marshal Jack Dillon from Dublin Special Branch. We're here to see DI McCormick in relation to a double murder last night in Desertserges."

"He mentioned you'd be coming down. Didn't expect to see you for another hour."

"Dillon was driving," Suel said, pleading innocence.

That brought a smile to the officer's face. "McCormick is out at the site. He left directions for you," he said as he reached behind for a sheet of paper with handwritten directions.

"We've got GPS on the phone," Suel said.

This time the officer chuckled. "Good luck getting it to work out that way. With all the hills and whatnot, the connection comes and goes."

"Wonderful," Suel said. He took the sheet and handed it to Dillon.

"It's about a thirty-minute drive," the officer said as he looked over at Dillon and smiled. "That's if you stay at the speed limit."

"We'll be sure to do that," Dillon said.

"Oh, American?" the officer said, picking up on Dillon's accent.

"Yeah, the powers that be brought me in to mind DI Suel."

The officer nodded. "Good luck with that."

"Full-time job," Suel said.

Back in the car, as Dillon pulled away from the curb, Suel read from the directions. "Take Castledon Court to the intersection and take a right. We pretty much drive parallel to the Bandon River."

"I suppose it would be too much to ask to have the roads identified," Dillon said.

"We've got directions. We don't need that."

Dillon took a right at the intersection, and Suel directed him onto the first left a few minutes later. The road became substantially more narrow, barely wide enough for one vehicle if it wasn't too large. Dillon reduced his speed to little more than a crawl.

Maybe five miles later, he slowed to a crawl as they met an oncoming car. Both vehicles pulled to the side, essentially driving on the shoulder, except there was no shoulder, just rocky fields and weeds on either side. As they passed the other vehicle, the driver, a woman, raised her index finger in a country wave.

Dillon did the same in response.

Twenty minutes later, Suel said, "I believe that's the Kilcolman Fishery." He nodded at a gorgeous brick home as they drove past.

"A fishery? It looks like someone's house."

"Yeah, it is, but it's an AirBnB place, and you fish on the Bandon River. Quite popular, I hear. Shouldn't be too much further." A minute later, Suel said, "That must be it up on the left with the Garda car parked in the entrance."

They pulled into a stone-lined entrance covered with a leafy vine. Dillon drove down onto an asphalt parking area where two cars were parked. The house itself was an elegant two-story stone structure with a slate roof and what appeared to be a lovely glass porch attached to the rear.

As they climbed out of the car, a man stepped out of the house. He was solidly built, not fat, with ginger-colored hair. He was dressed in casual clothes, in need of a shave, and wore latex gloves on his hands. Dillon guessed he had probably been called out in the middle of the night. "It's about damn time. How you doing, Paddy?" he said as Suel opened the car door.

"Jesus, Jamie, we would have been here sooner, but we got stuck behind horses and a wagon on your major county roads down here. This is my chauffeur, US Marshal Jack Dillon. Jamie McCormick, the lead inspector for the Bandon Gardai and crossing guard for the Bandon Nursery School."

McCormick stepped around to the side and shook hands with Dillon. "Don't believe a word this knacker tells you. Pleased to meet you. I've heard about you."

"Ignore whatever you were told. I'm actually a nice guy," Dillon said.

"So, your man Punchy Sheehan is still inside?" Suel asked.

"Yeah, come on in and see for yourself. I thought you might be the medical examiner. We've been waiting on them. They should have been here hours ago, but they're hauling two bodies from a car-truck crash. It must be pretty bad if it's taking them this long. Anyway, come on in, and you can see your man Punchy and his wife."

"His wife?" Dillon said and smiled. "He's not married. I think he's had two or three wives over the years and finally got the message. Women don't like him. He usually has some escort within reach. That's probably who the woman is."

"No, we checked out the passports. Same surname, wedding rings on the both of them."

"Really? Huh, I wonder if that just happened. Let's see what you got. Any idea who did this?" Dillon asked as they headed toward the front door.

McCormick shook his head. "If I had to guess, I'd say it was professional, no shell casings. We've dusted for fingerprints but haven't found much. Apparently, Sheehan arrived here last night. We talked to the owners, Thomas and Aisling Barry. They live in Bandon and were the ones who called us. They drove past a little after 11:00 last night and noticed the front door was open. Sheehan had rented the place for the next two weeks, paid in advance. If I had to guess, I'd say whoever did this was probably here for about thirty seconds. Did what he came to do and left."

"Watch yourself now," McCormick said as he opened the front door. "Your man is just inside. There's a box of gloves on the table next to the door as you step inside. Best to slip those on so you don't contaminate the scene. We've photographed everything, and I'll email that file to you, Paddy, as soon as I get back to the station and download the images."

THREE

Dillon and Suel followed McCormick into the entryway. Suel pulled two latex gloves from the box, handed them to Dillon, and pulled out two more for himself.

"There's your man, Punchy Sheehan," McCormick said and nodded at the body lying against the front wall behind the door. A hole was centered on the eyebrow above the victim's right eye. A trail of dried blood ran down the side of his head to his ear. "The wife is on the couch in the sitting room. Looks like whoever did this may have interrupted a bit of hanky-panky."

Dillon stared at the body on the floor for a long moment and shook his head. "That's not Punchy Sheehan," he said.

"Not Punchy?" McCormick said. "Sorry, lad, but we've checked their passports. Sean, bring those passports in here, will you? We'll have us a look," McCormick called to the man standing behind a black leather couch in the sitting room. "We checked their IDs and both of their passports and driver's licenses are from the

US. The passports and driver's licenses match one another and the individuals. Your man Punchy is named Dennis Sheehan, isn't he?"

Dillon nodded and said, "Yeah, Dennis Eoghan Sheehan. But he's sixty-five years old and weighs somewhere north of three hundred pounds. By the way, he's from Boston, Massachusetts, lived there his entire life. I don't know who that is on the floor, but it sure as hell isn't Punchy Sheehan."

"Are you sure?" McCormick asked just as the guy from the sitting room handed him two evidence bags. Each held a US passport.

McCormick handed the bags to Dillon. Dillon opened one of the bags and took out the passport. "Maureen Sheehan, born 10 October 1980. That makes her forty-one. She lives in Minnesota." He opened the other evidence bag and pulled out the passport. "Oh shit, Dennis Sheehan, born 11 May 1978. He's forty-three, twenty-two years younger, and at least a hundred and fifty pounds lighter than that bastard Punchy. I'm afraid we're looking at a case of mistaken identity."

"Oh, for the love of God! Are you serious?" McCormick said, shaking his head.

"You sure, Jack? I mean, if they were this quick making the hit, wouldn't they know who they were sent to kill?" Suel asked.

"Apparently not. Unfortunately, that's why we didn't have any knowledge of him coming into the country. He isn't Punchy. It's as simple as that. Christ, let's take a look at the woman."

"On the couch by the fireplace," the other Bandon cop said. He looked at McCormick and shook his head as if to say, 'What the hell?'

Dillon stepped into the sitting room and walked over to the black leather couch. As he approached, he noticed what had to be bullet holes, two of them, in the back of the couch. He stood behind the couch and looked down at the body. The woman was dark haired and naked except for the thong pulled down almost to her knees. She was hanging halfway off the couch with a wound through her right elbow, another in her right shoulder, and one in her right temple. An empty bottle of wine rested on the floor next to the coffee table. An almost empty wineglass sat on the far side of the coffee table. A broken wineglass with lipstick was on its side on the coffee table, close to the woman's body. Dillon guessed she probably knocked it over when the three rounds slammed into her, moving her off the couch.

Her left arm hung down to the floor, and Dillon walked around the couch to look. Sure enough, there was a diamond ring and a wedding band.

"It looks like whoever did this interrupted a bit of a private celebration," Suel said and shook his head. "Fecking idjits. Sheehan is a common Cork surname. What the hell? They were too lazy to check it out?"

"Well, it proves one thing. Apparently, there are some folks around who aren't going to be all that happy to see Punchy whenever he decides to arrive."

"Yeah, if he ever shows up. This could be a game-changer for Punchy. He may just decide not to come and walk away from the business here," Suel said.

"I suspect there's a fairly large amount of money he's already invested, and let's not forget, it's the doorway to the rest of Europe. We need to find out how we got the information on Punchy coming over. Was it a setup? Did someone pay for this couple's trip, knowing they'd be taken out? And what about Punchy? Just where in the hell is that worthless piece of shit right now?"

They heard a car door slam outside, and McCormick said, "It's about damn time. Hopefully, the medical examiner is finally here."

Dillon and Suel followed McCormick and his partner out the front door. The medical examiner's van was backed into the parking place next to Dillon's car. The rear doors were open, and two men were in the process of rolling a gurney out of the van. Two black body bags were resting on top of the gurney.

"Hi lads," a gray-haired man said. "Sorry it took so long to get out here, but we had a hell of a mess to deal with down south of town. A car accident, one of the vehicles caught fire. A sad state of affairs. I hear you got some big-name mobster inside."

As he spoke, his partner walked around to the side of the van and opened a small door. He pulled out two blue hazmat suits and walked back, setting one on the gurney. The other he unfolded and began to step into it.

"Mick, Devlin, this is DI Paddy Suel from Dublin and Jack Dillon, an American attached to An Garda Síochána," McCormick said. "They're down here to help with the investigation into our murder of the American gangster, only everything just went to hell."

"What do you mean, 'went to hell'? Is he still alive?" Mick, the older of the two, asked.

"No, unfortunately. But Dillon just told us that's not the gangster inside. It's just some poor knacker with the same name."

"What?" Both men stopped halfway into pulling on their hazmat suits and looked at Dillon. "Are you sure it's not your man? I thought there were passports and IDs identifying both individuals."

"There are," Dillon said. "Same name, but unfortunately, it's not the Dennis Sheehan we were all hoping for."

"You're sure?"

"Very. I met the bastard once. It's not him. The victim here is some twenty years younger and at least half the weight."

"Well, we'll still have to take them to the lab and do the examination. They're American?"

"Yeah, we got that part right," McCormick said and shook his head.

They examined the bodies for about forty minutes and then set them in the body bags, zipped them closed, and wheeled them one at a time out to the van. After a brief conversation, they climbed in the van and drove back to Bandon.

McCormick watched the van turn onto the road and disappear. Still staring at the now empty lane, he said, "We've got the two of yous staying in the Munster Arms Hotel. There's not much more we can do tonight. I'm not sure about the likes of ya's, but I could use some dinner and a pint. How's about we head back to town? You can check in. The room is reserved under the department name." He glanced at his watch. "We'll meet for dinner in the hotel. They serve a good meal. The Guinness is good, and we can go over what our plan is for tomorrow. We've still got two Americans murdered and no suspects."

"That sounds like a plan," Dillon said. "Paddy?"

"Fine by me. It'll be an early night, lads. We were on stakeout the last three nights. As a matter of fact, waiting for Punchy Sheehan to check into the Westbury Hotel. Needless to say, we came up empty-handed."

"Lot of that going around," McCormick said. "We'll lock up here and meet you in the dining room at 7:00. Sound like a plan?"

Dillon and Suel nodded and headed for the car. As he drove off, Dillon waved and pulled back onto the road. Suel gave a loud exhale and said, "I'm thinking the way our luck has been running, this wouldn't be the best time to buy a lottery ticket."

"Yeah, you can say that again. I'd say the Bandon department had high hopes they were going to be dealing with Punchy Sheehan's murder."

"Amazing," Suel said and shook his head. "Can you believe it? The same name and they're Americans. Punchy is supposed to be arriving, and it all blows up in our face. Talk about a cluster feck."

"We'll have to get to McCabe early tomorrow morning. I want us to be the ones to tell him. We're still going to be here for a day or two dealing with this investigation."

"Humf, we'll be lucky if it's only a day or two. Could be a week or longer," Suel said and shook his head.

"Jamie McCormick seems to have his act together. It will be interesting to see what he comes up with tonight."

"I'm thinking whoever did the shooting last night probably isn't local," Suel said.

"Why not?"

"It's a major hit, professional, or at least it looked that way. I want to ask McCormick tonight if they found cash on site. If so, that would suggest that whoever pulled the trigger did the job and got out of here. What did he say? It might have been thirty seconds start to finish. Looked like he and the wife were just getting started and there's a knock on the door or maybe they see a car pull in. Either way, your man opens the door and is shot.

Whoever it is steps into the sitting room, fires from probably five or ten feet, and puts three rounds into the wife.

"Maureen," Dillon said. "Yeah, no shell casings. You see any sign of an exit wound?"

Suel shook his head. "Not on the wife. Couldn't have been more than a few inches from your man when he fired. Small caliber, maybe a hollow point that raises hell inside the skull, but nothing large enough to exit."

"We'll see what those examiners come up with, hopefully, tomorrow," Dillon said.

FOUR

The Munster Arms Hotel, a three-story, cream-colored structure on Oliver Plunkett Street, was located in the center of Bandon. Dillon parked just down the street. They walked into the hotel lobby and headed for the front desk, actually a white-tiled counter.

"Good evening, gentleman. Do you have a reservation?" the woman behind the front desk asked and followed up with a smile. She was dark haired and blue eyed. She wore a long-sleeve black top. Dillon guessed her age to be late twenties or early thirties.

"I believe we've rooms reserved by Bandon Gardai," Suel said.

"Oh yes, they phoned us this morning. We've actually a two-bed suite reserved for you," she said, running her fingers across a keyboard. "I'll need to see some ID. It says here DI Paddy Suel and Marshal Jack Dillon?"

Suel took out his wallet and pulled out his An Garda Síochána card. Dillon pulled the lanyard from around his neck and placed his ID next to Suel's.

The woman leaned over and glanced at them, then flashed a quick smile. The printer behind her suddenly started up and printed off two sheets of paper.

"We offer a complimentary breakfast in our dining room. You're in room one-twelve, just up the stairs to the next floor and then take a right. Your reservation is for the next two nights. Should your stay be longer, just let us know. Any questions?" she asked as she took the two pieces of paper from the printer and placed them next to their IDs. She typed on the keyboard again and then reached down and set two keycards on top of the printed pages along with a hotel brochure.

"I think we're good for the moment. What time do you serve breakfast?" Suel asked.

"Our complimentary breakfast is available from 7:30 until 10:00 seven days a week," she said, following up with another quick smile.

Suel handed a keycard to Dillon, grabbed the brochure and the printed pages, and said, "Do you need us to sign anything?"

"No, you're all set. Enjoy your stay, gentlemen."

"Thank you," Dillon said, and they headed for the staircase.

Room 112 was on the second floor. The room was six doors down the hall. Suel inserted his keycard into the reader. It flashed green, and they heard the door unlock. Suel pushed it open, and they entered the room.

The room had two twin beds with a bedside table next to each bed. White pillows were leaning against the headboards, and a smaller, purple pillow rested against the white pillows. A small chest of drawers and a credenza affair were against the wall opposite the foot of the beds. A flatscreen TV was mounted on the wall above the chest of drawers.

"Home, sweet home," Suel said and tossed his suitcase on the first bed. Dillon set his overnight bag on the credenza, then walked over to the curtains and pulled them back. The window overlooked the main street below.

"You notice there isn't an elevator in this hotel?" Dillon said.

"Part of its charm," Suel replied. "To be honest, after working the last three nights and our interrupted sleep this morning, this bed is looking awfully comfortable. I'm going to sleep like a baby tonight."

"Promise?"

"What do you say to heading down to the bar for a pint? Jamie McCormick will be here in a half-hour. I don't feel like twiddling my thumbs up here for the next thirty minutes."

"Sounds good to me. I'll buy a round."

"I have a better idea. We'll just charge it to the room, and the Bandon Gardai can have the honor of buying us a pint."

"Then let's go," Dillon said and headed for the door.

The barroom was part of the dining room and was approximately half-full. They grabbed a table for four in the corner and ordered two pints of Guinness. Jamie

McCormick and his partner arrived about two minutes after the pints were placed on the table.

"Oh, at no surprise, I see you couldn't bear to wait, Paddy," McCormick said and pulled out a chair.

"Say, before I respond, we were never introduced. I'm Paddy Suel," Suel said and held out his hand to McCormick's dark-haired, green-eyed partner.

"Sean Lynch, nice to meet you," he said as they shook hands.

"Sean, I'm Jack Dillon. Nice to meet you," Dillon said and extended his hand.

McCormick waved the waitress over and said, "Teresa, two pints, please. Oh, and we'll be needing some menus as well."

"Back in a bit, Jamie," she replied and hurried off toward the bar.

"You a regular here?" Suel asked.

McCormick shook his head, "No, I've known her since primary school. She grew up a couple of doors down from our place. Her brothers and I were on the same hurling team. Nice girl, a nice family, actually. Say, I sent off the file with the scene images to you. Also sent a copy to DCI McCabe. We've been instructed to keep him in the loop."

"We'll be calling him first thing tomorrow morning to let him know this Dennis Sheehan isn't the knacker we were hoping," Suel said.

"Have you mentioned that to the owners? That it wasn't Punchy Sheehan?" Dillon asked.

McCormick shook his head. "No, we didn't mention anything regarding Punchy to them. As far as they know, it was some random act of violence. Some nutcase knocking on the door and murdering whoever answered."

"What about news outlets?" Suel asked.

"I believe at this stage they're unaware. That'll no doubt change by tomorrow morning."

The waitress set a pint of Guinness down in front of McCormick and another in front of Lynch.

Lynch raised his glass and said, "Here's to you, lads. Thank you for coming down. Sorry we didn't have your man."

"Amen," Suel said, and everyone clinked glasses.

"Is your department working on a press release?" Dillon asked once they'd finished the toast.

"Umm, so the press release," McCormick said and set his glass down. "Yeah, we've a lad working on that. Soon as it's approved, it will be released. I would guess that will be early tomorrow morning. There's bound to be a storm of media activity. A double murder is big news down here, so God only knows how the press will end up twisting it."

"Were you able to go through the place and check the luggage? I'm hoping maybe they brought laptops. Did they have any cash?"

"I think what you're suggesting, Dillon, is, were they robbed after being shot? From what we can determine so far, no, they were not robbed. Clothing was contained in two suitcases. Wait, let me rephrase that. Your man's clothing was still in his suitcase. His wife's clothing—"

"Maureen," Suel said.

"Yes, her clothing had apparently been in a suitcase and a garment bag. A number of items were hanging in the bedroom closet, three dresses, a couple pairs of slacks, two sweaters. What am I forgetting?" McCormick said to Lynch.

"Your woman had three pairs of shoes in the closet and undergarments in the chest of drawers. As far as a laptop goes, we didn't find one, and there was nothing like cords to charge a computer or even a travel adapter for electrical outlets. Oh, and your man's wallet was on top of the chest of drawers, umm two hundred and fifty euros in the wallet."

"Yeah, I'd guess our shooter didn't venture any further than the sitting room, shot the woman, and left," McCormick said. "Your man's suitcase had their return flight details, flying from Dublin to Amsterdam, Amsterdam to Atlanta, Atlanta to Minneapolis. I can't recall the airline at the moment. The flight was scheduled twelve days from yesterday, business class seats."

"Sounds like it was probably Delta," Dillon said. "How long did they book that AirBnB unit for?"

"Ten days. They had a reservation at the Maldron Hotel in Dublin the day before their departure."

Dillon thought for a moment and said, "I think that's the hotel right at the airport."

"Yeah, it overlooks terminal two," Suel said.

"So they journey down here and plan to stay for the better part of two weeks. Any idea why?" Dillon asked.

McCormick shook his head. "Not really. All I can guess is, they had a great bargain on the price, fifty euros a day. It's a lovely place, private. They could journey around the south of the country on day trips. I know they booked the place almost two months ago. The Barry's were thrilled to have renters for a two-week stretch. If they're lucky, it's usually a weekend couple, check in on Friday night or Saturday and leave Sunday."

"You looked at their passports, the travel?"

"Yes, both passports were issued two years ago. There was a three-day trip to Paris eighteen months ago and then the Dublin airport stamp three days ago. Other than that, apparently no travel outside the US."

"Sounds like they had planned this as their big trip," Suel said.

Lynch nodded and said, "We've someone set to check that. The Sheehan surname is fairly common down here, maybe family history, you know, famine people who made it to the States. Or maybe they just always wanted to come, and this was their big opportunity."

Suel shook his head and said, "Pity."

"Have you had a chance to look at the menus?" Teresa, the waitress, asked.

"Give us just another minute. Is there a special tonight?" McCormick asked.

"Every night is special with me, darling," she said and smiled. "Tonight, we're also serving Beef and Guinness stew."

"I'd better have that," McCormick said.

"Make it two," Lynch added.

Dillon and Suel nodded.

"So all four of ya's?" Teresa asked.

Everyone nodded, and McCormick said, "Better bring another round of pints as well."

"Coming right up." She gathered the untouched menus and headed toward the bar.

"Have you any idea where the real Punchy Sheehan is or when he might be arriving?" Lynch asked.

Dillon and Suel shook their heads. "At the moment, it's a blank page," Suel said. "I doubt he's in the country, but he could be, and we've no way of knowing. Obviously, whoever killed this couple last night was just as much in the dark as we are."

TO BE CONTINUED . . .

Thank you for checking out the sample of the next Jack Dillon Dublin Tale, <u>Mystery Woman</u>. Better grab a copy and see what happens . . .

BOOKS BY MIKE FARICY
CRIME FICTION FIRSTS

A boxset of the first four books in four crime fiction series:
Russian Roulette; Dev Haskell series
Welcome; Jack Dillon Dublin Tales series
Corridor Man; Corridor Man series
Reduced Ransom! Hot Shot series

The following titles comprise the Dev Haskell series:
Russian Roulette: Case 1
Mr. Swirlee: Case 2
Bite Me: Case 3
Bombshell: Case 4
Tutti Frutti: Case 5
Last Shot: Case 6
Ting-A-Ling: Case 7
Crickett: Case 8
Bulldog: Case 9
Double Trouble: Case 10
Yellow Ribbon: Case 11
Dog Gone: Case 12
Scam Man: Case 13
Foiled: Case 14
What Happens in Vegas… Case 15
Art Hound: Case 16

The Office: Case 17
Star Struck: Case 18
International Incident: Case 19
Guest From Hell: Case 20
Art Attack: Case 21
Mystery Man: Case 22
Bow-Wow Rescue: Case 23
Cold Case: Case 24
Cash Up Front: Case 25
Dream House: Case 26
Alley Katz: Case 27
The Big Gamble: Case 28
Bad to the Bone: Case 29
Silencio!: Case 30
Surprise, Surprise: Case 31
Hit & Run: Case 32
Suspect Santa: Case 33
P.I. Apprentice: Case 34
Rebel Without a Clue: Case 35
Puppy Love: Case 36

The following titles are Dev Haskell novellas:
Dollhouse
The Dance
Pixie
Fore!
Twinkle Toes
(*a Dev Haskell short story*)

The following are Dev Haskell Boxsets:
Dev Haskell Boxset 1-3
Dev Haskell Boxset 4-6
Dev Haskell Boxset 7-9
Dev Haskell Boxset 10-12
Dev Haskell Boxset 13-15
Dev Haskell Boxset 16-18
Dev Haskell Boxset 19-21
Dev Haskell Boxset 22-24
Dev Haskell Boxset 25-27
Dev Haskell Boxset 28-30
Dev Haskell Boxset 1-7
Dev Haskell Boxset 8-14
Dev Haskell Boxset 15-19
Dev Haskell Boxset 20-24
Dev Haskell Boxset 25-29

The following titles comprise the Jack Dillon Dublin Tales series:
Welcome
Jack Dillon Dublin Tale 1
Sweet Dreams
Jack Dillon Dublin Tale 2
Mirror Mirror
Jack Dillon Dublin Tale 3
Silver Bullet
Jack Dillon Dublin Tale 4

Fair City Blues
Jack Dillon Dublin Tale 5
Spade Work
Jack Dillon Dublin Tale 6
Madeline Missing
Jack Dillon Dublin Tale 7
Mistaken Identity
Jack Dillon Dublin Tale 8
Picture Perfect
Jack Dillon Dublin Tale 9
Dublin Moon
Jack Dillon Dublin Tale 10
Mystery Woman
Jack Dillon Dublin Tale 11
Second Chance
Jack Dillon Dublin Tale 12
Payback Brother
Jack Dillon Dublin Tale 13
The Heist
Jack Dillon Dublin Tale 14
Jewels To Kill For
Jack Dillon Dublin Tale 15
Retirement Scheme
Jack Dillon Dublin Tale 16
The Collector
Jack Dillon Dublin Tale 17

Jack Dillon Dublin Tales Boxsets:
Jack Dillon Dublin Tales 1-3

Jack Dillon Dublin Tales 4-6
Jack Dillon Dublin Tales 1-5
Jack Dillon Dublin Tales 1-7
Jack Dillon Dublin Tales 6-10

The following titles comprise the Hotshot series;
Reduced Ransom! Second Edition
Finders Keepers! Second Edition
Bankers Hours Second Edition
Chow Down Second Edition
Moonlight Dance Academy Second Edition
Irish Dukes (Fight Card Series)
written under the pseudonym Jack Tunney

The following titles comprise the Corridor Man series:
Corridor Man
Corridor Man 2: Opportunity knocks
Corridor Man 3: The Dungeon
Corridor Man 4: Dead End
Corridor Man 5: Finger
Corridor Man 6: Exit Strategy
Corridor Man 7: Trunk Music
Corridor Man 8: Birthday Boy
Corridor Man 9: Boss Man
Corridor Man 10: Bye Bye Bobby

Corridor Man novellas:
Corridor Man: Valentine

Corridor Man: Auditor
Corridor Man: Howling
Corridor Man: Spa Day

The following are Corridor Man Boxsets:
Corridor Man Boxset 1-3
Corridor Man Boxset 1-5
Corridor Man Boxset 6-9

THANK YOU!

Contact the author:
- Email: mikefaricyauthor@gmail.com
- Twitter: @Mikefaricybooks
- Facebook: Mike Faricy Author
- Website: http://www.mikefaricybooks.com

Published by

MJF Publishing